no FC 19

THE
FRAUD

ALSO BY BRAD PARKS

THE
FRAUD

Brad Parks

MINOTAUR BOOKS

NEW YORK

THE FRAUD. Copyright © 2015 by Brad Parks. All rights reserved. Printed in the United States of America. For information, address St. Martin's Press, 175 Fifth Avenue, New York, N.Y. 10010.

www.minotaurbooks.com

Designed by Omar Chapa

The Library of Congress Cataloging-in-Publication Data is available upon request.

ISBN 978-1-250-06440-0 (hardcover)
ISBN 978-1-4668-7047-5 (e-book)

Minotaur books may be purchased for educational, business, or promotional use. For information on bulk purchases, please contact the Macmillan Corporate and Premium Sales Department at 1-800-221-7945, extension 5442, or write to specialmarkets@macmillan.com.

First Edition: July 2015

10 9 8 7 6 5 4 3 2 1

In loving memory of Clement A. Price, the epitome of the gentleman scholar and the man who taught me where Newark came from.

Miss you, pal.

CHAPTER 1

It's the hypothetical question every parent considers at some point:

Would you give your life for your kid?

Would you dive in front of a speeding eighteen-wheeler to shove your daughter out of the way? Would you let your son take your heart when his number didn't come up soon enough on the transplant list? Would you place your head under the guillotine as part of some Faustian bargain wherein your child didn't have to?

Oh, I know what you're thinking, if you're a parent: yes, yes, yes, and yes. Even if it was just to spare yourself the agony of burying your own kid, you'd make that sacrifice every time. Or at least that's what you tell yourself you would do. What kind of selfish coward wouldn't?

But hold on a second. Don't answer yet. Because you still don't know everything. What if, just to increase the degree of difficulty, it was a baby who hadn't been born? A child who had not yet been named, whose gender you did not know, whose personality was a total question mark, whose eyes you had never gazed into, whose life had not taken shape in any meaningful way?

Would that change things? Make the decision tougher? Just a little?

Because, let's be clear, we're not talking about video game death, where you have nine more lives and all you have to do is press the reset button to cue up the next one.

We're talking about death everlasting. What Chandler called "the big sleep." What Rabelais called "a great perhaps." That thing where you lay down your mushy, mortal self, along with all your friendships and family ties, all your unmet ambitions, and all those bucket list items you still haven't kicked.

You trade it in for a baby you will never get the chance to meet, and then move on to . . . well, that's the real sticky wicket, isn't it? For whatever we may believe and for however strongly we may believe it, none of us really knows for sure. Maybe heaven. Maybe hell. Maybe nothing.

That's the dilemma. And in case you're still thinking it's too easy, let me give this triple lindy its final twist:

What if the question wasn't hypothetical?

My name is Carter Ross. I am a thirty-three-year-old newspaper reporter whose baby is almost fully baked inside my fiancée's womb. Up until now, I have led a charmed existence of upper-middle-class ease and American suburban comfort, a life where I have been able to avoid difficult choices such as this and blithely assume my continued survival.

But in forty-three hours, that's going to come to an end. Because in forty-three hours, I am going to find myself outside a room with two dangerous people in it. They're both armed. Neither is a stranger to killing. The moment I confront them, they're going to shoot at me. They will be firing from a few feet away, a distance from which they can't miss. I might be able to stop one of them from pulling the trigger. I will not be able to stop both. My protection will be nothing more than two thin layers of cotton.

And the only way to save my baby—who will be denied his first breath if I don't do something—is to walk in and take the bullet.

CHAPTER 2

There are certain young men nature wires for action. They are swift, lean, fearless, thoughtless. Good sense and impulse control have been sacrificed in favor of speed and acceleration.

The two young men huddled on opposite sides of a Newark, New Jersey, street corner, in the dark of a Newark, New Jersey, night, were two such specimens. They wore ski masks, the preferred headdress of criminals the world over. Their guns were drawn. They were about to make what could have been called a textbook approach, except textbooks were not written about this sort of undertaking.

The signal to attack was a quick, sharp whistle.

The first assailant angled in from behind the driver's side door, moving in a low crouch. The second came from the other side of the street, toward the passenger side door, in a run that was more upright.

The object of their assault, a top-of-the-line 2015 Jaguar XJ, was the lone car stopped at a red light that silently conducted traffic at the intersection of Mulberry and East Kinney streets.

The car's driver was a pudgy banking executive named Kevin Tiemeyer, weary from a late night out with colleagues. He had diverted his attention from the road in front of him to his iPhone, where he jabbed out a quick text to his wife: "Just left. Home soon. Love you."

He hit send. His wife would later tell the police she received it at 1:02 A.M.

The Jaguar's engine idled in a soft, low purr appropriate for a machine named after a great cat. The car was five months old and Tiemeyer loved it—loved the way it handled like an extension of its driver's will, loved the buttery softness of the leather seats, loved showing it off at the club.

His wife had fretted that they shouldn't be buying any new car, much less one with a $79,220 sticker price. The twins entered college next year. If he really wanted to replace his aging BMW with a Jaguar, fine, but couldn't he at least pick a less extravagant model? Or maybe a nice, low-mileage preowned one?

Tiemeyer told her not to worry so much, countering with an acronym the kids taught him: YOLO. You Only Live Once.

As Tiemeyer lifted his head from his iPhone, his peripheral vision registered the movement of the second man, the one coming in from the passenger's side. His reaction was instinctive and involuntary, an immediate racing of the heart and a dilating of the pupils. Those suddenly wide eyes took in the man's gun and ski mask, which was navy blue.

Then came three insistent raps on the driver's side window. Tiemeyer's head whipped around. Another gun. Another ski mask, this one black.

"Out of the car. Out of the car. Out of the car."

Black Mask delivered the order in rapid staccato. He had not bothered to pull open the door. He knew—from his rather extensive recent experience in this line of work—that the Jaguar, like nearly every luxury car manufactured for sale in the United States during the last ten years, automatically locked its doors the moment the vehicle exceeded five miles an hour.

It was a safety feature that, in this case, would do little to keep Kevin Tiemeyer safe.

"Let's go, let's go," Blue Mask urged.

Tiemeyer shifted the car into park. He took one last wistful gander at the beautiful crafting of the Jaguar's interior, shoved open the door, and swung his feet over to the pavement.

"Just relax," Tiemeyer said. "You can have the car."

"Damn right we can," Black Mask said, backing off slightly to give his victim room to disembark. "Now move it."

Tiemeyer stood.

"Put your hands where I can see them," Black Mask ordered.

Tiemeyer stood and raised his hands in the air. The sleeves of his suit jacket slipped down a few inches in the direction of his elbows, exposing the Rolex that adorned his left wrist.

"We'll take that watch, too," Blue Mask said, coming around from the other side of the Jag.

Tiemeyer stiffened.

"Wait, that's not . . . that's not part of the deal," he said.

"Hell it ain't."

"No, no. You take the car, that's it. That's—"

"This ain't a negotiation," Blue Mask said, tilting the gun sideways and taking a few more steps forward. "Give me the watch, fool."

"No, you don't understand. This . . . this was my grandfather's watch."

"Yeah? Well, it's mine now."

Black Mask had backed up further, jerking his glance between the two men, then up and down the street. It was still empty, but there was no guarantee it would stay that way. The Newark Police Department was overworked, but that didn't mean it was nonexistent. He started talking to his partner, "Come on, man. I told you last time, you can't keep doing this. Let's just—"

"Give me the watch," Blue Mask shouted, his eyes wide, his nostrils flaring. The barrel of his revolver was now a foot away from Tiemeyer's face, aimed at his forehead.

"Leave it," Black Mask said.

Attempting to exploit the rift, Tiemeyer started with, "Look, sir, can't we just—"

Blue Mask fired twice. Tiemeyer dropped, his expensive suit and his body crumpling simultaneously.

Blue Mask knelt by the man's inert form, unfastened the Rolex and pocketed it.

"Come on, let's go," he said.

From the small oval mouth hole of his black ski mask, the other man unleashed a stream of urgent profanity. He finished with, "Are you crazy?"

As both men scrambled into the Jaguar, Black Mask added, "You can't keep dropping bodies like this, man."

Blue Mask offered no explanation beyond, "He was disrespecting me."

It was said later that the only sin Kevin Tiemeyer committed was stopping for a red light in Newark.

That was not entirely true.

But given that the sentiment was uttered a few short steps away from his closed casket, it hardly seemed like the time or place to quibble.

CHAPTER 3

You don't stop for red lights late at night in Newark, New Jersey. At least you don't if you know what's good for you.

In some neighborhoods—I'll be kind to the city I love and call them affluence-challenged—stopping at a red light after a certain hour signifies one of two things. One, I would like to buy drugs, please sell them to me; or, two, I am stupid, please rob me.

And in case my big talk about taking bullets and saving babies has made me sound brave, heroic, or especially glutted with courage, I should probably correct that misapprehension straight off: I'm basically a chicken. Have been my whole life. Proud of it.

As a self-respecting, dedicated chicken, I regularly performed what my colleagues and I at *The Newark Eagle-Examiner* referred to as "the Newark Cruise." When you saw a red light, you slowed well ahead of time, giving yourself room to ease up to the light while still maintaining a rate of speed that would deter anyone from approaching your car. Your hope was that it turned green while you made your steady advance. If you reached the intersection with the light still red, you took a glance around to make sure nothing was coming and then you gunned the engine.

But you never stopped.

The nuances of this widely practiced piece of civil disobedience were explained to me on my first day at the *Eagle-Examiner* by a sagacious veteran copy editor, who had survived many a late-night drive home by putting minimal wear on his brake pads. When I asked him whether he was worried about getting a ticket, he just laughed. Back then, I was a twenty-four-year-old cub reporter, wide-eyed at the prospect of working for New Jersey's largest newspaper. I didn't understand what was so funny.

Nine years later, having scaled to the position of investigative reporter and acquired a bit of my own wisdom, I get it. Even on the rare occasions when Newark's Finest did stop you for running a light in the small hours, it was mostly to ensure that you weren't using the city streets as a pharmacy or that you weren't armed for an insurrection.

Once they determined you had neither guns nor drugs, they let you go. Police in Newark had better things to do at that time of day than ticket minor traffic scofflaws.

Red-light cameras, installed at the insistence of a crusading celebrity mayor a few years back, had complicated matters slightly. By forcing drivers to come to a complete stop, they turned numerous city intersections into a carjacker's version of a turkey shoot.

The other issue at play was the growing sophistication of vehicle antitheft systems. Whereas yesterday's car thief could mesh together a few wires and quietly misappropriate your motorized carriage without bothering you, the current generation must forcibly take it from you with the keys still in it.

The irony is lost on no one: two innovations meant to improve safety and deter theft have had the opposite effect, leading to the proliferation of a crime than is far more violence-prone and confrontational than the one it replaced.

It's the law of unintended consequences, and in Newark it remains well enforced. Over the past five years, carjackings in Essex County, which includes Newark, had more than doubled. It had gotten to the point where the county, with eight hundred thousand people, was on pace to finish with some five hundred carjackings for the year. That's an average of more than one a day, nearly three times as many as all of New York City despite having just one-tenth of the population.

What made Newark such a carjacking hotbed was at least partly genetic. The city was the grand theft auto capital of America during the eighties and early nineties. Boosting cars was in its DNA. Newark's delinquents were well-schooled on the subject of car-swiping, whether it was to resell, for a joy ride, or to have a "clean" vehicle in which to commit another crime.

But there was also a lot of geography at play. These days, cars have VIN numbers etched in all kinds of hard-to-reach places, making them difficult to unload domestically. Hence, the more sophisticated carjacking rings sold their merchandise abroad— mostly Africa and some of the more lawless parts of Asia.

The easiest way to get their product to that marketplace was via the Port of New York and New Jersey, which straddled Newark and Elizabeth. If you stole a car in Brooklyn or the Bronx, it could take you an hour—and two bridges—to get it there. That was a risk. If you stole it in Manhattan, you had to go through a tunnel. That was suicide.

If you stole it in Newark, you could have it loaded onto an ocean-bound container ship before the police even knew to start looking for it.

I don't want to say we at the *Eagle-Examiner* had been ignoring this particular criminal epidemic. We had done a few perfunctory stories about the problem, dutifully reporting the numbers. But at the clinging-to-life anachronism that is a state-wide daily newspaper, gone are the days when we had a fully staffed city desk and stuffed-to-the-seams suburban bureaus, ready to report on any threat to our readership. We had been forced to prioritize and up until one Tuesday morning, those priorities had not included deep inquiry into the subject.

The tragic shooting of a man named Kevin Tiemeyer during an apparent carjacking-gone-wrong was about to change that. It had happened too late at night—or I guess, technically, too early in the morning—to make it into any of that day's print editions.

But by the time the New York metropolitan area awoke, hungry for its daily helping of bad news, the shooting in Newark had become breakfast. And it had the look of lunch, dinner, and beyond, a meal that would be served until the public's appetite for it was fully sated or until we ran out of stuff to report, whichever came last.

As I hastily donned my workaday reporter's uniform of pleated slacks, a button-down shirt, and a patterned tie—all of which I carefully selected by closing my eyes and reaching into my closet—I listened to the latest on an all-news radio station. It began the top of the hour with the Tiemeyer story.

At this early stage, when the police had little information and were giving out even less, there wasn't much to report beyond the bare details of Mr. Tiemeyer's demise. He worked for United States Kinship Bank, better known as USKB, one of those huge banking conglomerates that seemed to have tentacles in anything that involved money. He drove a Jaguar. He was a married father of two who lived in tranquil Scotch Plains and had the misfortune to choose the wrong way home. A press conference was scheduled for later that morning. More details would be forthcoming.

I am aware there are critics of "the media"—two words some folks can't seem to say without a sneer—who would accuse us of sensationalizing crime simply to sell papers, attract Internet traffic, or drive ratings. These, after all, are the metrics with which we woo the advertisers who ultimately pay our salaries. I'm not naïve enough to deny that our news judgment is influenced by certain financial imperatives.

But I always remind these sneering detractors what's behind

those paper sales, Web clicks, and TV eyeballs. It's that a large portion of the public—AKA citizens, AKA people, AKA you and me and, yes, even those media-bashers—are more likely to tune in for bad news than for good news. We have the statistics to prove it,

In that way, the media is really just a mirror, one that reflects back at people the things they most want to see. Believe me, if puppies and flowers pulled ratings, that's all you'd see on your nightly news. But the fact is, many ships made safe transatlantic crossings in April 1912, but more than a hundred years later people are still yapping about the *Titanic*.

So I was unsurprised when I received a text from my editor, Tina Thompson, requesting an audience as soon as I saw fit to report for work.

"I still don't understand why he didn't just do the Newark Cruise," I texted back.

I received her reply as I drove in. "I know. Law-abiding citizens are the worst."

The newsroom was mostly empty when I arrived, not because I was particularly early, but because this has become its natural state in recent years. Where once this large, open space was filled with clusters of seasoned reporters vigorously making New Jersey safe for democracy, there are now vast seas of unused desks, vacated by staff reductions that never seemed to end.

The paper's corporate owner had recently announced plans to "downsize our footprint"—read: cram us somewhere cheap and sterile—and sell the building that had served as the *Eagle-Examiner's* home for more than half a century. It had yet to find a buyer. Apparently, there is little call for time-battered office space.

If and when we have to move, I will do so with sadness. But, in truth, only a little. The things I love about this business—the adrenaline rush of deadline, the feeling that the stories I wrote mattered, the privilege of putting out a newspaper alongside my lovably malcontented colleagues—will survive no matter where we happen to be plying our craft.

For the time being, my personal empire was still a desk in the far corner against the wall, where no one could sneak up on me. I annexed it a few years back when the veteran reporter who owned it took a buyout. Staff reductions do have their benefits.

Tossing my bag next to my chair, I stuffed a fresh reporter's pad in my pocket—TOPS is my preferred brand—and presented myself at the glass-walled office of Tina Thompson.

At the relatively young age of forty-one, Tina's sharp news instincts, intelligence, and drive had allowed her to rise to the lofty title of managing editor for local news. It was a big job, inasmuch as local news dominated the *Eagle-Examiner*. Among her responsibilities were the city desk, the suburban bureaus, and me.

She was also nine months pregnant with my child. If you think a man with my fancy vocabulary and expensive education ought to have been smart enough to avoid such a tricky arrangement, you've clearly never been introduced to Howard Gardner's theory of multiple intelligences. It's the idea that one can be gifted in one area while deficient in another.

On the bell curve of managing romantic relationships, I am several standard deviations below the mean.

I started talking as soon as I entered her room.

"Just to make sure I've got this right, we have basically been turning a blind eye toward the rising tide of carjackings that have been terrorizing this city for, oh, call it four years now," I said, selecting the chair closest to the door. "But the second a rich white guy from the suburbs gets killed, we're going to start hopping around like a one-legged man at an ass-kicking contest?"

Tina set down her midmorning beverage snack—some kind of gruesome-looking wheatgrass concoction—as she replied.

"Not to answer your question with a question, but let me ask you something: how many poor black guys get murdered in this city every year?"

"About a hundred, give or take."

"Very good. Now, how many rich white guys suffer the same fate?"

"I see your point," I conceded. "I just get tired of being so predictable."

"Okay, so come up with something different."

I had been thinking about this on the way in. "Let's broaden our reporting a little."

"Broaden it how?"

"Look, of course our hearts go out to the Tiemeyer family. What happened to him is awful and unconscionable and I can't even imagine what they're going through right now. But somewhere out there, there's another family who also recently lost a loved one in a carjacking. And they're going through the same thing. Yet because that loved one checked a different box on his census form, his death was more or less ignored. That family is probably waking up this morning, looking at all the fuss over someone else, and saying to themselves, 'What the hell?' Let's actually make them feel like our hearts go out to them, too. We'll give readers what they want about Kevin Tiemeyer, but we'll show them what carjacking normally looks like, too."

Tina shifted her weight. After a brief delay, her belly shifted with her. For a borderline exercise addict who welcomed refined sugars like Gandhi welcomed knife fights, it had been quite an adjustment to have a stomach that moved on its own. The benefits—the extra body in her curly brown hair, the glow to her skin, the prime parking at chichi grocery stores and so on—had not come close to compensating for the discomfort.

"Okay," she said after a brief pause. "Just don't get too frothy with whole black-white thing. Let's just let people draw their own conclusions—or not, if they chose to. As long as you play that part down the middle, I think Brodie will go for it."

By Brodie, she meant Executive-Editor-for-Life Harold Brodie. He was well into his seventies but showed no signs of relinquishing control of the paper. It was starting to occur to folks that perhaps his retirement party and his funeral would be simultaneous events.

"Okay," I said. "Who else is working this?"

"Investigative reporter Carter Ross, I'd like you to meet our carjacking beat writer, Carter Ross."

"Seriously?"

"Which one of our forty-seven layoffs did you not get the memo on? I've got Buster Hays going to the press conference later this morning and working the cops for a daily story. After that, it's all you, big guy."

"You can't even toss me an intern or two?"

Tina went to her computer and consulted the spreadsheet that told her what her reporters were allegedly doing. My species, which is to say experienced journalists who were above the age of thirty and made a living wage, was teetering on the brink of extinction. Most of the names on her screen were eager twenty-something interns whose paychecks barely covered the payments on their student loans.

"I could give you Chillax," she said.

Ah, Chillax. Some months ago, at the beginning of his time with us, this particular intern—actual name: Sloan Chesterfield—was being harassed to file a story by one of our famously over-stressed managing editors. The young man looked up and, invoking that noxious combination of the words "chill" and "relax," said, "Dude, just chillax, okay?"

He would never again be referred to by another name within the confines of the *Eagle-Examiner* newsroom.

"Yeah, I guess he'll do," I said.

"Good. By the way, did you get the crib assembled?"

Tina and I were still living apart. I had attempted to propose to her at least five times in the last nine months. I say "attempted to" because even though I bought the ring, cleared it with her parents, felt it with all my heart, and fell to one knee, she pulled me back to my feet each time. She said I wasn't allowed to ask the question yet.

This didn't hurt me. No. Don't be silly. Because I'm a guy and I don't have feelings. Or at least that's what I read in a magazine once.

Besides, she had promised to move in with me once the baby came. In this results-oriented world of ours, I figured that would constitute a happy ending. We had decided my two-bedroom house in Bloomfield was a better fit for our new family than her one-bedroom condo in Hoboken. Hence, I was in the final stages of turning my former junk room into a nursery.

"Yep," I said cheerfully. "Crib is all put together. Only ended up with five extra parts."

Tina looked stricken.

"Kidding," I assured her.

"And your phone is charged?"

I patted my pocket and nodded. Tina was now in her thirty-eighth week. Lately, the moment my battery dipped one bar below maximum, I went scrambling for a plug.

"How is C-3PO today?" I asked.

Like many couples, we had given our fetus a cute-to-us nickname. Tina had originally called him "Carter Jr." When I exercised veto rights over that one, she started calling him "Carter the third" instead. The shorthand for that became C-3, which soon morphed into C-3PO. At Tina's thirty-six-week checkup, our obstetrician, Carly Marston, told us the baby was upside down, so I briefly lobbied to change it to "Breach Baby." But by that point C-3PO had already stuck.

We did not have indisputable video evidence that he was a boy—we decided not to find out—but Tina was convinced she was carrying my male heir.

"He woke me up with a kick to the spleen this morning and I think he's broken about three of my ribs since then. We're going to have to sign him up for Ultimate Fighting lessons. Between that and having to pee every twelve minutes . . . speaking of which—"

She lifted herself from her chair. Tina was about five foot nine and still lithe everywhere except for her bulging midsection. She was starting to resemble a python who swallowed a pig, not that I planned to share this particular observation with her.

Instead, I went with: "So I'm not allowed to propose to you, but I am allowed to tell you how gorgeous you are, right?"

"You're the sweetest man alive even when you're full of crap," she said as she swept past me. "I read the other day where a pregnant woman was described as being 'great with child.' Let me tell you, there's nothing great about any of this."

CHAPTER 4

After watching Tina waddle out—and, no, I do *not* utter the word "waddle" in her presence—I turned my attention back to the newsroom, where I located the intern who would soon become my charge.

Chillax was long-limbed, probably about six foot three, two inches taller than me. His hair was longer, too. And whereas mine was neatly parted on the left side in a way that was pleasing in a Kiwanis Club kind of way, his light brown mop sort of flopped down his forehead until it half-covered his eyes and then curled in back. He had a good set of shoulders on him and when he wore short-sleeve polo shirts he made me feel like I really needed to spend more time at the gym. I'm quite sure he did not have trouble attracting the interest of the fairer sex.

"Hey, Chillax, what's going on?" I said as I walked up to him.

"Hey, what's up, brah?"

I am unsure what youthful genius decided that the word "bro"—which is already an effective truncation of the word "brother"—needed to be further morphed so it was pronounced like a woman's undergarment. But it was my hope this linguistic pioneer developed some affliction that was similarly annoying. Like a permanent hangnail.

"We've been assigned to work on a story together," I said. "There was a man killed in Newark last night during a carjacking."

"Yeah, dude, I just saw it on the Web site and I was like, 'No way, brah, that sucks.'"

"Like a Hoover," I assured him. "And our friends on the other side of the river have taken note, so it's pretty much you and me against every media outlet in New York on this story. Think you can handle that?"

"Tchya," he said, sitting up a little straighter and getting, uh, stoked.

"All right. There's a police presser in a little while that Buster Hays is covering. Why don't you work the human interest angle. Get us some background on who this guy was, get a sense of what the family is going through, get friends and neighbors saying nice things about him, that sort of thing. I want people to feel like they know this guy when they're done reading what we write."

There is no understating the importance of a good victim in any newspaper crime story. The fact is, violent crime is an abstraction to much of our readership. It is often written about using statistics—what's on the rise, what's dropping, what might be causing the fluctuation, and so on. I suppose such reporting has its uses, though in my observation, not many readers tear up over data points.

You need to shake them a little bit to make them realize crime was something that could and did happen to people just like them. You had to turn the victim from a faceless casualty into an actual human being.

"I don't have an address yet, but they live in Scotch Plains," I said. "You know how to use LexisNexis, yes?"

LexisNexis is one of those inventions that proves God loves reporters, a database that captures nearly every shred of public information available on private citizens.

"Yeah, dude, I'll LexisNexis the hell out of that," he said. "It's going to be you and me against everyone. It'll be like this time, back in college, I played lacrosse at Gettysburg—"

How surprising.

"—and we were going against Washington College for the Centennial Conference championship. We were down, like, thirteen to six and it looked like we were totally out of it. It was like, you know, unsurmountable odds."

It would have been even more impressive if the odds had been insurmountable, but I didn't want to interrupt his story.

"Anyway, Coach gave us this talk before the start of the third period that was, like, you know, all *Braveheart* and stuff. And then we went out and totally kicked their asses around the field and ended up winning fifteen-fourteen. Dude, we can do the same thing now. It's going to be totally sickety."

As a practiced reader of context, I was able to infer that "sickety" was a word with a generally positive connotation. My suspicion was confirmed when he held out a fist for me to bump. I tentatively knocked my knuckles against his.

"Pwsssh!" he said, spreading his hand like it had just exploded.

"All right, just go out there and get us some good color."

"Yeah, color," he said, running a hand through his hair. "Like . . . his house was brown, his yard was green?"

I just laughed. "Sorry. Color is newspaper jargon. It means details that make a person or a scene come alive. So if someone you're writing about is, I don't know, a hoarder or something. You don't come out and say they're a hoarder. You say their living room is filled with stacks of ten-year-old newspapers. Get it?"

"Oh, yeah, brah. Scoopsies."

"Scoopsies?"

"Yeah, you know, like when you scoop up the pill with your spoon and you're like, 'Raaaah, dude!' Scoopsies."

I stared at him for a moment. "Do you come with a Berlitz book?"

"Huh?"

"Never mind," I said.

"All right. Let's shred this mother."

We swapped cell phone numbers and made more noises about the mothers, fathers, and grandmothers we would crush, scoop, and shred. At some point, perhaps far in the future, Chillax would figure out that life was a bit more complex than a lacrosse game where someone was keeping score. But there was still time for him to come to that epiphany.

With Chillax on his way, I returned to my desk and set about working the other half of the story I had in mind. Which meant I needed a second carjacking victim.

The majority of these crimes do not end violently. I didn't know how far back in our archives I would need to go to find one that did. Unfortunately, my search didn't take long.

We had written a story two weeks earlier about a man named Joseph Okeke, a fifty-four-year-old Central Ward resident who was shot and killed during a carjacking on 15th Avenue. The make and model of his car were not mentioned. The story offered no other details, saying only that police were seeking more information about the crime.

The piece appeared on Page B3, which is where we put crime briefs. It totaled 117 words and appeared only in our Essex edition. There was no follow-up, nothing more in our pages to memorialize the life or death of Joseph Okeke.

This meant, more than likely, the crime was still unsolved, the perpetrators still on the loose. Law enforcement agencies were not in the habit of issuing press releases to notify the public they had made no progress on an investigation and likely never would.

But, just to make sure, I picked up the phone. Ringing the Newark Police would be a waste of my time, especially when it was being besieged by calls about Kevin Tiemeyer. So I dialed the number for the Essex County Prosecutor's Office instead.

Another unexpected advantage of working for the Incredible Shrinking Newspaper is that our large-and-growing diaspora of former employees has not, for the most part, vanished. It has simply gone into PR. A not-insubstantial number of the spokespeople at the agencies we regularly cover are former colleagues, and the Essex County Prosecutor's Office was no exception.

They were, in general, a pleasant lot to deal with, because they knew what we were after and how to help quickly. Also, we had logged enough hours together in the newsroom to enjoy a comfortable rapport.

Hence I started my call to the Essex County Prosecutor's Office spokeswoman with: "Hey, Kathy, it's your bed man."

Kathy Carter and I had a running joke about how a woman needed two men in her life: a "head man," who could listen to her and make her feel understood, and a "bed man," who could fulfill her more primal needs.

"Oh, baby, you know you couldn't handle this even if you could have it," she crowed. "How many times do I have to tell you, you're head man material, and there's nothing wrong with that."

"Don't underestimate me just because I'm a skinny white guy. I'm a double threat. Give me a chance."

She just laughed. Kathy was an attractive African American woman, but she was twenty years older than me and very happily married. Besides, I had all I could handle in that department at the moment.

"So what can I do for you today, my head man?"

"I'm calling about a carjacking in Newark from two weeks ago. Vic's name was Joseph Okeke."

I pronounced it in the proper Nigerian way, which I only

knew because Newark had a large ex-pat Nigerian population. For the record, it was: O-KAY-kay. I then spelled it for her.

"You sure you shouldn't be asking about a different carjacking?" she said.

"Oh, we've got someone working Kevin Tiemeyer. I just get tired of crime only mattering when it happens to someone of European ancestry."

"Well, look at you, Brother Carter. I always said you had some color in you."

"Yeah, so why is it I still can't dance?"

"Oh, honey, I said *some* color. You need a lot more color if you want to do that."

Now it was my turn to laugh.

"Okay, Joseph Okeke," she said, and I heard her keyboard clattering. "It happened in the four hundred block of Fifteenth Avenue at eleven fifteen P.M. Police and EMTs went to the scene and found Mr. Okeke unresponsive and bleeding from a head wound. Uh, let's see here, what else . . . no charges filed, obviously. . . . Huh, that's strange."

"Pray tell."

"I'm just looking at our investigator's notes, which are in the file," she said. The Essex County Prosecutor's Office had its own detective force that ran things down for attorneys as they prepared their cases. "It says, 'Insurance disbursement not made.'"

"Anything in there about why not?"

"Nothing I can see. But sometimes insurance companies like to play games, denying a claim for a silly reason or just delaying it enough that the people making the claim eventually get frustrated and go away."

"Can I ask your investigator what he meant?"

"It doesn't sound like he'd know anything. We don't really have anything to do with insurance companies. That's a civil matter. You might have a better chance with the surviving family.

These insurance companies, you wouldn't believe some of the stuff they pull, denying and delaying legitimate claims. If I was a young, crusading newspaper reporter with a lot of vinegar in me, I'd definitely do a story about it. Start with the family and see what they say."

"What kind of family did Mr. Okeke leave behind?"

I heard papers shuffling. "Uh, let's see . . . wife and three kids."

"Oh, man," I said, cringing even as I wrote it.

"Sounds to me like that's your best bet," Kathy said. "If there's an insurance company giving a widow a tough time, I'm sure she wouldn't mind giving them a little bad press."

Kathy was thinking like a reporter. I'm told by dearly departed colleagues it's a hard habit to break. Just because you took the girl out of the newspaper didn't mean you could take the newspaper out of the girl.

She continued: "Let's see . . . what else . . . police are looking for two suspects, both black males in their teens or twenties."

"Really? So there was actually a witness? Tell me more, tell me more."

The police hadn't mentioned that to us, naturally. Nor should they have. Being a known witness to a violent crime in a place like Newark put you on the short list to be the next man down. But Kathy knew that better than anyone. Witness intimidation was one of the biggest ongoing headaches at the prosecutor's office.

Kathy sputtered, now clearly remembering that the demands of her current vocation sometimes conflicted with the inclinations of her previous one.

"Come on, you know I won't put the guy's name in the newspaper," I urged. "I'm a head man, not a headless man."

She groaned. "I know, I know. I just can't have that come back at me. You know I love you, Carter, but I signed over my buyout check to cover college tuition. I need this job."

"Okay, okay," I said. "What kind of car did Mr. Okeke drive?"

She told me it was a 2015 BMW 328i, a sleek little sedan. Not that my reporter's paycheck has me window-shopping Beemers, but I could guess it was roughly a $35,000 vehicle.

It allowed me to make a few assumptions about this victim. As I said, Newark has a large and growing population of Nigerians. As a group, they were doing well for themselves. Their children, in particular, were knocking it out of the park. I'd love to know what portion of college scholarships that had been reserved for African American kids from Newark were being won by the children of Nigerian immigrants.

It was one more indication that while you couldn't ignore skin color, skin color alone did not explain the full extent of the struggles faced by African Americans whose families had been here since the days of slavery. To watch these first- and second-generation Nigerians—they sometimes called themselves "non-American blacks," though that term is controversial—come here and establish such a different trajectory for themselves suggested to me that whatever was going on was a lot more complicated than complexion.

"All right," I said. "Anything else?"

"Uh, let's see," she said, and I listened to her shuffle papers some more. Eventually, she said, "Not really. I'll tell you—and I don't mean to sound like I'm making excuses for anyone—but these carjackings, they're tough. We've had a task force working on this for a few years now and they've got some good people on there. But it's like a game of whack-a-mole. You shut it down one place and it just pops up somewhere else. And it's virtually impossible to guess where it'll happen next."

"Noted," I said. "And depending on which way this story goes, it might be good to get your boss on the record saying something like that. Much as it's fun to play rope-a-dope with you guys, that'd be a good perspective to have in whatever we write."

"Okay. Let me know if you want me to get him on the phone with you."

"Will do."

Kathy and I said our goodbyes and I leaned back in my chair. I let my eyes focus on nothing for a second or two.

In my line of work, we are around violence and its aftermath so frequently it's easy to become inured to its horrors. A certain thickening of the skin is inevitable, even healthy from a psychological standpoint. But I always promised myself I would never allow myself to become completely calloused.

So I spent a moment or two thinking about the terrifying last moments of Joseph Okeke: a life, fifty-four years in the making, destroyed in mere seconds; a family of five, shattered by its reduction to four; a sacrificing of human life for two thousand pounds of metal and plastic.

I've always believed my job as a reporter was to help make sense of the world, to explain its workings, to lend understanding to its complexities. I knew I was perhaps doomed to failure in this instance. There was no making sense of the senseless.

But I owed it to myself, to our readers, and even to the ghost of Joseph Okeke to at least try.

I sighed. Then I went back to work.

I had a witness to find.

CHAPTER 5

The four-hundred block of 15th Avenue turned out to be a short stretch of worn asphalt bounded by cracked sidewalks that glistened with shards of broken glass.

The neighborhood was the usual hodgepodge of new town houses, old multifamily homes, and vacant lots. Always vacant lots. During the early and mid-twentieth century, when it was a center of manufacturing, Newark's population peaked just above 440,000. Its current population was around 277,000. Sometimes I thought every one of those 163,000 lost residents was represented by a vacant lot.

If I have, so far, made Newark sound like some kind of desolate malefactor's playground, with thieves lurking around every darkened corner, I don't mean to. Any balanced presentation of the city must report that the majority of Newark citizens are nice folks, just trying to get along. And there has been a lot of hard work by some tireless heroes—teachers, preachers, cops, street activists, nonprofit workers, civic-minded businesspeople, philanthropists, and the like—who together have brought the city a long way from its nadir in the late seventies and early eighties.

During the daytime, when those people are enjoined in the task of making Newark a better place, when there are grandmas on the front stoops and schoolchildren in the streets, when the ordinary people are going about their regular business, I maintain you're as safe in Newark as you are in any city.

The problem is, the daylight hours eventually come to an end. That's when a certain subspecies comes out to run roughshod over the social contract. The stereotypes are, unfortunately, quite accurate: most of them are young men from single-parent or no-parent families that gave them very poor starts in this world; they have been failed by schools, churches, and the other institutions that might have saved them; and, let's not neglect personal responsibility here, they have also failed themselves with their attitudes and general outlook on life.

They lack respect for the statutes of a country they don't feel has given them a fair shake. They experience their first brushes with the law under the auspices of a juvenile justice system that they quickly come to view as a joke, one that gives them baby taps on the wrist for the very adult violence they inflict. They live in a culture where spending a stint in prison is so common it comes with virtually no social stigma and is, if anything, seen as a rite of passage into manhood. Therefore, they have little regard for the penalties that might deter them from wrongdoing.

As long as this subspecies is allowed to rule the night, Newark's recovery will only get so far.

There was a brief glimmer of hope a few years back when the city went more than a month without a murder—forty-three days, to be exact. It proved to be a mirage. That murder-free month was followed by a bloody summer. Then a looming structural budget deficit finally caught up with Newark, the city had to lay off 13 percent of its police force, and it was right back to the bad old days.

I go back and forth between having pity for the young men who cause this mayhem—because so many of the factors that have contributed to their circumstances are not their fault—and being really, really pissed off at them for all the damage they're doing to themselves, the people around them, and the city I love.

Naturally, being nocturnal creatures, they were all in hibernation as I cruised to a stop along 15th Avenue. I disembarked from my trusty-but-battered, six-year-old Chevy Malibu—so chosen because its value to carjackers only exceeded forty dollars when it had a full tank of gas—and looked around.

The north side of the street mixed vacant lots with new town houses in a way that reminded me of a gap-toothed grin. On the corner of the south side was a brick building that contained a storefront gospel mission and a bodega that would need renovation before it could even be considered shabby.

At the end of the block, hanging over the intersection at Tenth Street, was the traffic light that likely cost Joseph Okeke his life.

On the far side of the intersection there was a three-family house and yet another vacant lot. Given the sightlines involved, the witness I was looking for could have been a resident of the house. Or it could have been someone who happened to be walking along.

But more likely it was someone working in the bodega. It was called Goncalves Grocery No. 4 and its state of disrepair did not exactly fill me with the urge to visit Goncalves Grocery Nos. 1-3.

I pushed through a glass front door that had been scratched to the point of opacity and found the lone clerk sitting on a stool in a bulletproof box whose door he had left open.

The man was young and Hispanic, with a stocky build and a wide, dark brown face. He did not seem to note my entry, despite the clanging of some bells that had been tied to the door. His focus was on a glossy magazine with bold Spanish headlines.

"Hey there," I said and smiled.

He glanced up, then did a double take, because I wasn't what he was expecting. Then I saw the look, that suspicion mixed with wariness that I, as a well-dressed, officious-looking white man, often prompted in neighborhoods like this.

He mumbled something I didn't quite catch, but I decided to launch into my spiel anyway.

"Hi, I'm Carter Ross. I'm a reporter with the *Eagle-Examiner*. I'm working on a story about a carjacking that happened outside your store on a Sunday night two weeks ago. Were you working that night, by any chance?"

He just smiled at me thinly. And that's when I realized he had no clue what I was saying. I once again found myself cursing that I hadn't taken Spanish in school.

Being a reporter often calls on you to call upon hidden talents that you had never thought you'd have to bring to bear in your professional life. In this instance, it was a gift for improvisation that made me a formidable force in Ross family charades competitions.

If this kid had seen something, I could attempt to cajole a Spanish-speaking reporter out here to interview him. But I first had to figure out if it was even worth the trouble.

I walked across a linoleum floor that was worn through to the plywood in spots and grabbed that day's *Eagle-Examiner* from a rack of newspapers.

"I work," I said, then waved the newspaper in the air, "for this. *Comprende?*"

He nodded.

"I write articles," I said, pointing to one of the columns of text and then pantomiming writing motion.

"Two weeks ago," I said, holding up two fingers and then making them hop backward, like a time-traveling bunny. "On Sunday night. There was a man who was driving his car up to the traffic light outside your store."

I was gripping my imaginary steering wheel with two hands and making engine revving sounds. Then I applied my pretend car's brakes with a high-pitched, "*Vvvvvvv . . .*"

"When he stopped, two men with guns came at him," I said, forming my thumb and forefinger into the universal symbol for a firearm.

"They were carjackers," I continued. "They stole his car. Then they shot him. Bang bang bang. And he died. Did you see it happen?"

I emphasized the "you" by pointing to him and the "see" by gesturing to my own eyes. I had spoken slowly enough that I was sure he'd follow me, but he was still giving me this blank stare, like I might as well have been speaking an invented language that was a mix of Bahasa Indonesian and Vulcan.

Which wasn't right. I may look like a clueless white guy, but this wasn't my first bodega. No matter what their native tongue, the clerks had to know enough English to assist their customers, many of whom were monolingual African Americans. Older immigrants sometimes never learned any English beyond that, but the young brain is a sponge for language. Even if this fellow had just left Guatemala or Ecuador or wherever it was he had come from, he would have picked up some English by the time he made it this far north.

I thought back to a story one of the paper's sportswriters once told me. It was about a rookie from the Dominican Republic who had just been called up to the Yankees. All the reporters wanted to interview him, but he shyly explained that he *no habla inglés*. Then, a week later, the reporter happened to walk past the same player outside the team hotel. There was a flock of comely women gathered to flirt with famous ballplayers. Suddenly, the young man spoke near-flawless English.

This kid was playing me the same way. I just needed to give him the right inducement.

I sighed and said, "Look, we really need this story. What if I told you I'd give you a thousand dollars if you talked to me?"

He brightened immediately. "Yeah? You serious? Okay, Papi, what you want to know?"

"No, I'm not serious," I said. "I'm not even allowed to pay

for information. It's unethical. I just wanted to get you to admit you actually speak English."

"I never said I didn't, Papi. You're the one who started all that 'Me Tarzan, you Jane' stuff."

It took ten minutes of negotiation to determine he was, in fact, working during the night in question. And, while he wouldn't admit it at first, I was getting the sense he might very well have been the witness I sought.

But I wasn't going to press him for it immediately. Young Carter Ross might have done that. The Carter Ross who faced impending fatherhood with crow's-feet developing next to his eyes knew better.

This kid's first impulse when presented with an unfamiliar circumstance was to elude it. You don't back a sidestepper like that into a corner and force a confrontation. You dance him around the room first.

So I set a pleasant, meandering waltz going in my head and, slowly, got his story out of him. His parents had come from Ecuador during the early nineties, part of the first wave of immigrants from that country to settle in the North Ward.

A year after they arrived, they gave birth to their first child, the young man who now stood in front of me. He wouldn't give me his name, so as the conversation progressed, I started calling him Johnny. I told him it was in honor of Johnny Weissmuller, the guy who played Tarzan.

Johnny seemed to like his new name and it helped forge a little bond between us.

I learned after a few minutes that his English was actually better than his Spanish. The glossy magazine I had seen him reading was an effort to improve his faculty with a language that his parents had made every effort not to speak at home. He said he hoped to learn it well enough that he'd be able to teach his kids someday.

It was interesting he was already thinking about his children. I'm fairly certain I didn't when I was his age. That had changed—being one phone call away from fatherhood tended to do that to a guy. I subconsciously patted my phone in my pocket as Johnny continued talking.

Johnny didn't mind admitting his parents were here illegally. Having been born here, he was a full-fledged American citizen. And the day he turned eighteen, his father gave him $20,000 he had painstakingly scrimped and saved, a few bucks a day over the course of many years of day-laboring.

The father couldn't legally own property. The son could. Johnny used the money to buy Goncalves No. 4. They did not own the other Goncalves locations and it seemed, in any event, the original Mr. Goncalves was out of the picture. They had decided to keep the name for the same reason the previous owners had: it was cheaper than buying new signage.

The store was open from 7:00 A.M. until midnight every day, and between Johnny and his father, they split the 119 hours it was open each week. On Saturday, Johnny's father worked from opening to close. On Sunday, Johnny returned the favor. That way, each man got to take off one day a week.

They had been doing it that way for three years now. And they had saved up enough money that, when Johnny's little brother turned eighteen in a few months, they were going to buy a bodega for him, as well.

It was the American dream, thriving amid all the vacant lots and bulletproof glass.

And that's when I realized I had my angle on Johnny. For all his streetwise skepticism and *no habla* guardedness, there was optimism to him and his story. Unlike so many of the people around him, he believed tomorrow was going to be better than today.

He and his family were working hard to better themselves. Someday, his children would go to college. His grandchildren would go to medical school. People who think the Ecuadorians

33

are going to be any different from the Italians, Irish, Germans—
or any of the other great waves of immigrants who made places
like Newark their first stop—simply haven't been paying attention to their history books.

I steered us back in the direction of Sunday night two weeks
previous.

"Look, I can't pay you for your story, but I can tell you that
when we write about this sort of thing, it makes it harder for
people to ignore it. I'm not talking about the people around here—
you guys have no choice in the matter. I'm talking about law-
makers in Trenton, about rich people who think the problems of
the city aren't their own, about people who can make a difference
with their influence and their dollars. It doesn't happen instan-
taneously, but I'll tell you if you keep those people engaged long
enough, they help turn the tide.

"So," I concluded, "I guess the question you have to ask yourself is: What kind of city do you want to live in? What kind of
city do you want your kids to live in? You want to it be a place
where you get killed for driving a nice car or a place where the
good people fight back?"

He was nodding by the time I got to the end. "Yeah, Papi. I
get it. But you can't use my name. Those 'bangers know I snitched
and they come back and shoot up my store."

"What makes you think it was gangbangers who did it?"

He gave me a look like the answer should have been obvious. *Don't they do everything around here?*

"I wouldn't want to put you in that kind of danger," I said.
"Look, at this point, I don't even know your name, so I can't very
well put it in the paper. Let's keep it that way and you can talk to
me without worrying about things."

"Okay," he said, nodding again. "What you want to know?"

"What did you see?" I asked, hauling my reporter's notepad
out of my pocket so I could get it all down.

He pointed to the barred window behind him, one that gave

him a view of the whole intersection. "I watched the whole thing, Papi. This dude in this BMW rolled up and stopped and these two guys with guns jumped him."

"Did you get a look at the guys?"

"Not really. They had ski masks on. A black one and a blue one. There's a streetlight, so I saw them, but they never took off their masks."

That meant Johnny would make a pretty lousy witness if this thing ever went to trial. But that didn't make him useless from my standpoint. I wasn't there to convict anyone beyond a reasonable doubt. I was there to tell a story.

"Okay, so the guys jump him. What next?"

"They made him get out of the car."

"Describe the man for me."

Johnny paused to consider this. "He was older. Not, like, super old. But, you know, like middle-aged. He was black. Real black. Like Africa black."

"How do you know? African Americans are sometimes very dark-skinned, too."

"Yeah, but this guy dressed different."

"What was he, wearing a dashiki or something?"

"No, no. But you know, their clothes, they're not ghetto. They're like white people clothes, except they're cheaper-looking, you know?"

I nodded. It meant Joseph Okeke was probably buying knockoff designer stuff, which was available in abundance in downtown Newark. The garments were meant to look like Ralph Lauren or Tommy Hilfiger, but there was always something a little off about them. Even a sartorially disinterested person such as myself could see it.

"All right. So he got out of the car. Did he raise his hands like it was a stickup?" I asked. These kind of details would help me bring the thing to life on paper later.

"No. He kept them down."

"Did he look nervous or . . . how did he act?"

"I don't know. He just got out of the car. Then one of the guys, the guy in the blue mask, he came around to him and started pointing the gun at him. He started yelling at him. And the guy started yelling back. It was like they were having some kind of argument or something."

"What were they saying?"

"Couldn't hear it. The door was closed," he said, looking in the direction of his front door.

"Okay, what next?"

"Well, the guy in the blue mask, he just shot the guy. I was like, 'Oh, damn.' I mean, he didn't need to do that to take the guy's car, you know?"

"Then what?"

"I don't know. Soon as they started shooting, I ducked. I don't need to be catching bullets, Papi. I stayed down until I was sure they were gone."

I nodded, trying to envision the scene as Johnny had described it. I asked a few more follow-up questions, trying to elicit more details. Johnny wasn't being evasive. He just didn't seem to remember any. It sounded like the entire scene hadn't taken more than two or three minutes.

When I felt like I had gotten everything useful, I put my pad back in my pocket and made the offhand comment, "This is why I don't stop for red lights in Newark late at night."

And that's when Johnny hit me with this little nugget: "That's the weird thing, Papi. The light wasn't red. It was green."

"He stopped for a green light," I repeated. "You sure?"

"Yeah."

"Why would he do that?"

"I don't know," he said, and left it at that.

Stopping for a green light. Maybe there was some other reasonable explanation for it. The problem was, the only person who could say for sure was no longer around to do so.

CHAPTER 6

Blue Mask woke up not to an alarm or to a loud noise, but to a cat. The thing belonged to his great-aunt. It kept trying to curl up in the crook of Blue Mask's leg, which was located on the great-aunt's couch, which the cat very much viewed as being her property.

"Get off me," Blue Mask growled, jerking the cat off the couch with a sweep of his leg.

The cat landed softly on her feet and offered one disdainful meow before stalking off.

Blue Mask rolled off his side. There was a lump in his pocket that had been pressing—painfully, he now realized—into his hip. He sat up, rubbing away the ache from the lump.

He had been sleeping on his great-aunt Birdie's couch for three weeks now, ever since he maxed out of his latest sentence, a fifteen-month stretch for possession of controlled dangerous substances with intent to distribute. Or, in the shorthand of a criminal justice system overwhelmed by such young men, simply, "CDS."

It was his sixth such conviction as an adult and his second time going to prison for it. That, along with a trilogy-length juvenile record, had been sufficient that most of his family had given up on him.

There were only two people still willing to take him in. One was his sister. But he didn't like messing with her. She used to 'bang, just like him. She had since gone legit. And now she had this tendency to get all up in his business, telling him he should go back to night school and get his GED, ridiculous stuff like that.

That made Birdie his only other option. She was a small, withered woman who ate sparingly and had a nose that sort of looked like a beak. Hence the nickname. Birdie got up in his business, too. But she was older and more easily misled. Besides, she just wanted to lead him to Jesus. Blue Mask would take Jesus over night school every time.

The deal he and Birdie had struck was that he could sleep on her couch if he attended church with her on Sunday mornings and Bible study on Thursday night.

Oh, and he wasn't allowed to sell drugs anymore. But that was fine with Blue Mask. Thanks to his black-masked associate, who had recruited Blue Mask the day after he returned home from prison, he had found a much more lucrative occupation.

Working a drug corner in a place like Newark was no kind of get-rich-quick scheme, anyway. The margins were just too low. Selling a dime bag for six bucks when you bought it for five, you could bust your ass all night and be lucky to come away with fifty dollars for the effort.

But jacking cars? That was good money. He and Black Mask had split a $3,500 payout for the Jaguar.

It took more nerve, yeah. But Blue Mask was discovering he had plenty of that. He might not have understood exactly why, except during his latest stretch, one of the social workers had told him he had something called antisocial personality disorder.

Blue Mask was so intrigued he went to the prison library to learn more. Apparently, it meant he didn't feel remorse for his bad acts like most people did. He was what the literature referred to as a "sociopath." An outmoded term for it—the one Blue Mask liked better, because it sounded cooler—was psychopath.

Within that diagnosis, there was a range of possibilities. Some sociopaths were little more than unrepentant litterers and glib liars who never committed a serious crime. Others could shoplift or swindle old people out of their retirement accounts but would draw the line at physically hurting anyone. Others could go all the way to murder and not feel a thing.

Blue Mask now recognized he was one of those. And, what's more, he read an article that said he was probably born that way. It made jacking cars feel like a calling, one he hoped to be able to continue for as long as possible.

Already, in just three weeks, he was close to having saved enough to get his own place. It was in an apartment complex known not to get too particular about credit checks or employment requirements, so long as you could pay three months in advance. It was, for that reason, a pretty sketchy place. But Blue Mask was fine with it. As long as it had a bed—and lacked a damn cat.

Blue Mask swung his legs off the couch. He reached for the remote control and turned on the television, still rubbing where the lump had been.

Whatever station Birdie had been watching the night before was starting the top of the hour with a news update. Blue Mask was about to change the channel, until the screen flashed up with a familiar face.

It was the white dude. The one Blue Mask had shot the night before. He cranked up the volume as some scrawny Hispanic *chiquita* with a frowny face pretended to be concerned as she read from a teleprompter.

"Authorities are searching for two assailants, described as black males in their late teens or early twenties, and are asking anyone with information about this crime to come forward. The reward for information leading to an arrest is now at fifty thousand dollars after—"

Blue Mask couldn't even hear the rest. And it wasn't because he was suddenly nervous about being caught. No, no. He was too busy being thrilled.

Thrilled by the attention. Thrilled by the sense of power. Thrilled that someone thought catching him was worth fifty freakin' grand.

The first time he killed someone, that old African guy, no one had seemed to notice. He had seen a poster in the 'hood, announcing a reward of $10,000. That was all.

Chump change. Blue Mask much preferred it this way. But it did present him with a practical issue, one related to some merchandise he had to offload. Not the car, of course—that was already gone, to a place where Black Mask had promised no one would be able to find it.

It was the lump in his pocket: a Rolex watch, the one he had taken off the white dude. He had to fence it before things got too hot.

CHAPTER 7

With a better grasp on how Joseph Okeke died, it was time for me to learn more about how he lived.

The browser on my phone told me that Mr. Okeke last laid his head at an address just a few blocks from Goncalves Grocery No. 4. And so, having departed that purveyor of processed food products, I was on my way there when my phone rang.

Now, I am a newspaper reporter. I spend half my life talking to people—people who frequently chose to initiate contact by calling me. Sometimes I feel like my phone is an invasive parasite that has attached itself to my ear and refuses to let go. People phone me all the time, all day long. But did I think about any of the two hundred of them who might have a perfectly prosaic reason for doing so?

Of course not. Lately, every time my phone rang, some instinctive part of my brain started screaming: *This is it. It's daddy time! Go! Go! Go!*

It certainly didn't help that C-3PO was a breach. Tina had done some exercises to get the baby flipped around. Then the doctor had tried to turn him under guided ultrasound. Nothing worked. The little guy was stubbornly clinging to the butt-down position.

We had a C-section scheduled for next week. But Dr. Marston had given us a scary lecture about how we couldn't dawdle if Tina went into labor between now and then. In particular, if her water broke and the baby started coming out, there were two very real dangers.

One was head entrapment, which is exactly what it sounds like: the baby's body is able to slip out, but the head—the largest part of the baby—gets stuck when the cervix closes around it.

The other, even more dangerous, possibility was something called a "cord prolapse," which is what happens when the umbilical cord comes out first and then gets ruptured as the rest of the baby tries to come out behind it.

Dr. Marston warned us that cord prolapse can lead to "very negative outcomes." I'm sure most parents would leave it at that. But, being journalists, Tina and I asked what, exactly, that meant.

"It means you have less than ten minutes to get the baby out or it will die," Dr. Marston said.

"Oh," we said, both nearly feeling our hearts rip in two.

Hence, I was already short of breath as I fumbled to fish out my phone, my hands shaking so badly I was struggling to accomplish that simple act. I was sure it was Tina. Her water had broken. Her contractions were coming on fast and furious. There was a bulge of umbilical cord sticking out and—

Then I actually looked at the screen on my phone, which read, "Thang, Sweet 2."

My vitals instantly returned to normal. I considered not answering. Again. Sweet Thang was one of the interns who had briefly graced our newsroom with her youthful vitality. She had been given her molasses-laden moniker by some troglodyte on the copy desk because she was a bright-eyed, honey-haired, recent Vanderbilt graduate; and because our copy desk has a sense of humor.

She had two phones because she could talk down the battery of one in less than a day. During her time with us, we had been through a lot together. First, I nearly deflowered her (don't ask). Then we settled into a platonic relationship that included a near-death experience while reporting on a corrupt house-flipping scheme.

Sweet Thang considered me a mentor, and I let her maintain that illusion. The truth was, she had been a gifted natural reporter long before she met me. I had nothing to teach her. Her only weakness as a reporter—that she led with her heart, every time—was also her greatest strength as a human being.

She had since moved on to a calling to which she was perhaps better suited, joining the do-gooder brigade in Newark's nonprofit community. As was often case in that resource-deprived world, she wore as many hats as her head could fit, plus a few more. She served as spokesperson, marketing manager, events coordinator, donor wrangler, grant writer, envelope stuffer, and floor sweeper. She had been trying to get me to write a story about her employer for a while now. I had been avoiding her calls, strategically returning messages to her office voice mail when I knew she wouldn't be there.

It was certainly nothing personal, because I liked her a lot. It was just this allergy I had to doing puff pieces.

But with those reporter's skills of hers came a certain amount of tenacity. Her once-weekly calls had become twice-weekly calls. I had no doubt she would keep ratcheting up the pressure until I at least came up with a good excuse to put her off. And since I now had that excuse—a breaking story about the carjacking that was suddenly all the news in our fair region—I decided it was time to take her call.

At the last second before it went to voice mail, I answered with, "Carter Ross."

"Hey, Carter, it's Lauren McMillan."

"Hey, Sweet Thang! How's, the job going at, uh—"

I had blanked on the name of the nonprofit she now worked for.

"The Greater Newark Children's Council," she filled in. "We're doing fabulous, thank you. We just had our third annual Greater Newark Five-K and Kid's Fun Run—I sent you an invitation, by the way, but I didn't see you there—and we're deep into the planning to roll out our Brick City Baby Brick Buy. You know, buy a brick to support the babies of the Brick City? It goes toward prenatal care and new mother education. Catchy, isn't it?"

"Uh-huh," I said. My Malibu was closing in on a row of tidy, roughly ten-year-old town houses, one of which had until recently been home to Joseph Okeke. I hoped Sweet Thang would hurry up and get around to pitching whatever story she was selling so I could politely blow her off and get on with my day.

And then she obliged me. "But what I really wanted to talk to you about was our Chariots for Children campaign. It's a great program where people donate their cars to us and we help them maximize their tax write-off. And then we either rehab the car and use it in one of our programs or we sell it off. So it's a win-win slash win-win-win. But what we really need is some publicity. The Kars for Kids people have totally dominated the market, and we need to get word out there about Chariots for Children. We have this big media push starting next week and we were hoping you could kick it off by writing a story for Sunday's paper about the—"

"Yeah, that sounds great except I've got this big story right now and—"

That's when she dropped the bomb: "Uncle Hal said you'd be able to do it."

Her father and "Uncle Hal"—AKA Executive Editor Harold Brodie—were best pals. It was how Sweet Thang had gotten her internship in the first place. And it put me in something of a bind. Among the Ten Commandments of working for the *Newark*

Eagle-Examiner, "Thou Shalt Not Piss Off Harold Brodie" is very near the top.

"You, uh, talked to Brodie, huh?"

"Yeah, we chatted on Saturday. He and Madge were over for dinner at my parents' house."

Madge. As in Brodie's wife. The only first name I had ever addressed her by was "Mrs."

"Anyhow," she continued, "I've got a kid who would make for the perfect anecdotal lede. He's really sweet and he's just a love. Oh, and he's really photogenic, so don't forget to put in a photo assignment. We can start with interviewing him, because he's the kind of kid who the program will help. Then I'll show you where they rehab the cars. We have our own repair shop, which means more of your automotive donation ends up helping kids in need. Then I can hook you up with some donors if you want, so they can talk about how easy it is. We have this one woman, who—"

She continued prattling on for a while. I was now parked in front of Joseph Okeke's former domicile, which meant I was officially wasting time yapping with Sweet Thang. I had to get out of the conversation somehow. The problem, of course, is that Stalin had gulags that were easier to escape.

"Sweet Thang," I said at last.

"I know, I know, you have to go, sorry," she said. "You know me. I just get so passionate about helping these kids. So many of them come from families that have, like, nothing. But they're so bright and so full of energy, you feel like if someone just gave them a little bit of a chance, they'd—"

"Sweet Thang!" I said again.

"Sorry, sorry. Can I put you down for a visit to our place tomorrow morning at ten? I'll send you an e-mail with all the details. And I'll bring bagels. It'll be fun."

"Sure," I said. "I'll see you tomorrow morning. Ten o'clock."

I hung up and sighed. I decided to be proud of her, for being so good at her job. Because it beat the alternative: admitting that I had been thoroughly outmaneuvered by my former intern.

The erstwhile home of Joseph Okeke was among a row of adjoining town houses, all of which had their own tiny patch of a front yard. The yards were enclosed with these low, black iron fences.

They were mostly decorative. Almost anyone could hop over one. But they still served a subtle purpose. Criminals are like water: they seek the easiest path. Sometimes it didn't take much of an impediment to divert them elsewhere.

I opened the gate and strolled up the front walk. The unit appeared to be two bedroom, which made me wonder how a family of five was fitting into it.

As I rang the bell, I tried to anticipate what the Okeke family would be in the midst of experiencing. Their patriarch was now two weeks gone. They probably buried him a week ago. They were now in the part of the grieving process where the funeral was over, the extended family was gone, the neighbors had stopped sending casseroles, and things were getting back to what was supposedly normal. Except, of course, nothing felt normal anymore.

In my experience with grieving families, this was usually around the time the hurt really started to set in. To add to the pain, there may have been an insurance company trying to weasel its way out of its fiduciary responsibilities.

I rang the doorbell again, getting the sense it was empty. Then, from next door, a woman dressed in nurse's scrubs peeked out.

"He don't live there no more," she said, then added matter-of-factly; "he died."

"I know. I'm looking for his family."

"They don't live with him. You with the city or something?"

"I'm a reporter with the *Eagle-Examiner*. I'm writing a story about him. Did you know him?"

"Some."

I pulled out a notepad, took down her name, and went for the open-ended question approach. "I'm just trying to get a sense of what kind of guy he was. Tell me about him."

She considered this. "I don't know. He was pretty quiet, you know? We shared a wall but I never heard a peep from him. He was always very polite. He had lived here maybe three years? He and his wife were divorced."

Which explained the two-bedroom pad.

"What kind of work did he do?" I asked.

"I'm not sure. I know he went on business trips sometimes, because he'd tell me he'd be gone for a week or two and ask me to look after his place. I think he traveled back to Nigeria, but I don't know what he did there. He didn't talk about that much."

"What did he talk about?"

"His kids, mostly. He was really proud of them. Two of them were off at college. The other one is a senior at Arts High. That's where I went to school, so he would tell me about her a lot. She won a lot of awards for stuff. Maryam, her name is. He was always like, 'Maryam, she was student of the month. Maryam, she won the National Merit scholarship.'"

The woman had mimicked a deep bass voice and a West African accent for the last part, doing her best Joseph Okeke impersonation.

"What about the other two kids?" I asked.

"I don't know. One's a boy, the other's a girl. That's all I know."

"Do you know where they go to college?"

She shook her head. "I'm sure he mentioned it, but I'd just be guessing."

"Did the kids ever come over here?"

"No. I asked him about it one time and he said he and his wife had decided that the kids ought to have one home, not shuttle back and forth between two all the time. They wanted the kids to have as stable a life as possible. If he wanted to see them, he went over there."

"He and his wife must have been on okay terms, then?"

"I don't know. I never met her."

I looked down at my notebook, as if this would help me divine more information.

"What else. Any hobbies?"

"He was in Rotary. I know that. He'd talk about that sometimes . . ."

Her voice trailed off, then she added, "I'm sorry. I wish I could help more. I kind of have to get going to work now. I didn't really know him that well. I mean, we were neighbors and I liked him. We'd chitchat every now and then when we saw each other, but that was it. It's sad what happened to him. This city—"

She finished the thought with a headshake. Sometimes there was nothing more to say.

"I appreciate your help," I said, then let her go.

She had given me a solid start. And I was liking the picture of Joseph Okeke that was emerging. Here, of course, I was just being selfish on behalf of my story. As I said earlier, having a good victim is absolutely critical. Nothing ruined an otherwise heart-rending tale faster than an unsympathetic victim. If Okeke had been some man-about-town divorcé, trolling around in his BMW 328i while he blew off his family, it made him less of a tragic figure.

But that's not who he had been. He was an involved father, bursting with pride for his children. He was a businessman who was working hard to provide for his family. He was living a peaceful, quiet life.

And he was in Rotary. I liked that detail. Rotary had an element of business networking to it, sure, but it was a primarily a service organization. He helped others in his community.

It not only made him more sympathetic, it also made him more accessible to suburban readers: Joseph Okeke wasn't just another black guy who got killed in Newark, he was a Rotarian.

And, okay, maybe he wasn't the perfect victim. But he was an acceptable victim. I definitely could have done worse.

I returned to my car and worked my phone a little until I found Okeke's previous address, which corresponded to the current address of one Tujuka Okeke. It was closer to downtown, in an area of Newark known as University Heights.

It took less than ten minutes to get there. This is one of the advantages of traversing a city whose neighborhoods are 163,000 people short of peak population. Traffic in the middle of the day is usually pretty light.

What I found upon arrival was a detached, single-family home with a short driveway. It also had a fence around it, but this one was more than merely decorative. It was high enough to keep out the riff-raff, assuming the riff-raff weren't Olympic high jumpers.

There was one car in the short driveway. It was a Toyota, maybe three or four years old. Not as savory a piece of bait for a carjacker.

I parked just outside. Again, I tried to prepare myself for what might await. Mrs. Okeke was not, technically, a widow. But it sounded like the split had been . . .

Well, let's be clear: the term "amicable divorce" ranks alongside "jumbo shrimp" as an oxymoron. And yet it seemed Joseph and Tujuka Okeke had parted ways in as friendly a way as possible, at least civilly enough to allow what sounded like effective coparenting. And he was still the father of her children. She would have all kinds of conflicting emotions. I was willing to bet the mention of his name would bring tears to her eyes. The mention of his insurance company, meanwhile, might bring fire.

The gate had been left open, so I walked up the front steps and rang the bell. It was answered by a woman with jet-black skin and short-cropped graying hair.

"Ms. Okeke?" I said tentatively.

"Yes?"

"My name is Carter Ross. I'm a reporter with the *Eagle-Examiner*. I'm working on a story about Joseph."

She didn't cry. Instead, her face twisted at the mention of the name.

"I have nothing to say about him," she spat.

She gripped the door like she was about to give it a high-velocity ride back to its jamb. Then she thought better of it for a second and added, "Joseph is a fool. For what he did? He got what he deserved."

Then she slammed the door in my face.

Amicable divorce, meet jumbo shrimp.

I stayed on the stoop for another five seconds, my finger poised near the doorbell. Then I thought better. I wasn't giving up on Tujuka Okeke. But I was going to let her breathe a little bit.

Retreating down the steps, I returned to my Malibu and got it rolling back toward the newsroom. Clearly, postmatrimonial relations between the Okekes had not been as cordial as I thought. Still, I wondered if there was something more going on. What foolish act had he committed? And who deserves death-by-carjacking?

It was another small thing about Joseph Okeke—like stopping at a green light late at night—that set my easily addled brain to work.

CHAPTER 8

I was five minutes away from the office when my phone rang again. This time I managed to interrupt my daddy-delirium before it reached seizure stage and pulled my phone—more or less calmly—out of my pocket.

Then I saw where the number was coming from and started shaking all over again. It was someone in the newsroom.

This was it. Tina had doubled over with a contraction just outside the copy desk and grabbed the nearest phone to demand I take her to the hospital.

"Carterross," I said breathlessly.

"Carter, my boy, it's Harold Brodie. How are you today?"

Hearing our executive editor's voice, which kept getting higher and breathier as he worked his way deeper into his eighth decade, did little to soothe my nerves. Despite my multitude of journalism awards and a job status that was as close to tenure as a modern newspaper gets, I was still as afraid of Brodie as I had been as a rookie on probation.

Especially because I couldn't figure out why he was calling. I doubted Tina would ask Brodie, of all people, to inform me she had gone into labor. And he wasn't really the type to just pick up the phone and call reporters. As a long-ago military veteran—his first combat was at Antietam, I think—he believed in preserving chain of command. He always had the reporter's frontline editor deliver his wishes. This was the first time in my nine years at the paper he had ever called me directly.

"Hi . . ." I began, and then I paused. I had never quite summoned the nerve to call him by his first name, but didn't want to sound like a dork—or, worse, an obsequious kiss ass—greeting him by his last name. So I just added a "there." It came out: "Hi . . . there."

"I had a quick question for you, if you don't mind," he said.

"Sure. Shoot."

"You and Tina Thompson, you are . . . well, how would you describe your relationship? She is pregnant with your child but you are not married, is that right?"

Oh, lord. Where was he going with *this*? And could I get away with telling the executive editor to mind his own damn business? Then I thought back to that all-important commandment: Thou Shalt Not Piss Off Harold Brodie.

"Well, yes, sir, I'd say you've got things right."

"And you are betrothed?"

"I'm still working on that part, sir."

"I see. Well, I had a little proposition for you. Madge and I, we like to . . . well, back in the seventies, they used to call it 'swinging.' I'm not sure what the term is these days. But you're such a good-looking fellow and Madge has always been sweet on you. I was wondering if you'd like to come over and have a 'go' with her tonight while I get to know Tina a little better. I have to admit, I've always had a bit of a fetish for women at the very end of gestation. There's just nothing quite like the lactate-swollen bosom of an expectant mother. I bedded my first pregnant woman when I was barely more than a boy myself. Why, in my salad days, they used to call me 'mommy hopper.'"

I paused to be sure, then said, "Hi, Tommy."

Tommy Hernandez was our city hall reporter. He was twenty-five-years-old, of Cuban heritage, and as gay as backstage at the Tony Awards. How it was he had developed a spot-on impersonation of our arrow straight, Caucasian, septuagenarian executive editor was something of a marvel. He used it as a weapon whenever it suited him.

"Aw, man! I had been working on that one all morning," he whined. "Where did I lose you?"

"At 'swollen.' I feel like Brodie would have gone with 'engorged.'"

"The devil is always in the details," he said.

"No, the devil is you. Though I must say you are delightfully twisted."

"Thank you!" I could practically hear him beaming through the phone.

"Anyhow, does this call have a purpose beyond putting a seriously disturbing image in my head?"

"Yeah, actually, I wanted to make sure I wasn't stepping on your toes with something I'm working on."

"What's that?"

"There's a rumor the Nigerian government has decided that there's a sizable enough Nigerian population in northern New Jersey to establish an embassy here in Newark," he said. "We're not sure if it's a satellite to the main embassy in New York or if they're going to move their whole operation here. Either one is news."

"Yeah, sure."

"Anyhow, I was talking to Kathy Carter at the prosecutor's office about it and she said, 'What is this, Nigeria day?' And then she said you had talked to her about something related to Nigeria, but then she wouldn't say what because it was on background."

"Yeah, I was just asking about a Nigerian ex-pat who came down with a bad case of carjacking."

"Oh," is all he said. "And rumor is you're working on this with Chillax?"

"Yeah, why?"

"Because he's the most adorable intern in the history of interns, that's why. His face has that lost little boy thing going on, but his body is . . ." Here, Tommy made a noise that suggested he had just bitten into a really good steak, then finished with: "He is sooooo tasty."

"Yeah, and you're sooooo dreaming if you think he likes boys."

"I don't know about that. You know what position he played for his college lacrosse team, right?" Tommy said, but didn't wait before delivering the punch line, "Long stick middy."

I just shook my head. "How are things with Glenn, anyway?"

Tommy had been dating my cousin Glenn for the last eight months. My family had long suspected Glenn was gay—inasmuch as he looks like Brad Pitt yet had remained without a serious girlfriend for many years—but it wasn't confirmed until he and Tommy ended up hooking up at my sister's wedding. They had been together ever since.

"He asked over the weekend if we could take a break," Tommy said.

"Ouch. Sorry."

"I couldn't even take it that personally. I just don't think he's ever going to settle down," Tommy said. "But I'm not sure I can talk to you about it. You're not an impartial party."

"Okay," I said. "Well, switching back to Nigeria, why were you calling the prosecutor's office about the embassy thing anyway? What would they have to do with it?"

"Oh, this is the good part," Tommy said. "The only reason the whole thing came to our attention was that the land in question had a little problem with it. They were doing some site preparation but they had to stop work because they came across skeletal remains."

"Cool," I said. Macabre as it may be, there are just certain phrases that tweak a newspaper reporter's antenna. "Skeletal remains" is one of them.

"Yeah, well, we'll see. All Kathy would tell me is that the remains had been taken to the medical examiner and it was under investigation."

"Still. Could be good. Let me know, okay?"

"You got it," and then Tommy switched to his Harold Brodie voice, "and I'll try to remember that Tina's breasts are engorged, not swollen."

"Yeah, you better keep your voice down," I said. "If she hears you talking about her like that, it's your face that's going to end up swollen."

Despite my better judgment, I completed my drive to the newsroom, parked in our garage, and walked back into the office.

The reason for my visit as noontime neared was Buster Hays, our resident rumpled crank. Buster was our cops reporter. Except calling him a cops reporter was like calling Pavarotti a shower singer. Much as Buster annoyed me with his general grumpiness, he was an unparalleled virtuoso at working law enforcement sources. He understood how to speak their language, how to get them to talk to him, and how to wheedle things out of them they wouldn't say to anyone else. He had a series of well-stuffed Rolodexes that contained roughly forty years' worth of contacts, all of whom seemed indebted to Buster for one reason or another.

When Buster went to a press conference, he usually came back with at least a half-dozen tidbits that he had gotten on the side, stuff no other civilians knew. He seldom shared this information with readers, which was part of the reason the cops didn't mind giving it to him.

That might seem to be counterintuitive—what would a reporter possibly gain by withholding something from the paper?—but the real art came in leveraging off-the-record information from one source to get on-the-record stuff from another. Buster was a magician at it.

Alas, the only way to get Buster to share these extra crumbs of information he had gathered was to go into the newsroom, genuflect a bit, and then grovel. What kind of mood he was in dictated just how much you'd have to prostrate yourself.

I walked up his desk humbly, head down, eyes averted, as a harijan might approach the maharajah.

He was slumped in his chair, wearing one of his stain-splattered paisley ties, beating on the keyboard with savage ferocity. Buster's manual-typewriter-tuned fingers never had quite mastered the relatively light touch required by computer keyboards.

Before I could even open my mouth, he looked up and, in his hundred-and-toidy-toid-street Bronx accent, declared, "Beat it, Ivy, I'm busy."

I am actually not a product of the Ivy Leagues. But I had stopped correcting Buster on this misconception. At my alma mater, Amherst, we pity those graduates of the Ancient Eight and try to be quietly unassuming about the superiority of the undergraduate education we received.

"I didn't even ask you for anything yet," I protested.

"Yeah, but you're about to. I can tell by the way you're slinking."

I sat on his desk—which I knew he didn't like—and fired my first salvo. "If you don't help me, I'm going to tell Tina you called her fat."

"Go ahead. Your head will be rolling down the hallway before she even thinks about taking off mine."

Thwarted, I attempted the attract-the-flies-with-sugar approach. "Okay, okay. If you help me, I'll get you a sandwich from the deli down the street. Whatever you want."

"You trying to kill me? The pastrami in that place is older than I am."

Back to lemons. "Fine. You're forcing me to pull out the big guns. If you don't talk to me, I'm going to tell Chillax that for all your crustiness, you actually love nothing more than to mentor young people; and that therefore he ought to hang around you and tell you college lacrosse stories because you looooove college lacrosse stories."

Buster grimaced. He tolerated the interns even less than he tolerated me. And the fact was, with most of the reporters in their forties and fifties having been chased away, I was closer to his age than most anyone else around.

"Jesus, Ivy, you're like a bunion. Fine. The only thing I got that wasn't part of the presser is that they actually caught the demise of Kevin Tiemeyer on camera. For whatever good it did them."

"Why isn't that good?"

"The shooter was wearing a mask. Good luck putting that on a poster. 'Wanted: a black guy wearing a blue ski mask.'"

"A *blue* ski mask," I said.

"Yeah, what does that matter?"

I told him about the man who pulled the trigger on Joseph Okeke, who was also wearing a blue ski mask. It was, possibly, a coincidence. But it didn't feel that way. It felt more like there was a carjacker who was escalating his level of violence. The longer he went without being caught, the worse it was going to get.

"So what's your deal, Ivy, you're trying to be the Hunter Thompson of carjacking?" Buster cracked. Even though he reached maturity at a time when the so-called "New Journalism" was invented, Buster was a strict proponent of the old kind: everything was straight news, double-sourced, and written in inverted pyramid style with a minimum of imagination or creativity. He scoffed at anything narrative, experiential, or longer form.

"You know we've been ignoring this problem too long," I countered. "And if there really is a lunatic on the loose who gets his jollies shooting people while stealing their cars, that's something our readers ought to know."

Not even Buster could dispute that one.

"All right," he huffed. "I got a guy on the carjacking task force who said he'd notify me whenever there was a new hit. I think they want to turn up the heat on the county to give them more resources. I'll cut you in the loop."

"Thanks, Buster," I said. "Damn decent of you."

"A fifth of Ballantine's," he said, summoning the name of his go-to scotch brand. "My desk. Tomorrow morning."

CHAPTER 9

Blue Mask didn't know the guy's real name. No one, besides perhaps his momma, knew that. To everyone who dealt with him—which included no small part of Newark's criminal underworld—he was the Fence. Or just Fence, for short.

His place of business was alongside Chancellor Avenue in the South Ward, in an ancient concrete block warehouse that didn't have a front entrance. With that Rolex-shaped lump secure in his pocket, Blue Mask went around to the back and pressed the doorbell.

Five grand. Blue Mask needed to get his nut to five grand. Then he could get the hell out of his great-aunt Birdie's place and put down the deposit on his own. No more church. No more cat.

He was, as of his current accounting, at $4,217. That was the amount hidden in the brown paper sack he had stuffed in a high shelf in Birdie's kitchen, behind the cornstarch, in a place where a little bit of a thing like Birdie couldn't reach. It wasn't an ideal stashing place. But he couldn't figure any place better, and he didn't want to be walking the street with so much cash. Yet another reason he needed his own crib.

He had earned more than five G's in his three carjackings, of course. But a man had expenses. And needs. Especially a man who had spent his last fifteen months in prison.

But that was taken care of now. So he was focused on getting the most he could for the watch. A new Rolex went for, what, twenty? Twenty-five? Blue Mask didn't know. But he figured a used one would go for ten. Which meant he might be able to work Fence for three grand. Maybe five.

The door buzzed. Blue Mask entered. Halfway down the hallway, there was a window—probably bulletproof—with a small slot. Blue Mask stood in front of it. The slot opened. From inside, he could see the Fence, a black guy so obese that he even had fat rolls on the back of his neck.

"Yo, 'sup, Fence?"

"Ain't got time for small talk, young 'un. What you want?"

"Got a Rolex, yo."

Blue Mask went into his pocket, pulled out the watch, dangled it where Fence could see it.

"Yeah. So?"

"It's a real one," Blue Mask said.

"What do I care?"

"Wanna buy it?"

"Lemme see it."

Blue Mask held it closer. Fence's first response was to belch. His second was to say, "I can't sell that."

"What you mean? It's a *Rolex*."

"Let me ask you something, young 'un, what time is it?"

Blue Mask was automatically reaching into his pocket to check the time on his cell phone.

And then he stopped himself. He got the point.

"Yeah, see?" Fence said. "Maybe—maybe—if it was a new model, I might be able to unload it on some Wall Streeter looking for a status symbol. But there ain't no call for no busted ass old model like that."

Blue Mask just stood there.

"You ought to start rippin' off people with better taste," Fence said, laughing at his own joke.

Fence started closing the window slot.

"Wait, wait," Blue Mask said. "It's gotta be worth *something*."

He hated the desperation he heard in his own voice. But he also didn't have a choice. He didn't know anyone else who took merchandise like this. And going downtown and trying to sell it on the street was not an option. There were too many "Rolexes" there already. And if, on the off chance, he got stopped by a cop who knew it was a real Rolex—and who started wanting to know where this one came from—things could get bad in a hurry.

"I could melt it down for the gold," Fence said. "Give you three hundred for it."

"*Three hundred?* Come on, man, it—"

The window slot began closing again.

"Fine, fine. Three hundred."

Blue Mask shoved the watch through the slot. Moments later, three wrinkled hundred-dollar bills came back out.

"Next time, go after some lady and get yourself something sparkly," Fence said. "Brothers don't wear no watches no more. But ladies always like jewelry, you feel me?"

CHAPTER 10

Since I was in the newsroom anyway, I decided to check in on my unborn child and future wife.

When I met Tina Thompson nine years earlier, she was the nightside assignment editor and I was interviewing for a job at the *Eagle-Examiner*. Through some unusual circumstances, we ended up working together on a story that resulted in the resignation of a powerful state senator.

I wish I could report that my initial attraction to her came when I stared deep into her eyes and my soul recognized its own mate. Alas, I'm not a Hallmark card writer. I'm a guy. So mostly what drew me to her was that she was smoking hot. It was only slightly later that I discovered she was also feisty and fun, smart and—I know this makes me something of a newspaper nerd—incredibly good at her job. What can I say? Competence is sexy.

I'm also drawn to challenging women, and in that regard I really hit the jackpot with Tina. She's like the LSATs, MCATs, and GMATs all rolled into one.

I would have thought that nine years after our first meeting, she would be wearing my ring on her finger, not telling me to keep it stowed in my pocket. But at least so far, events had conspired against that.

For a number of years, back when we were both unpregnant, she wanted me to be the father of her baby—but nothing else. I kept pressing for an arrangement that involved more than just insemination. She refused, citing the demands of her job and a history of wrecked relationships. We dated other people, even as she continued to press for procreation.

Eventually, she gave up on the idea of parenthood with me or anyone else, declaring that motherhood had passed her by. Then a seemingly innocent dinner at her house, along with the unintentionally sloppy administration of her birth control pills, wound up with her getting pregnant. I was still debating whether I should someday tell the kid he owed his existence to a leg massage that got out of hand.

Since then, we have returned to our historic roles. I keep pressing for a committed relationship. She keeps putting me off. I realize this sort of makes me the girl in this whole scenario. Yet I'm secure in my manhood and have not let her hesitance deter me from thinking we'll eventually be together. The way I see it, I beat out roughly thirty million other guys on the night I was conceived. I've had a winning attitude ever since.

Tina had just returned from the eleven o'clock story meeting and was still trying to find a comfortable position in her desk chair when I appeared in her doorway.

"Hey, how are you feeling?" I asked.

"You already asked me that today. I told you, you only get to ask once per each twenty-four-hour period."

"No, I asked how C-3PO was feeling," I corrected her. "Your well-being is still unexplored territory."

"Well, I'm fine, thank you."

"Can I get you anything? Water? Juice? A nonprocessed food snack?"

"No. Stop being nice."

Much as certain indigenous groups believe having their picture taken will rob them of their spirit, Tina acted as if accepting help from a man would imperil hers. It should be stated she was a firstborn child.

"Want to do Indian take-out at my place and then have a sleepover?" I asked. "You can inspect the crib and make sure it holds together."

"Can't. I'm putting the paper to bed tonight."

Tina was one of our three managing editors, along with Rich Eberhardt and Chuck Looper. They rotated responsibility for the paper's production. On a normal night, when no major news was breaking, it involved staying until ten or so and then being on call thereafter. It didn't lend itself to romantic dinners.

"I thought it was Eberhardt's turn tonight."

"Yeah, and then he got a vicious case of food poisoning. He's on the shelf for today."

"And Looper is—"

"Golfing in Arizona, I think. Brodie has volunteered to help pick up the slack until Looper gets back from vacation and Eberhardt is back on his feet, but I'm on tonight and I can't ask Brodie to cover for me because you have a hankering for chicken tikka biryani."

I shook my head. "Look, I know every other important person at this paper seems to be a man over the age of sixty so they might not understand the implications of your condition. But have any of them noticed that you're about to bring forth life? What are they going to do when you're on maternity leave?"

We had yet to discuss the exact contours of Tina's leave. The paper had a generous policy that allowed new parents to take up to three months paid leave. But I knew Tina was worried how her high standing with corporate might be compromised if she disappeared for that long. Even though we were supposed to be living in more enlightened times, Tina had the fear—shared by working women everywhere—that maternity leave would count against her.

This had caused me to worry that she was going to take a

three-month leave and cut it short after three days. Every time I talked about how lucky we were to have such a kind employer—between the two of us, we could stay at home with Baby Boy Ross for his first six months—she changed the subject.

I pressed on. "And while I'm bringing up subjects you're trying to avoid, we really need to start moving some of your stuff over to my place. At least some clothes. It's going to get a lot harder once C-3PO makes his arrival."

She absentmindedly rested a hand on her belly.

"Yeah," is all she said and she stared out the glass wall of her office into the newsroom beyond.

"What?" I said.

"Huh? Nothing."

"No. It's not nothing. You're gazing off into the distance with a contemplative look. I'm a highly trained newspaper reporter, you know. I notice things like that."

"It's nothing," she said again. "Have you heard from Chillax lately?"

"And now you're dodging my question. Didn't I just mention I'm a newspaper reporter?"

"Yes, but I'm not one of your sources, Carter Ross. I'm your girlfriend. So drop it, okay?"

I have to admit, I was so warmed that she described herself as my girlfriend—most of the time she resisted labels that might suggest attachment—I let it go.

"All right, fine," I said. "To answer your question, I dispatched Chillax to Scotch Plains this morning and haven't heard from him since."

"Could you please make sure he hasn't fallen in a hole or something?"

"Yeah, you got it," I said, and shoved myself away from her door frame, against which I had been leaning. I had my shoulder turned to walk away when she spoke up.

"Hey, Carter. I'm sorry about dinner. You know I wish I could spend time with you tonight, right?"

"Yeah, sure," I said, smiling at her. "And you know I love you."

She smiled back. I quickly glanced around to make sure no one was watching, then blew her a kiss.

My stomach was starting to do its predictable 12:15 P.M. rumble and as I left Tina's office I scanned the newsroom for Tommy Hernandez, my partner in pizza. Not seeing him, I settled into my desk and dialed Chillax's number.

After two rings, I heard, "Hey, dude."

"Hey, Chillax, it's Carter Ross."

"What's up, brah?"

I clenched my teeth. It was an effort to unclench them enough to be able to speak. "I was just calling to see how things were going out there."

"It's good, brah. I'm outside the dude's house. There's, like, a billion TV trucks here. You'd think the president was holed up inside. It's pretty boss."

I realized he was using "boss" not as a noun or verb, but as an adjective. I took it to mean that the young man was impressed by the spectacle spread before him.

"Have you gotten any good stuff?" I asked.

"Not really. The word is that a family spokesman is going to give a statement sometime this afternoon. But no one knows when."

"What about the neighbors?"

"I think we've scared them all away. Any time someone walks by, they get jumped by all the TV people. I'm talking tigers on raw meat. It's totally Animal Planet."

"Did any of them give us any insight into Mr. Tiemeyer before they got devoured?"

"Nah, brah. But I got a little bit of color for you."

"Lay it on me."

"I'm not going to say he was a fat slob who needed to lose weight," Chillax said, parroting my earlier description of what color was. "I'm going to say he recently stopped using a lawn service and had started mowing his own lawn to get more exercise. And he and his wife had stopped going out for dinner three or four nights a week and cut it back to one."

"Okay. That's good. What else?" I asked.

"Not much. You asked for color. This dude's color was, like, neutral off-white. I mean, he played golf. Woo-hoo. What rich white guy doesn't? I got a bunch of the 'Oh, he was such a nice person,' and 'Oh, everyone liked him.' But I don't think anyone in this neighborhood really hangs out, you know? It's like Mc-Mansion heaven out here. I think the only reason the neighbors mentioned the lawn-mowing thing is that they didn't realize white people knew how to mow lawns. They act like that's why Mexicans were invented."

"Yeah, I hear you," I said, somewhat surprised to hear Chillax voice such a social conscience.

"Really, the only thing the neighbors knew was that he grinded out a lot of hours at work. It wasn't unusual for him to come home late. That's all I got."

Young Chillax's energies needed to be better directed. He was clearly wasting his time where he was. I knew I was going to eventually get good stuff on Joseph Okeke. If he didn't come through with an equal measure of Kevin Tiemeyer, our story would be unbalanced.

Then my eyes fell on Buster Hays, still doing violence to his keyboard. Buster was the master of using a little bit of information to get more information. That's what we had to do here.

"Okay," I said. "So you said he played golf. Was he a member of a country club or something?"

"Yeah, Fanwood."

Fanwood Country Club, named after the town next to Scotch Plains, was no Baltusrol or Pine Valley—two of New Jersey's most famous courses. But it was a nice place. And it was a place where people would know Kevin Tiemeyer and might be a little more forthcoming with us than his neighbors, who were being blinded by klieg lights as they spoke.

Back in the days when we had four or five reporters available to work any big story, we could simply dispatch one of them to Fanwood while Chillax continued to babysit the house. These days, we had to be more creative.

"Okay, here's what we're doing to do," I said. "If and when the family spokesman comes out, the TV stations will be all over it for us. I'll make sure someone on the desk grabs the quotes. Meanwhile, you head over to Fanwood and get some of his buddies to fill your notebook. Get a good anecdote or two about him on the golf course but then also talk to them about what they're thinking and feeling. Are they avoiding Newark now? Are they planning on making their next car purchase a Ford so they won't be such juicy targets? I want to know how this crime is impacting them."

It would be perfect: the golf-playing masters of the universe suddenly feeling their own vulnerability, shaken over the loss of one of their own.

"You got it, brah."

I cringed again. "Oh, and Chillax? You might want to refrain from calling any of them 'brah.' They might think you're talking about something their wives buy at Victoria's Secret."

"Huh?" he said.

"Never mind. I'll talk to you later."

I hung up, stood up and strolled over to Tommy's desk. Tommy had movie star good looks, with thick dark hair; big, puppy dog brown eyes; the perfect amount of facial scruff (just long enough to be noticed, not so long that he looked homeless); and olive skin that was the recipient of an exfoliating-and-moisturizing regimen that a straight guy like me could not begin to understand.

His clothes were also well-considered. On this day, he was wearing skinny jeans that probably cost more than the blue book value of my car and a carefully wrinkled button-down shirt that had darts on the side to give it a tailored look. Tommy still lived with his parents. He wore his paycheck.

I summoned my best Southern accent. "You know, boy, I don't know what you're trying to pull off with that shirt. The only place a man ought to have darts is at a bar."

Tommy didn't take his eyes off his computer screen. "This from a guy who dresses like 1996 never ended."

I switched back to my own voice. "You haven't even looked at me yet."

Tommy shifted his glance my way and gave me a deliberate up and down. He sighed and declared, "You're very Prince of Denmark today."

"What does that mean?"

He rolled his eyes. "Prince of Denmark, as in *Hamlet*—one of the great tragedies of all time."

I should have known better than to try and get into a fashion war with Tommy.

I went back to Southern. "Boy, we should have banned your kind from the NFL while we still had the chance."

"A sport where everyone wears tight pants and every play begins with a man putting his hands under the butt of another man who is bent over? Oh, honey, it's too late to ban us. We've been there since day one."

We enjoyed a snicker at the expense of homophobes everywhere.

"Anyhow, I know you've got Nigerians and skeletal remains

on your hands, but are you hungry? I just looked at the time and it's a quarter past pizza."

"I'd join you if I felt more confident I was going to get this story," he said. "But at this point, I'd put the odds of that about equal with the chance of you winning *Dancing with the Stars.*"

I ended up dining alone.

CHAPTER 11

Midway through my second slice of pizza—and three-quarters of the way through a life-giving Coke Zero, always my beverage of choice—I got a call from Chillax.

"They kicked me out, brah," he said.

I wiped my chin with my napkin. "What do you mean, 'they' kicked you out? Who kicked you out?"

"I went to Fanwood Country Club and was hanging out in the parking lot talking to some dudes and then this dude from the club came charging out and was like, 'You can't be here. This is private property. Blah, blah, frickin' blah.'"

"And who, exactly, was this dude?"

"I don't know. He said he was the general manager."

"All right," I said. "Just hang there for a little bit. I'll be there in twenty minutes."

On my way out, I grabbed a copy of that day's paper, which would make for useful leverage in what I anticipated would be my negotiations with Fanwood Country Club's general manager. It has been said the pen is mightier than the sword. In my experience, the product of hundreds of pens—when printed in a form that is disseminated to hundreds of thousands—is mightier still.

As I drove out of Newark to points west, I plotted the rest of my afternoon.

First, I would get Chillax on track. Then I would return to Newark, where I would find Maryam Okeke in some place not near her fuming mother. My hope was that the daughter would have had a better relationship with her father than the mother had with her ex-husband, and that she would be able to tell me enough about her dad to allow me to assemble a decent biography on the man.

My best chance was probably to snare Maryam as she left school. Arts High School was just up the hill from the *Eagle-Examiner* offices. I could get her after the final bell rang. Maybe she would divulge what transgression her father had committed that made him "deserve" his fate.

I also had to work the Rotary angle. Not that I expected resistance there. As community minded businesspeople who liked attention for their good deeds, Rotarians welcomed having their names in the newspaper. They were easy marks.

It was no more than three minutes after I had this all worked out when my plan started to unravel. I was on Route 22, just past a well-known strip club—motto: "All we wear is a smile"—about to enter the roadway's less-seedy, big-box-retail-choked stretch, when traffic came to a halt.

I wish I could report I handled this with the sanguinity of a Buddhist monk in a coma. Alas, I reacted in a way perhaps more typical of my Jersey heritage: by silently wishing death on everyone in line ahead of me.

When that didn't work, I gripped my steering wheel until my knuckles turned white.

Strangely, this also failed to have any impact on what had now coalesced into an unyielding column of brake lights. So I waited until I had inched up to the next chance to depart the roadway, which I availed myself of.

Any real Jersey Guy knows at least five ways to get where he needs to go, because chances are the first four are clogged with people who have forgotten where their gas pedals are. Yes, some of those routes could be a little circuitous. But for those of us who are infrequent bedfellows with patience, the liberty of movement more than compensated for the extra mileage we put on our automobiles.

Especially in my case. My Malibu's odometer has not budged past 111,431 for at least eighty thousand miles now.

I was so relieved to be free, I'm not sure I registered that a white Ford Fusion had pulled off behind me. Or if I had noticed it, I thought it was just another not-quite-Buddhist joining me on the path to a more meaningful enlightenment.

It was when I turned off Route 28, a popular Route 22 alternate, that I really noticed him.

He had also turned off. He was laying back a bit, trying not to be obvious about it. But we were now the only traffic on roads less traveled, cutting through the greener parts of Union County.

At first, I thought maybe I was just being paranoid. So I tested him by picking a random street and making a left.

When I turned, he turned.

I eased off the throttle a little bit. He did the same. Any Jersey driver restless enough to bail on a traffic jam typically maintains a following distance of approximately three gnat eyelashes. Yet this guy was suddenly in no hurry.

With the sun glare on his windshield and with the distance he maintained I wasn't really able to see the driver. The license plate was also hard to make out. I thought I caught the letters SME. The numbers all seemed to be 8s, 0s or 6s, which made them difficult to differentiate.

I was starting to get at least curious, if not concerned. Who went around following newspaper reporters other than the mentally ill or the terminally bored? Don't get me wrong, I had been harassed from time to time, threatened more than once. But that was usually either right before a story's publication or shortly after it came out, not when I was still trying to figure out which end was up.

Plus, it's not like I was sitting on some powder keg of information here. At least not that I knew of. Kevin Tiemeyer and Joseph Okeke seemed to be little more than decent guys from different neighborhoods who liked fancy cars and paid for it with their lives.

Maybe I was just spooking myself. Time to find out for sure. I had reached a subdivision I had been to before. Its primary road was a large loop that emptied back out onto the road I was currently on.

So I made the turn. The driver in the Fusion with the SME license plate, who I had already started calling Sammy in my head, kept going straight. As he passed directly behind me, I caught a glimpse of him. Sammy appeared to be a dark-skinned black man who was either bald or had very short hair. But he was not driving close enough or slow enough for me to see his face.

I took the wandering road through the subdivision, already chiding myself for having indulged my overly active imagination. Then I reached the exit and rejoined the road I had been on.

And there he was again. He must have pulled over and waited for me. Either he knew the subdivision, like I did, or he had a GPS that showed him I would soon be coming out the other side.

He was being even more cautious now, having let another car come in between us. I thought about jamming on the gas, knowing I could now lose him without any trouble. But that would do little to sate my curiosity as to who Sammy was in the first place. So I sped up—but only a little—and, when I reached the next light, turned right. As soon as I was out of sight of the intersection, I pulled over to the side. Unless Sammy was willing to become Captain Obvious, he would have to pass me.

Sure enough, he cruised past me about thirty seconds later. He hadn't accelerated to more than about twenty miles per hour, so I got a good long look at him as he past.

What struck me, immediately, were his cheeks. They bore deep, vivid scars. I couldn't pretend to know what the scars signified. But I did know that all of the main ethnic groups in Nigeria still practiced scarification to some degree. Which meant I could make a reasonable guess as to where Scarface Sammy was from.

I could have followed him—turnabout being fair play—except I didn't know what I hoped to accomplish in doing so. All I could do was keep an eye out for him in the future. It's not like he would be hard to spot, now that I knew what I was looking for. Even if he changed cars, he couldn't change his face.

Unless, of course, he was wearing a blue ski mask.

CHAPTER 12

Scarface Sammy knew he had been made.

And he was furious. He felt like pulling the Beretta out of his glove box, taking aim at something—a stop sign, a building, *anything*—and firing off a few rounds.

Mostly, he was just in disbelief. In his line of work, one that frequently involved what might be called predatory behaviors, following people was part of the job. And he had learned there were certain facts about it—and certain fictions.

The fictions are supplied by Hollywood and by the dozens of detective shows that populate screens large and small. They depict people successfully following their targets, always four cars back, never losing them despite highway on-ramps and railroad crossings and alternating merges and all the obstacles the road can throw at you. If the targets realize they're being trailed, a thrilling car chase ensues. But those are portrayed to be the only possible outcomes.

The facts? Well . . .

Real Life Fact Number One: following people is actually a lot harder than the movies make it out to be. Especially in moderate to heavy traffic, and especially if you're doing it by yourself. Forget lagging back by however many car lengths. Most of the time, even if you are doing your damndest to glue yourself to the target's bumper, it's all you can do just to keep up with him. You're constantly getting cut off by other cars, or by lights that turn red at the wrong time, or by other circumstances far beyond your control.

For that reason, you sacrifice subtlety in exchange for a better chance at success. But that's not really a problem, because . . .

Real Life Fact Number Two: almost no one realizes they're being followed. Most people go about their days in well-practiced oblivion. They drive to their jobs, to their friends' houses, to their kid's school—or wherever—in a state of consciousness that, from the standpoint of the person following them, can be difficult to distinguish from a coma. You practically have to walk up to them, knock on their windows, and announce, "Hey, you notice I'm following you, right?"

Sammy thought back to where he had gone wrong. He had been watching Tujuka Okeke's house, no different than he had been doing for weeks now. And then the man in the Malibu showed up.

A white man in a tie, driving a lousy old car, a Malibu, yet walking like he owned the whole neighborhood. Sammy's curiosity had been piqued immediately.

The man spent a few seconds talking with Tujuka Okeke, but only a very few. Like he was delivering a message of some sort? Or perhaps receiving one? And then he departed just as quickly as he came.

To Sammy, who had been sitting on the Okeke house for more than a week now, this was the most interesting thing he had yet seen. It very well might have been exactly what he was looking for. So he decided to follow the man.

First, they went to the offices of the newspaper—what was Malibu man doing *there?*—and then to a pizzeria. And then suddenly he was heading west to . . . where exactly?

Sammy never got the chance to find out. Somehow, the man in the Malibu—who was, apparently, not as catatonic as most of the people Sammy followed—had figured out Sammy was there.

He had even gotten a good look at Sammy's face. It was humiliating to Sammy. He fancied himself as better than that.

Sammy had to drop his tail before he could figure out who Malibu man was or what he wanted. But Sammy knew he would eventually figure it out.

To be sure, his employer would be interested. And if his employer was interested, that meant Sammy was interested.

And have no doubt . . .

Real Life Fact Number Three: Scarface Sammy always got his man.

CHAPTER 13

Being a good little intern—to say nothing of an unhurried one—Chillax had stayed just outside Fanwood Country Club. He had pulled out his lacrosse stick and was using one of the brick pillars that marked the entrance to the club as a backboard, whipping a ball off its brick facing and catching it in one quick motion.

I rolled the window down as I came to a stop.

"Sorry I'm a little late. Traffic," I said, opting not to mention Scarface Sammy. There was too great a chance Chillax would tell someone else—because it was, like, totally epic, brah—who would end up telling Tina, who would promptly reassign me to the copy desk until she determined the threat level was lower or until C-3PO graduated from medical school.

"It's okay, brah," he said. "It gave me a chance to practice. Alumni game coming up. Gotta keep my skills sharp."

I'm sure the club manager would love that. "All right. Why don't you follow me inside. I'll do the talking."

As I put the car in gear and entered the playground of the 1 percent, I immediately felt conspicuous. A dented Chevy Malibu is great camouflage for driving through Newark. At Fanwood Country Club, it is like a lanced boil on the face of Miss America.

Especially in a parking lot like the one I soon pulled into. Lexus, Range Rover, Mercedes, Lincoln—the place was a carjacker's paradise.

Not more than thirty seconds after I arrived, a nattily dressed young man in a golf cart pulled to a stop just behind my trunk. He had a haughty air about him and I could tell he was sneering at my Malibu. I immediately disliked the guy. Only *I* can sneer at my Malibu.

"I'm sorry, sir. Are you a member here?" he asked as I got out.

"No, I'm a guest of the Underwoods," I replied.

The subtle *Fletch* reference sailed so far over his head I thought I saw it land on the eighteenth fairway behind him.

"Uh-huh," he said, his lip still set in a disparaging curl. "Can I help you with your clubs?"

"I don't use clubs," I said. "I move the golf ball with my mind."

This clearly stumped him. I brought both hands to the sides of my head, as if summoning deep concentration. "It's called tele-kinetic golf," I added. "I'm surprised you haven't heard of it yet. It's all the rage in Sedona these days."

I was either convincing or too crazy to be bothered with, so Mr. Haughty moved his line of inquiry to Chillax, who had gotten out of his car—a Honda that was nearly as misplaced as my ride.

"Can I help you with your clubs, sir?"

"He's my caddy," I said quickly.

"I thought you said you don't use clubs."

I sighed as if I was losing my patience. "Well, not that *you* can see. You have much to learn and I don't have time to teach you." Then I looked at Chillax. "I want to will some putts into the hole before the Underwoods arrive. Come along, Noonan."

The nod to *Caddyshack* was also lost. On everyone. Aren't kids exposed to the *film de' art* classics of the eighties anymore?

Mr. Haughty studied us for a moment, then decided to let us be someone else's problem. "Very well, sir. The putting green is that way."

I tucked that day's paper under my arm and made for the clubhouse. As we walked, Chillax whispered, "You know my name isn't Noonan."

"I just claimed to have telekinetic powers and you're worried that I made up your name?" I asked.

He didn't reply. We walked up an impressive set of brick steps into the clubhouse, where I soon ascertained the location of general manager Earl Karlinsky. It was beneath the main floor of the clubhouse. In the basement. Where the help belonged.

Karlinsky was sitting behind a desk. He had a full head of bristly gray hair. He wore a jacket with the club emblem, a matching tie, wire-rim glasses, and altogether too much of a musky scented cologne. I surmised he had been dousing himself with it so long that his nose had been desensitized to the smell. Either that, or he took baths in it.

I was aiming for polite-but-firm in my approach, so I didn't mince words.

"Hi, Mr. Karlinsky, my name is Carter Ross. I'm a reporter with the *Eagle-Examiner*. I understand you told my colleague here he wasn't welcome at your club."

Shooing away a shaggy-haired kid probably came quite naturally to Earl Karlinsky, who spent half his summer bossing around caddies who looked just like Chillax. I was a more formidable presence, if only because I had long practice handling obstinate bureaucrats like this guy.

"Hello, Mr. Ross," Karlinsky said. "Yes, this young man was in the parking lot without announcing himself."

"Well, his name is Sloan Chesterfield, so now he's announced. We're here working on a story about Kevin Tiemeyer, who was tragically kil—"

"Kevin Tiemeyer! What makes you think we have anything to do with that?"

Karlinsky was suddenly sitting up a lot straighter in his chair, as if it had just been plugged into a wall socket.

"I never said you did," I said. "We're just looking to interview people who knew Mr. Tiemeyer so what we write in the paper about him isn't callow and uninformed. All we're trying to do is honor the memory of one of your members, so I would greatly appreciate it if you could let Sloan spend a few hours here. I assure you he'll be quite courteous and only talk to those who don't mind talking back."

It was, I felt, a reasonable request, respectfully submitted. Karlinsky quickly folded, then unfolded his hands. Even that small amount of movement sent another wave of musk wafting my way.

"I can appreciate what you're doing, but I'm afraid this is just not a good time," he said. "This has been very upsetting to our membership and I can't have—"

That's when I pulled my newspaper out from under my arm and slapped it on his desk. Again, politely but firmly.

"Open the sports section. Page D-Eight, please."

"O-okay," he said. "I'm not sure what this has to do with—"

"Third column. Midway down. The results of the Fanwood Country Club member-guest, A flight and B flight, low gross and low net, men, women, and mixed."

"Yes. And?"

"And that little strip of agate type is at least a hundred dollars' worth of free advertising for your club. We've given you the same courtesy for every tournament you've contested for at least the last fifty years, if not longer. We're talking about probably a hundred thousand dollars in publicity."

"Yes, I see," is all he said.

Sensing my advantage, I pressed: "So what do you say we

both play nice and you treat Sloan like a guest for the next few hours? As I said, we're just looking to be able to say a few nice words about Mr. Tiemeyer."

Karlinsky adjusted his glasses again. Then he did something I absolutely did not expect.

"I'm sorry, I'm going to have to ask you to leave," he said.

For a moment, I could barely believe what I had heard. Was the guy really kicking us out? Seriously?

I pretended to be unruffled. But, really, I was pissed.

"Got it," I said. "So what you're saying is, you'd like me to call our sports editor and tell him exactly how welcoming Fanwood Country Club is to *Eagle-Examiner* reporters. I'm sure he'd be interested to know so he can treat your next club championship results with roughly the same amount of hospitality. And I'm sure you'll enjoy explaining to your members why those results are no longer appearing in the paper."

"If I must," Karlinsky said. "Now, you can either show yourself out or I can call the Fanwood Police. It's up to you."

I just stood there, pondering my options from a list that only included lousy choices. If I chose a confrontation, I wasn't going to win. This was a private club. We had no right to be here if we weren't wanted. I didn't need to waste time waiting for a cop to tell me as much.

"Very well," I said, then turned to Chillax. "Let's go."

I had other means of getting into Fanwood Country Club, whether Earl Karlinsky wanted me there or not. Chillax trailed me out into the parking lot.

"Brah, that was awesome. Are you really going to call the sports editor?"

"I wish I could," I said. "Unfortunately, we're the good guys. We don't get to be small-minded and vindictive, even when it seems like fun."

"But you said—"

"It was a bluff. He called it. I lost."

Chillax accepted this defeat philosophically—they taught that at Gettysburg, right?—and I soon sent him on his way back to Scotch Plains. I, meanwhile, began my drive toward Newark and, hopefully, a rendezvous with Maryam Okeke. I knew I should have been looking ahead to that, not behind at the fiasco at Fanwood Country Club. But the whole episode just bothered me.

I was making a reasonable request of a man who ought to have been happy to do a favor for a reporter at the state's largest newspaper. Nothing I was asking for would cast the club or its membership in an unfavorable light. And yet Earl Karlinsky had run us off like we were there to take pickaxes to the eighteenth green.

Then there was his curious outburst when I first mentioned the name Kevin Tiemeyer. *What makes you think we have anything to do with that?*

It was difficult to imagine what a country club in the Jersey hinterlands had to do with a carjacking in Newark. But, as I neared the city, I couldn't chase the suspicion that Earl Karlinsky was hiding something.

CHAPTER 14

In a school system that, sadly, still has too many lumps of coal, Arts High School is a real diamond. It requires an application and an audition, and only the more motivated students will put themselves through that process. That small bit of self-selection does marvels. The ones that make it through feel like they've accomplished something special by being there.

The school's gothic facade decorated the south side of Martin Luther King Boulevard—the former High Street, to those who knew the city long ago—and that's where I planted myself as the school bell rang.

If I had gone on school property, I would have had to inform the school administration that I was there and tell them why, a time-sucking headache. As a result, I was careful to stay on the sidewalk.

As students began pouring out, I flagged down three kids, none of whom knew Maryam Okeke. It was the fourth, a chubby girl of perhaps sixteen or seventeen, who brightened at the mention of the name.

"Oh, she's my friend, hang on."

She didn't ask who I was or what I wanted. Unlike my experience in the bodega, this was one of the times when being a well-dressed, officious-looking white man was very much to my advantage. She had simply assumed I was legit and had pulled out her phone. Her fingers flew across her keypad at the speed of teenager. Few things could make a thirtysomething feel decrepit faster.

"I told her there was a white guy out in front of the entrance looking for her," the girl said. "I think her last class is up on the third floor. She'll probably be down in a minute or two."

"Thanks. But how do you know she got your—"

Then I heard her phone chime. Someday, perhaps, we will all have chips implanted that will allow us to exchange brain waves with each other, and that will become the fastest method of human communication. But until that happens, nothing is going to beat high school girls texting each other.

"She'll be right down," the girl said. "See ya!"

Sure enough, I waited no more than two minutes before I was being approached by a young woman of African heritage. She was medium height and curvy, with a wide face and long braids. She had a light smattering of adolescent acne on her cheeks.

"Hi, I'm Maryam," she said, with no trace of Nigerian accent. "You were looking for me?"

I introduced myself and asked her a few perfunctory questions—how to spell her name, how old she was, and so on. As my luck had it, she had just turned eighteen, so I wouldn't have to worry about getting permission to use her quotes. The age of consent was a marvelous thing.

Then I got down to my purpose, and I went straight at it. I told her I found it sad and wrong that the death of white Kevin Tiemeyer had attracted so much more attention than the death of black Joseph Okeke, and that I wanted to make that right— albeit a few weeks too late.

At the mention of her father, there was no change in her expression. He was dead and buried and so, apparently, were her emotions about him. Or maybe it was just that a crowded sidewalk outside her high school—surrounded by her peers—was not a place she was going to choose to show them.

"So, really, I just wanted to learn a little more about him," I finished. "You know, be able to tell people about who he really was."

I don't know if my speech about racial justice had moved her or if she was just a guileless teenager who didn't mind helping a reporter. Either way, she replied, "Okay. What do you want to know?"

"Let's start with what he did for a living?"

"He was a businessman."

"What kind of businessman?"

"So he did stuff with, like, cell phone towers and cell phone equipment? He was kind of a go-between for U.S. companies that wanted to sell and install their stuff in Nigeria. But I don't really know."

"So we could say he was in the telecommunications business," I said, trying to be helpful.

"Yeah, that would be good."

I had my pad out by this point and made a show of jotting that down. Sometimes I did this not because I particularly needed to stop to write anything—I had long ago mastered the skill of taking notes while talking—but because I wanted a pause in the conversation. Silences were a powerful tool during interviews. Sources often felt compelled to fill them, often with words that otherwise might not be said.

But Maryam just waited patiently for me to finish.

"I take it he was born in Nigeria?" I asked.

"Yeah."

"When did he come over here?"

She told me it was 1997, shortly before she was born. Maryam's older siblings, a sister and a brother, were born in Nigeria. But Joseph wanted at least one of his children to be born in the U.S.A. And since his business involved selling U.S. technology overseas—thus creating jobs here in America—it made it easy for him to get a green card.

"Obviously your mom came over at the same time if you were born here?"

Maryam nodded. I shifted into what I knew was a potentially touchy subject. But I have learned potentially touchy subjects are easier to finesse if they feel like they're in the flow of conversation.

"So when did your parents split up?"

"When I was twelve," she said. "He still lived with us for, like, a year or two, but that wasn't working, so he got his own place when I was, I don't know, thirteen or fourteen?"

"Did you still see him a lot?"

"Oh, yeah, pretty much every day. Unless he was traveling or something. He'd come over and help me with my math homework or whatever. He had dinner with us a lot."

I liked that detail and the image it produced: Joseph Okeke and his daughter, their heads bent over some algebraic equation.

"Your parents got along okay, then?"

"Yeah, I guess."

"You guess?"

"Well, they'd . . . I wouldn't call it fight. But I'd overhear them having some serious conversations about tuition. My brother is at Duke and he gets financial aid and scholarships, but it's still expensive. And then next year, with me, they'll have two tuitions to worry about. They talked about it a lot. Education is really important to them."

My mind briefly wandered to the day when I might have the same worries. The saving grace was that, as a fairly high-ranking editor, Tina made a lot more money than I did. Also, she was a saver. She had probably set up a 529 Plan shortly after her first positive pregnancy test.

"But in general they got along a lot better after he moved out than before," she continued. "They're just one of those couples who is happier when they each have some space." She said this with a world-weariness beyond her eighteen years.

"I talked to your mom earlier today and she seemed pretty pissed at him about something," I said, again just trying to keep things in the natural flow. "I asked her about what happened and she said something like, 'He got what he deserved.' Do you know what that's about?"

Maryam shook her head. "That's just my mom. Sometimes she'd get really pissed at him for, like, no reason."

Somehow, I doubted it was *no* reason. It was just a reason I had yet to uncover and Maryam was ignorant of. Had Joseph Okeke taken a girlfriend? Had he fallen behind on child support? Whatever it was, Tujuka Okeke probably didn't want to bad-mouth her children's father in their presence. It showed commendable maturity.

I debated whether I should ask Maryam about the insurance issue. There was a chance she knew all about it and could enlighten me as to what was happening. Then again, Tujuka might have been keeping it from her daughter, knowing a teenager who just lost her father already had enough stress in her life and didn't need more. And, no, as a reporter I wasn't strictly bound to honor that. But just because she was eighteen—and, legally, an adult—didn't mean I had to treat her like an adult in every way.

More questions from me elicited a similar amount of nothing, or at least nothing compelling. She said he traveled a lot for business, but I knew that already. She said he liked to read, everything from crime fiction to military histories. She said again that education was important to him, so important that after moving here he had earned an MBA online from Strayer University, even though he really didn't need one.

I inserted occasional pauses into the conversation, pouring

my attention into my notebook, scribbling nonsense in the hopes Maryam would say more about a given subject. But, just like she had the previous times, she was content to stand there as what remained of the Arts High School student body filed past her on their way home.

Nothing else in our conversation really grabbed me until the end of a discourse about how much her father liked golf. Joseph's father—Maryam's grandfather—had been a greenskeeper at a course outside Lagos, one that catered to British colonists before Nigeria was granted independence in 1960. Joseph had grown up playing the game and still mashed a mean five iron. He made his children learn how to play, because it was the game of American business.

"He was so excited a few weeks ago," she said. "He got this invitation to play at this fancy place."

"Oh, yeah? What place?"

"Fanwood Country Club," she said.

"Fanwood," I repeated, feeling that little tilt in my head that happens when someone has given me a piece of information whose import goes beyond the obvious. "Small world. I was actually just out there earlier today."

"He just raved about it," Maryam said.

"You don't know, by any chance, who invited him there?"

She shook her head.

"Has he ever mentioned the name Earl Karlinsky?"

She wasn't sure. But as we wrapped up our conversation and swapped cell phone numbers, I couldn't chase the possibility from my mind: what if Joseph Okeke had also known the inhospitable and perhaps mendacious Earl Karlinsky?

I didn't know what, exactly, it would mean if he did—except that I had more to learn. I had already planned to interview some Fanwood Country Club members about Kevin Tiemeyer, if only to rub it in Karlinsky's face.

This newest revelation had just moved that agenda item to the top of my list.

I am not, by nature or by preference, the most organized person in the world. My desk in the newsroom is covered with irregularly shaped stacks of papers and notebooks, the contents of which may or may not be related to the same subject. My books at home are neither alphabetized nor indexed. I eschew most forms of collating, classifying, or categorizing.

But I am absolutely fastidious when it comes to keeping track of my sources. If someone gives me their phone number or e-mail, I save it in my phone's contact list, even if I think there is only a one in a million chance I'll ever need it again. I then store every other relevant piece of information I know about them—their employer and job title, their professional affiliations, their educational background, the names of their spouse and children, whatever may be relevant in the future.

I will also record a quick log line about the article for which I interviewed them ("Ludlow Street murders," or "Windy Byers story," or what have you). It all goes into the notes file for each contact and I have rolled up somewhere in the neighborhood of two thousand names during my time at the *Eagle-Examiner*.

Hence, as soon as Maryam left me to attend to her duties as yearbook editor, I whipped out my phone and pulled up my contacts. I searched the phrase "Fanwood Country Club," knowing that I would have listed such membership in my notes.

Three names popped up. By far the most promising was Armando "Doc" Fierro. I actually smiled when I saw it.

He was perfect. He was, in Malcolm Gladwell's *Tipping Point* parlance, a connector. He would know Kevin Tiemeyer if only because Doc was the kind of guy who made it his business to know everyone. He had been a campaign manager, cabinet member, close advisor, and all-around whiz kid for a long-ago governor. He had since served on a stunning number of official commissions, blue-ribbon panels, and boards of directors, all of which were based on his extensive latticework of personal relationships. He was now the owner-operator of a small firm that did a mix of lobbying and consulting, with a little public relations on the side—which is why he cultivated a relationship with me.

He had gotten the nickname "Doc" not because of any medical or advanced degrees, at least not that I knew of. Legend was that long-ago governor was confronting a problem and told someone, "Take it to Doctor Fierro, he'll get that fixed up right." People in the administration started calling him Dr. Fierro, which quickly got shortened to Doc.

He was smart, gregarious, and charming, as guys like that tended to be. I had quoted him at least half a dozen times in the paper, and there were probably twice as many stories where he had helped me by making an important introduction. He was also, as they say in the old country, fond of the drink. He didn't need much excuse to tilt one back.

I briefly debated whether to call or e-mail and decided to go electronic. I mostly just wanted to find a legitimate way to get inside the doors at Fanwood Country Club so I could snoop around. If I did it over e-mail he'd ask fewer questions as to my motives. I typed:

> Doc,
> Working on a story and hoping you can help me. Also, I'm developing a terrible thirst and the rumor is your bartender at Fanwood now has one of my favorite beers on tap. In the name of efficiency, can we take care of both these urgent matters simultaneously? 5:30 tonight? Let me know.
> Best,
> Carter

With that taken care of, I moved to my next item of business, setting my search function to work on the phrase "Newark Rotary."

Alas, nothing came up. Somehow, I had been toiling nine years for Newark's finest and only newspaper, yet never come across a single Rotarian in the city. I guess there does not tend to be much of a need for hard-hitting investigations into misuse of the Rotary Happy Dollars fund.

I monkeyed around on the Web for a bit and found that the current president of the Newark Rotary Club was named Zabrina Coleman-Webster. The name was unusual enough that I was able to trace her to Lacks & Ragland, an accounting firm that had offices on Academy Street in downtown Newark. She was listed as an associate with the firm.

In the company directory, I located her direct dial line. I was about to call it when I stopped myself. The address listed was just a short stroll down the hill from Arts High, no more than maybe ten minutes. I started walking instead.

Conducting cold call interviews was sort of like sex: thanks to modern technology, there was a way to do it over the phone, but it was infinitely better to do it in person.

CHAPTER 15

In recent years there have been a proliferation of companies like Lacks & Ragland that have found Newark. They're midsized firms that don't want to have to pay Manhattan rents, but still desire access to public transportation—which Newark has in abundance—and close proximity to New York. They tend to be quite happy in Newark, as long as the city's incessant dysfunction doesn't scare them off.

Lacks & Ragland occupied all five floors of a small building on Academy Street that had been attractively renovated sometime in the recent past to include hardwood floors, exposed brick, and other features suitable to young upwardly mobile professionals.

I announced myself to a grumpy security guard who pulled himself out of that day's edition of the *Eagle-Examiner* just long enough to lift up the phone on his desk and mutter into it.

He listened for a moment, grunted a few words at me—they may have been "she'll be right down"—then turned his attention back to the paper. His lack of courtesy and attentiveness bothered me not in the least. I was just happy to see someone engrossed in our product.

As I waited, my phone dinged with an e-mail:

Carter,

I, too, feel a thirst coming on. 5:30 it is.

Cheers,

Doc

I had just stowed the phone back in my pocket when the elevator doors slowly eased open to reveal an African American woman in a red skirt suit. She was nicely proportioned, fortyish, and had straightened her hair, which she wore shoulder length.

"Hi, Zabrina Coleman-Webster," she said, smiling and walking toward me.

"Carter Ross."

"How can I help you?"

"I'm working on a story about Joseph Okeke."

Saying the name was like flipping a kill switch on her smile.

"Oh, Joseph," she said, in a way that was almost like a sigh. She put a hand over her heart, slumped her shoulders, and cast her eyes down. She held that pose for a few seconds, her own small moment of silence.

Then she straightened up. "Why don't you come upstairs? We can talk in the conference room."

"Thank you. That would be great."

I stepped into the elevator and she punched the button for the fifth floor.

"I'm sorry," she said. "I'd take you to my office but the associates have to share. Only the partners get their own."

"I understand. It's no problem."

The door slid shut just as slowly as it had opened. The elevator had apparently not been renovated along with the rest of the building. It groaned and creaked underneath us as it summoned the momentum to begin its journey.

As soon as it finally got underway, Zabrina said, "So how did you know Joseph and I were dating?"

I resisted—barely—the urge to blurt, *You were?!* I was glad she had her attention focused on the lighted numbers above the door that were tracking our upward progress, because it meant she didn't see my jaw drop.

Once I composed myself, I said, "Oh, well, you know how gossipy Rotary people are."

"I thought we kept it pretty quiet. You must be a good reporter."

"Just lucky, mostly," I said, which was truer than she knew.

At least now I understood Tujuka Okeke's disgust with her ex-husband. Sure, they were divorced. But this might have been the first time he had found comfort in the arms of another woman. Even if Joseph remained devoted to his family, Tujuka would have resented the intrusion and the possible disruption to their well-oiled coparenting routine. Plus, just because she didn't want him anymore didn't mean she wanted someone else to have him. Jealousy and reason are only intermittent pen pals.

I wondered if Maryam knew about her dad's squeeze. I suppose it was possible for a father to hide a girlfriend from a daughter he didn't live with. Maryam obviously hadn't said anything about her dad dating; but, then again, I hadn't explicitly asked her, either. It made me ponder what else she had left out.

"It had really only been going on for a little while," Zabrina said, filling the silence I had given her in ways Maryam had not. "I mean, the attraction had been there for a while, I guess. He's a very handsome man. Have you ever seen a picture of him?"

"No," I said, as we arrived at the fifth floor.

She pointed to the conference room, which was directly opposite the elevator. "Wait in there. Let me just grab my phone."

I walked into the conference room. It was standard-issue corporate, which meant it gave me a minor case of the creeps. Your typical reporter is a free-range animal who needs large, open spaces in which to graze. It does not thrive in captivity.

"This is Joseph," Zabrina said as she returned to the room, closing the door behind her. Holding out her phone, she showed me a photograph of the two of them that appeared to have been taken at a Rotary Club meeting. Joseph had his arm tightly clamped around Zabrina's shoulder. He was dark-complexioned, with short hair. I recognized the cheekbones and the wide set of the eyes, both of which he had passed to his daughter.

"Isn't he gorgeous?" she added.

As a rule, I tend not to be the greatest judge of the gorgeousness of other dudes. This probably explains why my first date to the Homecoming Dance was named Kara, not Karl. But I felt like it was only polite to summon some enthusiasm. "Oh . . . yes," I said. "He's a . . . a fine-looking man."

"Yeah, and it doesn't hurt that he had his own job and made his own money," Zabrina added. "Let me tell you, there are not a lot of single black men in Newark who can say that. Trust me. I grew up here."

This was mildly surprising. There are not, to my knowledge, a profusion of black female accountants. There are even fewer black female accountants who grew up in Newark.

Sensing an opening to pry into her past—and wanting to get her talking freely before I turned the conversation to her erstwhile boyfriend—I said, "Do you want to sit?"

"Oh, yeah, sure," she said. She sat at the head of the table. I selected the corner next to her, the one that faced the door.

"So obviously you decided to stay close to home," I said.

"I don't know if you could call it a decision. I was the typical dumb ghetto girl. I got pregnant at sixteen, dropped out of high school. I thought my baby daddy was going to support us."

She laughed at the absurdity of the idea. "He was gone before the baby was even born."

"It's a pretty long way from single teenaged mom in Newark to the conference room of Lacks and Ragland," I said. "How'd you swing that?"

"Eventually I grew up. It just took a while. I think my boy was about eight when he said, 'But, Mama, why do I have to go to school? You didn't and you're doing fine.' We were living in Section Eight housing. I was working two jobs that both paid minimum wage. And I was like, 'Baby, I am *not* doing fine.' That's when I decided to get my GED. Then I just kept going. I got my associate, then my bachelor's, then my accounting degree. I realized I was his biggest role model, so I wanted to show him what his mama could do. I passed my CPA exam the same month my son graduated high school."

"Wow," I said. "That's quite a slog."

"Yeah," she said, leaning back in her conference chair and crossing her legs.

"How long have you been working here?"

"Six years," she said.

At that point, I felt like she was properly warmed up. Or maybe it's more accurate to say I realized she was a natural and unabashed sharer: someone who freely laid out the details of her life to a stranger. She had walked a certain path, one filled with both mistakes and triumphs. But she owned every single step and misstep. It was hard not to like someone like that. And I say that not just because it made the job of the journalist easier.

I pulled out my notepad, opened to a blank page, and said, "So tell me about you and Joseph."

They had met shortly after she joined Rotary, at a time when they were both embarking on major life transitions.

She had just taken a job at Lacks & Ragland, the beginning of her ascension to the bourgeoisie. He was in the throes of a divorce that would finally free him from a marriage that hadn't really survived its trip to America.

He was kind, thoughtful, and well-read, and she liked him

103

immediately. But dating wasn't really in the picture for either of them.

Then, slowly, the picture changed. Over the course of a few years, they fell into a pattern where they often sat at the same table during Rotary meetings. She was rising through the ranks, first becoming the chapter treasurer, then its vice president. He was an active member who had spearheaded their most recent scholarship drive. He never missed a meeting unless he was out of the country on business.

Soon she recognized she missed him when he was gone. And that when he was there, she would seek out his table. He seemed to be doing the same. Finally, he asked her if she wanted to have coffee sometime.

"At first I didn't even get that he was asking me on a date. It had been so long since a guy had even tried to date me. In the 'hood, the guys are mostly like, 'Hey, baby, you want to git wit dis?'"—she affected a cocky head shake while pointing to her crotch, then interrupted herself with laughter—"It's like I didn't even know dating existed."

Coffee led to lunch. Lunch led to dinner. They eventually introduced the other to their kids. I mentioned I had met Maryam, which caused Zabrina to take on a briefly maternal glow.

"She's such a good kid," Zabrina said. "And so smart. Did you know she was a National Merit Scholar? That kid is going someplace. I wish my son had his act half as together as that girl."

Not wanting to get into an examination of Zabrina's offspring, I steered the conversation back to Joseph. It sounded like each escalation of the relationship only happened after the appropriate measure of time. They were two grown-ups with busy lives and enough scars that no one was sprinting into anything. But there was an inevitability to it, at least in the version Zabrina was giving me.

About eight months ago, they had started spending the night

at each other's place. It was understood that maybe, someday, they would move in together. They talked about having a Newark pad and then going in on a place down at the shore once Zabrina saved a little more and Joseph got out from under tuition payments.

And maybe, at some point in the future, they would make it legal. There was no hurry on either end.

She was just telling me about how they were planning their first vacation together when a constipated-looking white man with a bad suit and a worse haircut opened the door without knocking.

"You have the Sawyer audit done yet?" he demanded. Then he registered my presence, and, as an afterthought, added, "Sorry to interrupt." He said it in that sorry-not-sorry way.

"Hello, Benn, good afternoon," she said, which only emphasized his brusqueness. "Yes, it'll be done before I leave today."

"Good. We need it," he said, then departed without another word.

As soon as the door closed behind him, Zabrina said, "That's Benn, with two n's, because it's short for Bennington," she said. Then, after a beat, she interjected, "Yeah, I work for a jerk."

I laughed. "Lots of people do."

"I know, I just . . . the way they treat me is like I'm half a person. I've got my degrees, just like them. But because I got my degrees online when I was in my thirties, it's like they don't count around here. Like, I'm sorry I'm a single mom who didn't go to college straight out of high school and kill my brain cells in a fraternity basement like you did. I'm sorry I can't talk about whether my school's football team is playing in a bowl game. But, you know what? My degree is just as good as yours. And I passed the CPA exam just like you did."

"Yeah," I said, just to say something.

"They're glad they have Zabrina From The 'Hood, because

they can be like, 'Look, we're all diverse. We got a black woman working here. We got a true Newarker working here.' But when it comes time to talk about who's going to get a promotion or make partner next, Zabrina From The 'Hood doesn't exist anymore."

"You could go to another firm," I suggested.

"I know, I just . . . my mother is here. My brother is here. My grandmother is still alive. I've got aunts and uncles. Newark is home, you know?"

I nodded. There were places that really did embrace diversity, not just tokenism. A firm like that would love to have Zabrina Coleman-Webster. But, ultimately, I wasn't here to offer career advice. She'd either punch through the glass ceiling here or not.

"Going back to Joseph," I said. "When was the last time you saw him?"

"The night it happened. He had actually just left my place. He was going to spend the night, but then he remembered he had left some papers at his place and he had a meeting first thing, so he decided—"

She got quiet for a moment. Zabrina From The 'Hood was a tough specimen, one who jumped over barriers of a magnitude that a suburban-bred, Amherst-educated WASP like me could only imagine. That's not some version of white guilt talking. That's just the truth. The only people who couldn't recognize that growing up poor and black in Newark was a fundamentally different version of the American experience were . . . well, they were constipated-looking jerks named Benn.

She pulled herself together and resumed: "He decided he wanted to get them that night. He was on his way home when he . . . when it happened. I didn't even know about it until the next night. The police notify next of kin. They don't notify girlfriends."

"How'd you find out?"

"I knew something was wrong. We would normally text each other during the day and when I didn't hear from him I started calling him. And then when I didn't hear from him I finally called Tujuka."

"Wow, you must have been pretty desperate to do that."

"Why?"

"Well, calling your boyfriend's ex . . . I mean, I can't imagine you and Tujuka get along all that famously."

"Oh, we're fine," Zabrina said. "I think it helps that we're both single moms. We sort of understand where the other is coming from. I told her right off the bat that Joseph's commitment to his kids came first. From that point on, we've been good."

I wasn't so sure they were as good as she thought they were, given the way Tujuka slammed the door at the mention of her dead husband's name. But I asked, "When you called, what did she tell you?"

"I was like, 'I'm sorry to bother you, but have you heard from Joseph? I can't get a hold of him and I'm starting to worry.' And that's when she told me that Joseph had been shot during a carjacking. The police didn't know any more than that. And from what they're telling Tujuka, they probably won't ever know. Unless they recover the car. But I'm sure they won't."

"Did the police talk to you at all?"

"I don't even think they know about me. Like I said, Joseph and I kept things pretty quiet."

I let that breathe for a moment, to see if she would add anything else. But nothing came out.

"Have you been out to the intersection where it happened?" I asked.

"No. I'm not sure I . . . I just haven't been all that interested."

"I talked to a witness out there who said it looked like Joseph stopped for a green light. Can you make any sense of that?"

Her face went blank for a second, then she said, "Not . . . not really. Except, maybe, well . . . he was terrible when it came to distracted driving. He was always sending texts and e-mails while he drove. I got on him about it constantly. Maybe he just didn't know it was green? But—"

She forced out a sizable exhale. "Wouldn't that be something? I've been trying to get my head around the idea that he died simply because he forgot some papers at his town house. To think that he died because he was stopping to send an e-mail?"

There was no more to add to that thought. I saw Benn The Jerk, walk past the conference room, peering his head in as he did so. Zabrina saw it, too. Our time was running short.

"The only other question I had was actually about Joseph's insurance policy," I said. "I don't really have this nailed down yet, but I'm hearing that his insurance company might be giving Tujuka the runaround about paying out. Do you know anything about that? Did Tujuka mention anything?"

"Sorry. We haven't really talked since the funeral," she said.

"All right. I'll let you get back to work then."

Zabrina just rolled her eyes. I knew I could—and probably would—talk to her again. For now, she had given me plenty.

"Hey, while I'm thinking about it, would you mind e-mailing me that picture of the two of you together?" I asked.

Going back to the importance of having an acceptable victim, photographs always helped. It made them that much more human.

"Sure," she said. I gave her my e-mail address and she mailed me the picture on the spot. We swapped cell numbers, then said our goodbyes, and parted ways.

As I rode back down the too-slow elevator, I looked at the image that was now on my phone. One of the things that makes photographs so powerful is that they capture a moment in time; and while the photograph stops, time moves ahead.

It means, oftentimes, the person viewing the photograph knows things that the people in the photograph don't.

So as I gazed at a photograph of two lovers, I did so with a sense of its tragedy. Neither was a youngster. But they still thought they had at least a half a lifetime in which to enjoy each other. They never knew how short their time really was.

Then again, I suppose none of us do.

CHAPTER 16

The smell of beef stew greeted Blue Mask as he returned to his great-aunt Birdie's house, wafting its way from the kitchen into the living room.

Blue Mask hated beef stew and hated Birdie for making it. He knew it meant he'd end up having to run out to McDonald's later. Between that and the Rolex setback, it would put him that much further away from being able to move out.

He closed the door softly behind him. He could hear Birdie in the kitchen, singing an old gospel song to herself: "Jesus has done so much for me. I cannot tell it all. I cannot tell it all!"

He didn't want to have to talk to her, answer her questions about what he had been up to, or listen to her latest thoughts on what Bible verse applied to a wayward young man such as himself. He wanted to get his three new best friends—Ben Franklin, Ben Franklin, and Ben Franklin—up with the rest of his stash in the highest cabinet and get on with his day.

Birdie stopped singing and called from the kitchen, "That you, baby?"

Blue Mask shuffled into the kitchen, his hands stuffed in his pockets. His right was placed protectively over the bills.

"Hey, Birdie," he mumbled.

He would have to wait until she went to the bathroom or retired upstairs for a few minutes so he could hide them. Then he'd get with Black Mask. Talk about doing another job. Maybe that night. *That* would get him over five grand.

"I'm making stew," Birdie said. "Gonna get a good dinner in you. Beef and potatoes and carrots. Gonna get some meat on you. You're too skinny."

"Uh-huh."

Like Birdie was one to talk. She couldn't have weighed more than ninety-five pounds. Most of it was gristle.

For a moment or two, he just watched her, alternating between stirring beef stock with an old wooden spoon and chopping vegetables with a dull knife. She wasn't leaving. He wanted her to leave. He gripped his bills a little tighter.

"Oh, honey, the most blessed thing happened today," she said. "You think Jesus isn't good, but I keep telling you, Jesus is good all the time. I was just getting all my ingredients in place and I went up into that cabinet over there, and you would never believe what I found. There was a paper sack with over four thousand dollars in it. Can you believe? Four thousand dollars! Just sittin' there! I never seen anything like it in all my life."

That's when Blue Mask saw the cornstarch sitting on the counter. His eyes shot up toward the shelf where his stash was hidden. In front of that cabinet, there was a stool, which Birdie had obviously used to reach it. He had never seen the stool before.

Blue Mask felt his heart pounding. Antisocial personality disorder may have hindered his attachment to fellow human beings. It did nothing to interfere with his attachment to money.

"I couldn't believe it, just couldn't believe it!" Birdie continued. "It was like the Lord himself put it there. And so I prayed to Him, I said, 'Jesus, Lord, you have brought this bounty into my life, now tell me what I'm supposed to do with it.' And I was prayin' and prayin' and then, God as my witness, the phone rang. And it was Pastor. I swear to you it was Pastor. And I said, 'Pastor, you got to get over here right now, because I think the spirit is working through you real strong today.'

"So he came over and I showed him the money and he just started laughing. And he told me, 'Birdie, you wouldn't believe it, but the boiler in the church basement broke yesterday, and today the man came over and said it was going to cost five thousand dollars to fix. And I was just starting to fret over where I was going to find that kind of money.' And we just laughed and laughed and laughed. The Lord provides. He really does."

She went back to singing, "Jesus has done so much for me. I cannot tell it all. I cannot tell it all."

Blue Mask finally managed to stammer out: "So what . . . what did you do?"

"What do you mean, what did I do? I gave him the money."

"You *what*?" His volume was increasing.

"I gave him the money."

"Birdie, that was *my* money."

Birdie stopped stirring the stew, stared at him hard. "Young man, where did you get money like that? You keep telling me you can't find a job but suddenly you've got four thousand dollars? You been selling drugs again?"

"No! I worked for it."

Birdie hadn't broken her glare.

"Odd jobs," he said.

Finally, she let out an incredulous, "Uh-huh."

Blue Mask took his hands out of his pockets, started waving them around, his agitation growing. "Birdie, that's my money. You got to get it back."

"What do you mean, 'get it back'?"

"Go to Pastor, it's my money and tell him he needs to give it back."

"I'm not doing that. I already gave it to him. Far as I'm concerned, that's the Lord's money now."

"But it wasn't yours," Blue Mask said, yelling now.

"Well, it sure wasn't yours, either. You can't tell me with a straight face you got out of prison three weeks ago with nothing and now you got four thousand dollars from working odd jobs. I don't know how you got that or what you did for it, but as far as I'm concerned it was wicked money and now it's blessed. The Lord has taken it for His own work and I think He was right to do so."

"That's my money," he bellowed.

"No, it's not," she said, just as fiercely. "Pastor said he's going to make his whole sermon about it on Sunday. You and I are just going to sit in the front row and hear all about it. If you want to confess what you done to get it and come clean, that's between you and God. But you are not getting a nickel of it back."

Blue Mask didn't really think about what transpired next. It sort of just happened naturally. His hands shot out and wrapped themselves around Birdie's twig of a neck. And then they squeezed.

Birdie twisted and flailed for a bit, trying to hit her great-nephew with the wooden spoon she had been using to stir the stew. All that really accomplished was to fling a fine spittle of broth on his clothes and parts of the kitchen floor. She tried to scream, but the sound came out choked and garbled.

Through it all, Blue Mask kept squeezing. He squeezed until Birdie stopped flailing. Then he squeezed some more, until he was sure life had departed her.

CHAPTER 17

For the second time that day, I found myself heading out to Fan-wood Country Club. Unlike the first time, I had an invitation that would see to it I wasn't immediately booted off the grounds.

That improvement in circumstances had sufficiently im-proved my mental state such that, when my phone rang, it didn't immediately plunge me into a baby-charged panic. I even stayed calm when I saw the number was coming from the *Eagle-Examiner* newsroom.

"Carter Ross."

"Carter, my boy, how are you? It's Harold Brodie."

Sure it was. Just the fifty-years-younger, gay, Cuban version. And I wasn't falling for it this time.

"Hal, you wrinkly old coot, I'm doing great, buddy. And I've been considering your little proposition from before. Tell Madge to put on some slinky little number and I'll come over dressed up like a plumber. We can do a little fantasy role-playing. She'll tell me she has a leaky sink and then I'll pull out the biggest wrench she's ever seen and make sure she has the cleanest pipes in the whole neighborhood, if you know what I mean."

"What are you—"

But I wasn't letting Tommy get a word in. "I'll probably spank her a little bit, because she's been such a bad girl and I know she likes it rough. And then, of course, one of her neighbors will come over to borrow a cup of sugar and the three of us will finish off the job together."

Tommy wasn't saying anything, so I added: "You can watch if you want. Maybe grab some pom-poms and cheer us on from the sidelines in a cute little pleated skirt? I know deep down inside of you there's a little girl just crying to get out. What do you say, Hal? You game?"

There was still silence on the other end. I could tell Tommy was trying to come up with a retort, but he had been rendered speechless by my masterful plot summation of approximately three-quarters of the pornographic movies made between the years 1977 and 1992.

Then the silence was broken with a high-pitched howling, the likes of which I had never quite heard before.

"Is this your idea of a joke? You're way out of line, Carter Ross. Way out of line! Who do you think you are, talking about my wife in such a licentious, disrespectful manner!"

I felt a prickle of alarm. There was no way Tommy would risk raising his Harold Brodie voice to such a high volume in the newsroom. The old man would hear it. Plus, I couldn't imagine Tommy using the word "licentious."

And that's when the prickle turned into a full-size, stainless-steel, Vlad the Impaler–style spike ripping through my gut. And I finally realized:

This wasn't Tommy.

It really *was* Harold Brodie.

In an instant, my mouth and my brain received a jolt of energy that had them both working in overdrive but, sadly, not in concert. The result was that my brain began barking out instructions—like a coxswain with a megaphone sitting in the front of a rowing shell—as my mouth began trying to furiously paddle its way out of trouble.

"I'm very, very sorry, sir. I didn't think it was actually you. I thought it was . . ."

Don't say Tommy's name. Don't say Tommy's name. Be a man. Go down with the ship.

"Someone else, someone else who was just pretending to be you. So I didn't mean anything personal by it. Trust me when I say I have no desire for Mrs. Brodie whatsoever—"

Attention, moron: you just insulted the man's wife.

"Not that she isn't a very lovely woman, sir. I don't want to insinuate that she's unattractive in any way. I'm sure there have been many, many plumbers who would have liked to—"

Danger! Danger! Disengage mouth immediately!

"Uh, anyhow, I just mean that I would like to stress that I have total respect for you and for your marriage and I never meant to insinuate that you have any fantasies regarding cheerleaders, either dressing up as one or . . ."

Stop talking. Stop talking. Stop talking.

"I'm just saying I have nothing but respect for you, and for Mrs. Brodie, and I was just making a terrible, terrible joke, for which I'm very, very sorry."

The hole I had dug for myself was already deep enough that the antifracking people were going to start coming after me. Having finally gotten to the apology, I figured I'd stop myself before I made it all the way to the Earth's molten core.

All I could hear on the other end was Brodie's breathing.

In. Out. In. Out. In retrospect, I can say it took about fifteen seconds. In the moment, it felt like it lasted longer than the fifth grade.

Finally, he spoke in a measured tone: "I was just calling to see how you were coming on that Chariots for Children story. Let me make this very simple for you: that story will be on my desk by five o'clock tomorrow. If it's not, we're going to have a long chat about your sick, sick sense of humor. Do I make myself clear?"

117

"Yes, sir. Very clear. Perfectly clear. And I'd like to say again that I meant absolutely no disrespect to you or your—"

But I was already talking to an empty phone line.

My mortification had only subsided slightly as I neared Fanwood Country Club. But I had to buckle down and concentrate.

The dollar-fifty word for what I was doing was "compartmentalize." Like most guys, I did it quite well. It was the male gender's consolation prize for being congenitally incapable of multitasking.

I had two objectives. One was to gather more string on Kevin Tiemeyer. The other was to see if I could ascertain how Joseph Okeke had secured his recent invitation to play at the club—and whether it had anything to do with Earl Karlinsky. I reasoned that if I could find out who Okeke's playing partners had been, one of them might know.

As I passed through the brick pillars that guarded the entryway to the club, I noted with bemusement that one of them was scarred with several dozen small, white pockmarks from where Chillax had used it as a backboard.

There was no sign of Mr. Haughty as I pulled into the parking lot. Then again, it was now after golfing hours. The only members coming into the club now were heading to the bar like me. So they didn't need help getting unloaded. Quite the opposite, in fact.

I escorted myself into the main clubhouse and around to the back, where the bar was located.

There, sitting on one of the stools in front of a monolithic slab of polyurethane-covered wood, I found Doc Fierro. He had not waited to begin his cocktail hour.

"Hey, what's happening?" he asked, his smile already loosened by whatever amber-colored liquid was in his highball glass.

"Dr. Fierro, a pleasure, sir."

We shook hands in that way that men comfortable with themselves do. Which is to say, neither of us tried to prove anything by crushing the other's hand. The bartender appeared and I ordered a Flying Fish HopFish IPA. Doc and I touched classes and I savored my first sip. For anyone who doesn't think craft brewing when they think New Jersey, I urge them to try Flying Fish's fine line of beers.

"This is actually my second trip to your fine club today," I said as I brought my glass back down to the table. "I was out here earlier with one of our interns. Your general manager took umbrage to our presence and ran us out."

Doc looked a bit startled by this. "Why?"

"I don't know. We're trying to give Kevin Tiemeyer some nice posthumous press and your guy was acting like we were out here to do a hatchet job on him."

Doc ran a finger along the edge of his glass. "I guess maybe at his next performance review the board needs to reemphasize the section of his job description that begins with the words, 'public relations.'"

"No kidding. What's his deal, anyway?"

"I don't know. Small penis, maybe?" Doc said, then sipped his drink. "So, Kevin Tiemeyer, huh? I kind of figured you might be asking about him. Poor bastard."

"You knew him?"

"Sure."

"And?"

"Good guy," Doc confirmed. "I divide the members here in two broad categories. There are guys that you're happy to have be a part of your foursome. And then there are guys that, when the starter says, 'Oh, Mr. So-and-so is going to be joining you,' you just sort of roll your eyes. Luckily we have a lot more of the former than the latter. Kevin was definitely in the first group. He liked to chew a cigar while he was playing, which was a little gross. But he was good company."

"How was he as a golfer?" I asked, not because I particularly cared about Tiemeyer's pitching and putting but because I wanted to see if I could work Doc around to telling an amusing story or two. In the business, we call it mining for anecdotes. And I would like to consider myself a seasoned pitman.

"He played what we call Army golf," Doc said. Then, in a marchlike cadence, he added, "Left, right, left, right."

"Did he ever, I don't know, unexpectedly win a member-guest or something?"

"Not lately, that's for sure," Doc said. "Not many people around here would know this—I only know because I'm on the board—but he had recently asked for his membership to be suspended for a few months."

I took a sip of my beer. "Didn't realize you could do that."

"We only let people do it once every few years. You can't let them do it every year, or else every Florida snowbird would go inactive for three months during the winter and it would play hell on club finances."

"Did he give a reason?"

"Not that I heard," Doc said.

As I considered this, Doc announced he needed to hit the men's room. The Kevin Tiemeyer file now had a definite pattern to it. According to Chillax, Tiemeyer stopped going out to dinner as often and started mowing his own lawn. Now it comes out he had gone inactive at his country club. Maybe he really was just on a diet. Or trying to save some money. Or maybe it was part of some larger lifestyle change. Was he going vegan? Or quitting drinking? Or training for a marathon?

Whatever was happening, it felt like it was important for fleshing out the Tiemeyer side of my story. There was just something about a man being interrupted in the midst of an ambitious self-improvement plan that I found poignant. And if it touched my heart, I'm sure it would touch a reader's, too. I'd have to run it past Chillax and see how it meshed with the rest of his notes.

I tilted my glass back for another dose of hoppy deliciousness, only to smell a gust of musky scented air coming from my right.

It was brought in by Earl Karlinsky, in all his emblem-jacketed, overscented, self-important glory. Fanwood Country Club's general manager had parked himself just off my right elbow, between my bar stool and where Doc would have been sitting if he weren't in the bathroom. It was a pronounced invasion of my personal space, which I suppose was the point.

He was holding his head high and, being as I was sitting, he had a slight height advantage. He used it to peer down at me through the bottom of his glasses.

"Mr. Ross, I thought I told you, you aren't welcome here," he said in a voice even a porcupine would have found too bristly.

I lifted my glass in a mock toast. "Ah, but it appears I am here all the same," I said.

"You have to leave. Now."

"No, actually, I don't," I said, pleasantly. "*Salut,*" I said, and took a sip of my beer.

And then Earl Karlinsky grabbed my wrist, the one whose hand was gripping the beer, as if he was going to physically drag me out of the place. He forced my wrist down to the bar top, spilling some of the beer.

Now, I am not one for physical confrontation. I believe humanity has evolved any number of better ways to settle disputes, from mediation all the way down to rock-paper-scissors.

That said, I am not a small man. Nor am I stranger to the kind of exercise that makes a body suitable for action. And I am sure as hell not in the market for being pushed around. Plus, he spilled my beer.

In a calm, deliberate voice, I said, "Get. Your hand. Off me. Now."

He was still glaring at me, like I was some easily intimidated eighteen-year-old caddy. I stood, so I was now taller than him, and may have stuck out my chest a little.

That was when Doc reappeared. "Is there a problem here?" he asked.

Karlinsky released my wrist and turned to Doc. "I'm sorry, Mr. Fierro. But Mr. Ross was here earlier today and I made it very clear to him that he was not to be on the premises. He has to leave."

"Uh, Carter is here as my guest," Doc said.

"I explicitly told him that he was not welcome here," Karlinsky said, apparently not hearing what Doc said.

"Earl," Doc said, a little more forcefully, "I'm telling you as a member of this club and as a member of its board of directors that Carter is here at my invitation and he is welcome to stay here as long as I or any other member wants him here. I think you're forgetting your place."

Karlinsky stiffened, having apparently heard Doc this time. He knew he was beaten. At a private country club, general manager trumps rabble-rousing reporter. But board member trumps general manager. He gave me one last scornful glance, then departed.

"Seriously, what's going on with him?" I asked.

Doc just held up one pinky, the internationally recognized symbol for a small penis.

But I once again found myself wondering why Karlinsky was so threatened by the presence of someone whose only job it was to seek the truth.

As we settled back into our drinks, Doc began shunting me toward acquaintances and golfing buddies of Kevin Tiemeyer, who soon became the subject of many mournful toasts. Not that it was doing my story a whole lot of good. I was getting the usual empty platitudes people say about the deceased.

One of these days, I would figure out what it was about dying that turned people into saints. Had I been talking to these same guys about Tiemeyer two weeks ago, when he was still alive, I'm sure they would have told me Tiemeyer was a relatively ordinary schmuck: a decent-enough guy who was trying his best despite being as mistake-prone as the rest of us.

But now that he was dead? Kevin Tiemeyer was suddenly a man who everyone loved; who had no enemies, foreign or domestic; and who never said a bad word about anyone.

It's the last one that gets me every time. Because, I'm sorry, this is New Jersey. We say bad words about *everyone*.

Nevertheless, the best I could get beyond clichés were superficial factoids about him, his foibles and peccadilloes. In addition to his cigar-chewing, he was a bit notorious for giving himself four-foot putts and back nine mulligans. On the plus side, he had an apparently inexhaustible supply of dirty jokes and was quick to buy you a drink after your round.

Tiemeyer was clearly well liked, though I was getting the sense he was not especially well known. No one claimed to be his best friend, or to socialize with him away from the club. And no one was close enough to him to be able to say what his recent makeover might have been about.

About an hour and two beers in, I excused myself for a trip to the men's room. As soon as I was out of eyeshot, I quickly hooked around the corner, down the stairs. They led to the locker rooms and, more important, the pro shop.

When I was a rookie reporter in the housing projects and tenements of Newark, I can remember feeling like my learning curve was a long one. The environment there was so different from the one I had been raised in, it took a few years to really learn the ways of the 'hood.

Let's just say snooping around a country club came a little more naturally to someone with my upbringing. And I had been around enough of them to know the pro shop usually contained the starter's desk, which at a busy place like Fanwood served as the nerve center for the whole operation.

The starter was the guy who made the reservations for tee times. He paired people up with their favorite caddies, took into consideration who might like playing with whom when making foursomes, fretted over pace-of-play, and generally kept things running smoothly. He also—and this was crucial, from my current standpoint—wrote everything down.

Which meant there would be a record of Joseph Okeke's day at Fanwood. All I had to do was find it.

From an ethical standpoint, what I was about to attempt was not . . . well, I wouldn't go so far as to call it gray. I would also not call it the glistening, virginal white of a wedding dress. It was maybe slightly off-white. A nice clamshell, perhaps.

A reporter with a respectable broadsheet newspaper like the *Eagle-Examiner* cannot misrepresent himself in order to gain information, nor can he break a law to obtain it. I rationalized that I had been invited to enter the club—and, hence, was here legally— and that no one had told me I couldn't have a little look around.

So I felt I was on firm enough ground as I walked down a hallway, past the oil-painted portraits of past club presidents who presumably had made the turn to the ultimate back nine. On the floor, there was thick carpeting that nicely hushed my footfalls. After two beers on an empty stomach, I knew I probably wasn't being as quiet as I'd like. Still, the carpet made me feel like I was in stealth mode.

I reached the entrance to the pro shop and paused. The door had four glass panes in its upper half, so I could see the other side was dark and empty, as one would expect at that time of day. I tentatively turned the door handle.

It was open. Softly, I entered.

Then two things happened: the lights came on automatically, activated by a motion sensor; and a pressure sensor in the welcome mat announced my entry with an earsplitting *bee-baaaah* chime.

So much for stealth mode. I halted, in case someone came charged out of a back room to politely but pointedly inquire about my presence. But no one came.

Moving a little faster now, I walked past standing racks filled with clothing, all bearing the Fanwood Country Club emblem; then past racks of drivers, putters, and other implements of golfing mayhem; then past boxes of balls that were soon to be littered about the woodlands and waterways of Fanwood's eighteen-hole track.

Around the corner, at the front of the pro shop, near a door that led outside to the putting green, I found the starter's desk. I reached it by pushing through a swinging half door.

The desk itself was chest height. It was neatly kept: scorecards stacked in a small bin, free tees in one circular container, those damnable stubby pencils in another.

The only other objects on it were a computer keyboard and monitor, both of which had wires leading down to a terminal on the floor. I checked the shelves that had been built in underneath, hoping to find a thick book jammed with hand-written pages, like they would have done it in ye olden days of yore. Alas, all the shelves contained were towels with the club logo silk-screened into them.

It was the computer or nothing. I just hoped the thing wasn't password protected, or this was going to turn into a very unsatisfying expedition.

The computer's screen saver had been engaged and was busy scrawling never-ending geometric patterns across the monitor. Its keyboard, which wore the dark brown stains of too many fingers over too many years, was probably the first dirty thing I had seen at Fanwood. The mouse was similarly grimy.

I put my hand on it and gave it a quick upward shove. A quarter second later, the screen saver blinked off to reveal the virtual desktop, which was every bit as uncluttered as the actual desktop in front of me. The operating system was Windows 7, which I might have scoffed at, except that our computers in the newsroom were still running Windows 98.

There were a half-dozen shortcuts running down the left side of the screen. The one that immediately caught my eye was the one with an icon that looked like a golf ball. It was called Start-Pro Green.

Two clicks later, the application had opened. I was just starting to scroll through the menu options when a noise nearly stopped my heart: that *bee-baaaah* chime.

Someone was coming, someone who would almost certainly know I did not belong snooping through the club's computer. I ducked, making myself as small as I could behind the desk. I wished I could tuck myself in the shelves, but, one, they were filled with towels, and, two, it would make too much noise.

I didn't have much of a view, but it turned out I didn't need my eyes to know who had entered the pro shop. Just my nose. It was Earl Karlinsky. The man had once again been preceded by his odor.

And that wasn't the only reason I was holding my breath. Had he thought it strange that the light in this normally darkened area was on? Would he notice that someone had logged on to the computer? Could he smell me the same way I could smell him?

His feet brushed softly against the deep carpet as he walked briskly through the room. Then he paused. He was no more than ten feet from me on the other side of the desk. I heard him trying the handle of the door that led outside.

Locking up. He was just locking up, making sure everything was safe and secure. It was part of his routine, something he did automatically, without much thought, before he, I prayed, left for the night.

It sounded like the door handle had not yielded. Someone had already locked that door. Satisfied, he turned back around. I heard his shoes squish on the carpet as he pivoted. Then he departed the same way he came, leaving behind only his musk-tinged wake.

Slowly, quietly, I exhaled, counted to twenty, then stood up. The computer was still waiting for me. I shoved the mouse again, though this time I noticed my hand was shaking.

Calming my jittery mind, I returned to my systematic study of the menu items. On the fifth tab over, I found a search function. I pulled it up, typed "Okeke," and hit enter.

Only one entry came up. He had played a little less than a month earlier—a week and a day before he had been killed, to be exact. The start time for the round was 2:08 P.M. It would have been a nice afternoon round that, perhaps, preceded dinner at the club.

He had just one playing partner. I had expected the name might mean nothing to me. Instead, it was a name that meant everything:

It was Kevin Tiemeyer.

CHAPTER 18

You learn about all sorts of things in prison: mainly, things that make you a better criminal.

How to sell drugs in a way that won't make you as vulnerable to police buy-busts. How to mangle a gun so it becomes untraceable. How to buy a woman, a baby, an endangered species.

Even how to get rid of a body.

On that last front, one of the more interesting facts Blue Mask had learned, courtesy of a former cell mate, was that there were few better places on the East Coast to dispose of an unwanted corpse than the New Jersey Pine Barrens.

The Pine Barrens are the state's largest tract of open space, more than a million acres. And thanks to the foresight of a governor named Byrne—who understood that America's most crowded state might someday appreciate a little room to breathe—development was no longer allowed there. The few houses that remained were slowly emptying out.

That's part of what made the Pine Barrens such a good receptacle for a body, according to Blue Mask's cell mate. The other part was simple science. The man had said the soil was so acidic, from untold eons of fallen pine needles, that it greatly accelerated a body's decay. After a few months, the acid ate through everything. Even the bones. There would literally be nothing left of it.

That's if he could get there. The only problem was, Blue Mask didn't have a car. Birdie didn't have one, either.

Blue Mask considered what to do about this problem as he began tidying up the kitchen. He poured the stew broth down the drain. Then he tossed the vegetables in the trash. Then he cleaned the dishes, just like Birdie would have done. He didn't want anything to look out of place, should someone happen to drop by.

Once he was done, he turned his attention back to Birdie's corpse.

She had been one of those women who was constantly in motion—always cooking, cleaning, or just puttering around. To see her so completely still was something of a novelty.

There were dark marks on her neck where Blue Mask's hands had been. Her head was tilted back. Her mouth was agape. Her eyes were wide open, staring up at the ceiling with that deathly incomprehension that life had ended.

Eventually, Blue Mask made up his mind he was going to have to do *something* with her.

First thought: the basement. There had to be somewhere down there he could stash her. An old trunk? Maybe a garbage barrel?

But there would be the problem of smell. Even if he kept the lid on, she would eventually start to stink up the place, wouldn't she?

The attic? No. Same deal.

If he tied her up in a couple of heavy-duty plastic garbage bags, would that do the trick? He had no idea.

Problems. Nothing but problems. Why did she have to give his damn money away to that preacher? Why couldn't she have just made macaroni and cheese instead of stew? He could have saved up his five thousand and been gone.

He needed to get the body out of the house. The more he thought it through, it was the prudent course of action. Birdie was an active socialite. Between the church and the senior center, she was doing something pretty much every day. If she stopped showing up for things, people would come looking for her.

He could tell them he hadn't seen her, of course. Old people lost their minds and wandered off all the time, right?

Except Birdie wasn't senile and everyone knew it. He knew he needed to make certain if they got a search warrant they weren't going to find her. If they did, it wouldn't take them long to start looking real hard at her ex-con great-nephew. Cops loved to pin stuff on guys with rap sheets even when they didn't do it.

If only he had a car. He could just toss the body in the trunk, drive south until he made it to the Pine Barrens, dig a shallow grave, and let the soil take care of the rest.

Then, finally, what should have been obvious finally occurred to him: he didn't have a car, true, but he sure knew how to get one.

He certainly had a lot of practice at it lately. He could even say, without bragging, that he was getting good at it.

He pulled out his phone and dialed Black Mask.

He heard: "Hello."

"Yo, it's me."

"What you want?"

"We gotta do one tonight."

There was pause. "Says who?"

"Says me."

"I don't give a damn what you say. It's—"

Black Mask almost said a name, then stopped himself. His employer had been explicit: never, ever use names over the phone. Even using disposable cell phones it wasn't safe. Black Mask continued with: "It's the people with the money who I listen to. And they ain't said nothing to me."

"Yeah, well, I need a car," Blue Mask said.

"Yeah, so?"

"So let's get one."

"Dawg, you ain't listening. The people with the money say we do a job, we do a job. They say when we do it, they say where we do it, and then they pay us. That's how it works. You wanna get paid, right?"

Blue Mask felt his frustration building. "Yeah, but I need a car *now*."

"Then that's on you, dawg."

That's when Blue Mask realized: yes. Yes, it was. He didn't need help. Not from Black Mask. Not from anyone.

He could do this himself. All he had to do was wait for darkness.

CHAPTER 19

There were times when I felt like being a reporter was a lot like being an electrician. It was all about looking for contact points.

An electrician sought them out because that's where a circuit was completed, allowing the current to flow. For a reporter, contact points—or intersections, or crossroads, or whatever you wanted to call the place where two things connected—were often where stories came together and found their flow.

That was true whether you were talking literally or metaphorically; whether you were referring to differing ideologies, policies, problems—or, in this case, people.

Joseph Okeke and Kevin Tiemeyer had come into contact on a golf course. Some kind of circuit had been completed that day. I didn't yet know what the circuit was, or what purpose it was supposed to serve, or what larger system it was part of. But less than a month later, both men were dead, victims of carjackings gone wrong.

And that did not seem like happenstance. A carjacking was supposed to be a random event, a wrong-place-wrong-time-wrong-car, sorry-you-got-hit-by-lightning kind of thing. It did not seek you out because of your relationships, and certainly not because of your golf pairings. It should have been no more predictable than winning the lottery.

Except, of course, this being New Jersey, there was always the possibility someone had rigged the drawing.

But who? And how? And when? And to what exact end?

Did Earl Karlinsky have something to do with it? Or was his hostility toward me—and his peculiar edginess toward the subject of Kevin Tiemeyer—unrelated to a round of golf that had taken place at his club a month earlier?

I wasn't at a point where I could even dream up the answers, but I was going to have to find some, and quickly. My article was supposed to run in Sunday's paper, which meant I needed to have it done by a reasonable hour on Saturday. And I couldn't exactly turn in some gee-whiz thumb-sucker of a story about two guys from different background who were killed in unrelated carjackings if the carjackings were not, in fact, unrelated.

After returning to the bar, where my slightly extended absence had not been noticed, I made some casual inquiries as to whether anyone had seen or interacted with Joseph Okeke during his visit to Fanwood. It made sense a tall, ebony-skinned African man would have been noticed in a place where the membership was not noted for its abundance of melanin. But no one claimed to have seen him.

Eventually, I felt like I had wrung out all the moisture I was going to get from this particular washcloth. I offered my thankyous to Doc Fierro, whose remarkable liver seemed to be having little trouble keeping up with its workload.

Mine was feeling taxed and I had stopped at two beers, which I had consumed over the course of two and a half hours. This, according to a chart I recalled from a long-ago high school health class, meant I was sober enough to drive.

On my way out, I was momentarily blinded by a bank of lights that had been set up next to the clubhouse, where one of the local television stations was doing a stand-up. Karlinsky must have been outvoted on that one. Either that or he didn't have the same objection to cameras as he did to notebooks.

I can't say my reaction to them was quite as charitable. In my ranking of Things I Like, local TV news has a slot somewhere between infectious diseases and bedbugs. Except, of course, you can't inoculate yourself against them and no amount of fumigating seems to get rid of them.

It's nothing personal. On an individual level, most of them are quite acceptable. But when you put them all together and made them chase the same dwindling ratings, it became a race to reach the lowest common denominator.

There were times when I worried the newspaper business might be heading that way. One newspaper I knew had slashed all of its reporters' salaries but offered a deal wherein they could make up what they had lost via incentive pay tied to the number of clicks their stories received online. So, basically, the only way the reporters could pay their mortgages was if they wrote stories that popped up when teenage boys googled things like "Taylor Swift naked."

The fallacy, of course, is that all clicks are created equal. Let the record be clear that they're not. Quality matters. It mattered when all news was printed on dead trees. It continues to matter now that it's all binary code sliding through the well-oiled tubes of the Interwebs.

I tried to give this particular TV news crew a little credit and not make assumptions about them. Maybe they were attempting to elevate the discourse.

And then, as I walked past, I overheard a frosty-haired blonde report, with all due earnestness, "and the members here at Fanwood Country Club say he *never* said a bad word about *anyone*. Back to you, Andy."

I'm fairly certain, out of courtesy to my fellow media professionals, that I kept my response muted. But if someone were to take the initiative to put that footage into a audio enhancer and crank up the background noise, the last thing they would hear was a newspaper reporter making a scoffing noise.

.   .   .

My first order of business, after I got in my car, was to find a road-side pizzeria. Some people drink coffee to sober up. Not being a fan of that concoction, I have found grease and crust to be an adequate substitute.

Luckily, in the Garden State, such establishments offering these salves are never far. Once there, I ordered and then consumed two slices of sausage. Back in the car, and feeling more level-headed, I checked in with Chillax, whose voice mail informed me I had selected the worst way to reach him, and that he much preferred texts or e-mails. Being as I much preferred to actually talk to a human being, that left us at a standoff that would have to be resolved at a later time.

It was now a little after eight o'clock, an acceptable hour for a reporter not on deadline to call it a night. But I felt like I had one more phone call in me, and I knew who I wanted to be the recipient of that call: Zabrina Coleman-Webster.

I am a member of the One Great Source school of reporting. In most stories—or on most beats—there is one source who will become your go-to, the sage voice who helps you assemble all the pieces into a more cogent whole.

The trick, of course, is knowing when you've found that person, and cultivating them properly once you do. I was hoping, as I dialed her number, that Zabrina might be it for this story.

"Hello?" she answered. I could hear the television on in the background.

"Hey, Zabrina, Carter Ross with the *Eagle-Examiner*."

"Oh, hey."

"Sorry to bother you again. Am I catching you at an okay time for a quick question or two?"

"Yeah, sure. Shoot."

"I was wondering if Joseph ever mentioned the name Kevin Tiemeyer."

There was no immediate response. "Hang on," she said, muting the volume on the TV. Finally, she said, "Did you say Kevin Tiemeyer?"

"That's right."

Another pause was followed by: "No. Not that I remember. Is that a name I should know?"

"Well, if you've been listening to the news today, he's the banker who was killed in a carjacking last night."

"Oh, yeah, I knew it sounded familiar. But what does that have to do with Joseph?"

"Almost a month ago, a week and a day before Joseph was killed to be exact, they golfed together at Fanwood Country Club."

"Oh," she said. "That's strange."

"Yeah, I know. That's why I'm trying to figure out what happened that day. Did Joseph mention anything about it?"

"I remember him saying he was going to play Fanwood. He was excited about it. I don't think I asked who he was playing with. Joseph had a lot of business contacts. If he found out one of them was a golfer, he usually played with them at one point or another. He was always looking for an excuse to go out."

"Was Tiemeyer a business contact?"

"I don't know. Maybe."

"Did he say anything about how he and Tiemeyer knew each other?"

"No. I never heard that name before today," Zabrina said. "Joseph and I didn't talk a lot about work. Well, actually, that's not true: I talked about work all the time. I probably talked the poor man's ear off. But he didn't say much. He'd mention stuff now and then, but it's not like he told me about every minute of every day, you know?"

Which meant Zabrina's chances of becoming my One Great Source were looking dim. But I took a stab with another question anyway: "Did he ever mention the name Earl Karlinsky?"

"Karlinsky," she repeated. "Now, I do know that name. But help me out: who is Earl Karlinsky?"

"He's the general manager at Fanwood Country Club."

"Oh, yeah, now wait a second," she said. "That definitely rings a bell. Yes, yes. You know, I had forgotten about this until just now, but Joseph said that a Mr. Karlinsky approached him after his round and asked him if he wanted to sell his car."

"That's . . . kind of odd."

"I know."

"What did Joseph say about it?"

"Oh, he loved talking about that car. I don't think he minded. It struck me as a strange thing. But Mr. Karlinsky said he had been looking for a late-model BMW and he wanted to know if Joseph would be willing to part with his. He asked Joseph all kinds of questions about the car."

"What kind of questions?"

"Oh, like what features did it have, what add-ons had he gotten with it, that sort of thing."

Which are the kind of questions you might ask someone whose car you were planning to buy.

Or whose car you were planning to steal.

I hustled Zabrina off the phone before I unloaded a whole lot of unsubstantiated babble on her. But it turned out she was a pretty good source, after all—without even knowing it.

Because my brain was already whirring on this.

Was *that* the circuit being completed at Fanwood Country Club? Was Earl Karlinsky somehow marking club members and their guests for carjacking?

I thought back to my first reaction to strolling through that parking lot: that it was a carjacker's paradise. Karlinsky must

˙have seen it that way, too, and then eventually decided to profit from it.

No sane human being would attempt to pull off armed carjackings at the gates of Fanwood Country Club. If you looked at a ratio of dollars budgeted to violent crimes committed, the Scotch Plains–Fanwood Police Department was probably about a hundred times better resourced than its Newark equivalent. And that was a conservative estimate.

Karlinsky was simply finding good targets in Fanwood. He could walk through the parking lot, casing it for new vehicles with a high resale value. He probably knew which members worked in Newark regularly and which ones didn't.

From there, it was just a matter of slapping a tracking device on the vehicles that fit the profile he was looking for. Then, his associates in Newark—and I was assuming Karlinsky was part of a crew that pulled this off—would plug into the data from the tracking device. They could wait until the time was right and then strike.

It was modern carjacking, a method that took the randomness out of the equation. Why hang around all night on a street corner in Newark and wait for the right vehicle to come along? It was much more efficient to pick the vehicle ahead of time, know where it was at all times, and strike when you were good and ready.

Or at least that's how I was imagining it all. My problem now, of course, was that outside of my own wild speculation, I had nothing in the way of hard evidence to prove it. I had a round of golf between two men and a conversation between one of those men and a golf club's general manager. The rest was conjecture, nothing I would put in the newspaper.

But it was only Tuesday. There was time to solidify it. The first thing to do was prove this was no coincidence. If there had been a rash of carjackings among Fanwood members, it would go a long way toward supporting my theory.

I quickly tapped out an e-mail to Doc Fierro, thanking him for his hospitality and asking him if he wouldn't mind sharing with me a Fanwood membership list—which I would, of course, treat with all due discretion. If he balked, I would tell him why I needed it. Doc would recognize the greater good I was trying to achieve.

Once I established a correlation between Newark carjackings and Fanwood Country Club's parking lot, I would then have to prove that Karlinsky was the causative element. I didn't know exactly how I'd do that.

But, again, it was only Tuesday. There was time.

Having driven home and gotten myself more comfortably attired, I was just winding down toward sleep when my phone blurped with a text message. I had been on the couch of my tidy, two-bedroom Bloomfield abode, reading Sue Grafton's latest (I had finally made it to *W*, and it made me hope the letter Z would never come). Deadline, my black-and-white domestic short-haired cat, was on my lap, doing his best to imitate a puddle of goo.

The text was from Tina. And, like most things coming from Tina, it surprised me: "Can I come over?" it read.

I wrote back: "Of course. I'll be up."

Setting my phone down on the coffee table, I asked Deadline, "I wonder what that's about?"

He indicated his intense interest in this conversation by keeping his eyes screwed shut and holding the remainder of his body perfectly still. I ran my thumb along the path between his eyes and up to the top of his head until his purrs began making his whole body vibrate. Make no mistake: Deadline is the most easily contented roommate, male or female, I've ever had.

I returned to my book for another thirty minutes or so until

I heard Tina's footsteps on the front porch. She didn't need me to open the front door—I had given her a key to my place, without much fanfare or commentary, a few months earlier—but I still poured Deadline off my lap so I could get to my feet and greet her.

The woman who entered my house sort of looked like Tina. She had Tina's protruding midsection and Tina's pregnancy-thickened curly brown hair. It's just her face that had turned into a reddened, blotchy mess. You didn't have to be the *Eagle-Examiner's* ace investigative reporter to know she had been crying.

"Hey, what's the matter?" I asked.

She rushed toward me, another unexpected development, and buried her nose in my neck, wrapping her arms around my shoulders. Her body was heaving in a distinctly nonrhythmic fashion and I could feel her tears against my skin.

As a keen interpreter of nonverbal cues, I sensed that she was upset. I still had no idea what was going on. But being that I have long experience playing the part of the Confused Male—sadly, it doesn't involve much acting most of the time—I just held on to her and let her shake for a while. I ran my hand along her head and rubbed the spots on her back that had been sore from the second trimester on.

"Can we sit down?" she asked finally.

"Of course," I said, and led her over to the couch, where I assisted in lowering her onto its surface. She depressed the cushions enough that Deadline sort of just rolled against her side, like he was being drawn by her gravitational pull.

"Can I get you a tissue?" I asked.

She nodded. I went into my bathroom and retrieved the whole box. Back when this was strictly a bachelor pad, I never kept tissues in the house—they are, to my mind, completely redundant with toilet paper and/or paper towels. But I had been made to understand this viewpoint was less than fully civilized.

"What's going on?" I asked after I handed the tissues to her and settled into the couch next to her.

She blew her nose several times, leaving the spent wads resting on the shelf created by the top of her belly.

"Brodie had a heart attack," she said at last.

"Aw, Jesus," I said, because I was momentarily incapable of saying anything more cogent.

"He was just out near the copy desk, jingling the change in his pocket, looking over people's shoulders, creeping them out a bit—the usual things he's done ten thousand times. I was out there helping Gary with a headline and the next thing I knew someone was saying, 'Brodie, are you okay?'

"I looked over and he had his hand on his chest and the weirdest expression on his face. I've never seen anything like it. He was totally bewildered about what was happening. And then he just collapsed. It's like someone shot him or something. His eyes were rolled back in his head. It was so scary and horrible. He was practically right next to me."

As Tina spoke, I was just staring at a spot on the floor, thinking about Brodie. He had been with the paper for nearly fifty years. For the last quarter century or more, he had commanded it as executive editor. He was our unquestioned leader.

But he was more than that. He was our heart, our soul, our conscience. We all looked to him—for his guidance, his experience, and his wisdom, yes; but also for the joy that he brought to newspapering, day in, day out.

It was a trait we desperately needed. In a world where deadlines are measured by the minute and never stop coming, there is an incredible burnout factor. But even more insidious than that is complacency. After enough years, there's this tendency to forget the importance of what you're doing. After all, what's one more murder? One more plane crash? One more scandal?

Brodie never lost his enthusiasm for the big story. It's like it was new for him every time. He understood that we had a sacred trust with readers: they paid attention to us and bought our paper because we worked our asses off to get things right, with every issue we put out, and he wanted to make damn sure we followed through on our end of the promise. There was something about seeing a seventysomething-year-old man charging around like his ass was burning that lit a fire under the rest of us.

I thought back to one of the first run-ins I ever had with him. I had to earn the trust of some gang members I needed to interview, so I smoked pot with them. I was still stoned as I walked into the building, where I bumped into Brodie smelling like I had just come from a Cheech and Chong marathon. Far from being upset with me, he was delighted—absolutely delighted—that one of his reporters had gone to such lengths to get a story.

That was Brodie. He was, above all else, a *newspaperman*. At a time when the breed is becoming extinct, maybe that made him unfashionable. But if that was the case, I aspired to be just as out of style as he was.

It was at that moment that I understood, with a renewed sense of appreciation, how much I looked up to the man.

Tina broke the silence with: "I feel like I watched him die."

"Is he . . . ?" I started, but couldn't finish the sentence.

"We don't know," she said. "We called an ambulance, of course. Some of the copy editors started doing chest compressions immediately. But it didn't . . . I mean, I just don't know. He's at the hospital now. We called his wife to let her know. She was on her way."

A sob tried to overtake her. She swallowed it, turning the whole thing into an audible gasp.

"I'm sorry," she said. "I kept it together the whole time in the newsroom because I felt like everyone needed me to stay strong. I mean, we had a paper to get out, you know? If nothing else, Brodie wouldn't want anything to mess with that. That's everything he stood for and I wanted to . . . to honor that. So I made sure we hit the mark with the first edition and that everything was fine. And then on the way here, it just hit me like crazy. I mean, I already feel like I'm out of control with these pregnancy hormones and—"

"You don't have to keep it together for me," I said.

"Thanks," she whispered.

We stayed like that for a good long while, leaning against each other. Every once in a while, we'd say whatever happened to be on our minds. Thoughts about Brodie. Thoughts about the fragility of existence and the gift that it was. Thoughts about the new life stirring inside her.

But mostly we just sat. By the time we got up to go to bed several hours later, the box of tissues was spent.

CHAPTER 20

When he was a kid, playing Little League baseball in Newark, Blue Mask had been like this with his uniform.

Everything just so. Checked in the mirror. Tucked and re-tucked.

He would put it on at six thirty in the morning for a two o'clock game. The excitement consumed him. He couldn't wait to get on the field. The anticipation was almost better than the game itself. Almost.

Blue Mask realized he felt the same way about jacking cars. Another sign that this was what he was meant to be doing with his life.

And maybe he looked ridiculous, walking around the house with his blue ski mask pulled down and his gun tucked in his waistband, four hours before he was going out. He didn't care. It's not like Birdie was going to say anything.

He enjoyed feeling like a kid again. Pacing around. Looking at himself in the mirror. Playing out things in his mind. Scripting what he'd say to the driver. Imagining the look on the driver's face.

Maybe he'd shoot the guy. Maybe he wouldn't. Depends if he felt like he was getting the respect he deserved.

He made himself wait until ten o'clock, then charged out into the street and then . . .

Well, what? Black Mask had always been the one to say where they went and when. Black Mask said which car to hit—almost like he knew the thing was coming.

Blue Mask's only job was to wait for the whistle and then go.

For a few minutes, Blue Mask felt like an idiot. He had spent so much time thinking about the actual act, he hadn't thought out any of the other stuff that led up to it. The planning. The strategy.

No big deal. This was just a small setback. He rolled the ski mask off his face, wearing it like a hat instead. He pulled his hoodie over his head, mostly to hide the mask. Then he left the house and started walking.

His first move was to get out of the neighborhood. He noticed Black Mask never did jobs near where he lived. That was smart. The cops in Newark did this community policing thing, which meant they all stuck with a certain area of the city. The idea was that they got to know the thugs in their own sector. If there was a crime, they always started with the known suspects. Blue Mask wanted to go to a part of town where he'd be unknown.

That meant downtown. It was where there were more likely to be expensive cars anyway. Plus, there were more traffic lights there.

He stalked around for a time, spending some time on Washington Street, then on University, then on Halsey. Nothing felt right. Either the light was green or the car was wrong or he wasn't in position in time.

Eventually, he settled on Washington Street and set up on one corner. There was a shuttered storefront with a small vestibule that gave him both concealment and visibility: he could see the intersection but not be seen by any passing cars.

It was now after midnight. Traffic had gotten noticeably

lighter over the previous hour. Most of the cars out were beaters that would probably break down before he could get Birdie's body out of town.

Finally, he caught the gleam of a new car just as the light turned yellow. It slowed to a stop rather than risk running the light. But it was Chevy. He wasn't here to jack no damn Chevy.

Another fifteen minutes passed before there was another half-decent opportunity. He thought, at first glance, that it was a Lexus. But, no, it was a Toyota that just sort of looked like a Lexus.

He was starting to think about giving up and just grabbing whatever came along. He sure didn't want to have to sleep with Birdie's body getting all stiff in the kitchen.

Then. Finally. Cadillac. White. The car was a few years old. Still, it was a Cadillac. There had to be some value there. He didn't know quite who he'd sell it to. Black Mask had always taken care of that part. But Blue Mask would figure out something. He had contacts of his own.

The ski mask went down. The gun came out. The light was holding red.

Blue Mask sprinted toward the driver's side door, the gun barrel pointing the way. The other jobs he had done with Black Mask, the drivers had played their part nicely—getting out the car, hands up, letting them just take the vehicle.

This guy wasn't going as easily. He was a black man. A big fellow, but soft-looking. Blue Mask saw his mouth go wide, then his eyes, just like the others.

But then he stomped on the gas pedal. The others hadn't done that.

Still, there was this small hesitation, a split second for the fuel injectors to spray fuel into the piston chambers, another split second for the spark plugs to ignite the gas, another split second for the car to transfer the energy from that small contained explosion to the drive shaft.

In that brief time lapse, Blue Mask fired two shots through the window, loosely aimed at the man's face. The glass did not shatter. It just acquired two shallow craters where the bullets entered. Blue Mask couldn't tell if he'd hit anything beyond it.

Then the car was gone. Some tragic fraction of a second too late, it had accelerated across the intersection. For perhaps two hundred more yards, Blue Mask watched the Cadillac careen down the street. Then it jumped the curb and hit a light stanchion, coming to a crunching stop.

Blue Mask ran after it, his gun still drawn. The driver must have blacked out and lost control of the vehicle. Or maybe the guy's head had been blown off and that was just the car driving on its own. Blue Mask figured he'd yank whatever was left of the driver out of the vehicle, maybe put a kill shot in him, and be on his way.

Then the driver's side door opened. Blue Mask was still a hundred yards away. He was amazed to watch the driver emerge with a hand clamped on his neck. He was a burly fellow, all right. He took one or two halting steps, leaned on the car, then cast a wary glance over his shoulder.

Then he saw Blue Mask and started staggering away, toward a nearby alley, with surprising speed for such a big guy. Maybe he knew he was running for his life.

As Blue Mask closed in, he considered going after the driver. But no. If the gunshots hadn't attracted enough attention, the sound of the crash would. It was time to get out of there.

Blue Mask reached the wreck. The bumper had a small V in it. The driver's side window was now mostly gone, with just a few jagged glass edges clinging to its frame.

But there was no time to worry about aesthetics. He hopped in the still-open driver's side door, sat in a leather seat marred by glass pebbles and blood, and closed the door behind him. He shifted into reverse to get the car away from the light stanchion, then into drive to get away.

There were no sirens approaching, no other drivers or pedestrians around to sound any alarm. After a mile or so, Blue Mask pulled over, stole the license plates of an old Saturn, and tossed the Caddy's plates in a Dumpster.

He cursed when he surveyed the damage to the Cadillac. But maybe it wouldn't hurt the resale value too much. The bumper could be pulled out. The window could be replaced.

It certainly was drivable. And it would get him down to the Pine Barrens and back. He could have Birdie buried by dawn. That was what mattered.

CHAPTER 21

I woke up the next morning with this feeling of dread, like the awful aftertaste of the night before had yet to leave my tongue.

Tina was still in bed when I dragged myself out of it. She had slept fitfully, like usual. It is the horrible irony of the final trimester that a woman who wants nothing more than to sleep can't seem to do it. People like to say it's the body's way of preparing itself for the marathon of sleep deprivation that is to come. I think it's just one more cruelty nature visits on pregnant women.

Naturally, Tina's struggles meant I had slept poorly, too. Though I was just smart enough not to complain. I like my face unslapped.

The encouraging news, which Tina received via an early-morning e-mail that she drowsily checked while in bed, was that Brodie had made it through the night. He was far from out of the woods—they were just starting to assess the damage—but he had survived those crucial first twelve hours. Apparently, it took a lot more than just a heart attack to take down our executive editor.

I was stepping out of the shower as Tina entered the bathroom.

"Can I pee?" she asked.

We were not at the point of our cohabitation that we were

comfortable urinating in front of each other. And, come to think of it, that was a point I hoped we would not reach for a while—like, a hundred and fifty years or so. I realize not all couples in this great, urinating nation of ours feel the same way. I say: keep some of the mystery intact, America.

I vacated the bathroom for a moment. When I heard the toilet flush and the shower turn on, I thought it safe to reenter.

"I can't believe I'm going to have to put the same underwear back on when I get out of here," she said.

I decided this was not the moment to badger her about her failure to have moved any of her stuff into my house. (See previous reference to: face, unslapped.)

"I'd offer you some of mine, but somehow I don't think they'd fit."

"No, the sad thing is, they probably would," she said. "The only problem is this will end up being the day I go into labor, and the nurses will ask me if my wife is planning to attend the delivery."

"You could always go commando."

"No, *you* could go commando. Trust me when I say a woman in my condition cannot. You don't want to even know what's oozing out of—"

"You know, why don't I just let you enjoy your shower?" I said.

She laughed and let the water run for a while. As I shaved, my thoughts meandered back to Earl Karlinsky. I knew I needed to catch him in the act, whatever that act happened to be.

A friend of mine tells a great, perhaps apocryphal, story about Jimmy Breslin, the famed New York *Daily News* and *Newsday* columnist. This dates back to the early eighties. Breslin was already a legend—his piece about the ditchdigger at John F. Kennedy's funeral is perhaps the most venerated newspaper column of all time—but he was not the type to rest on his Pulitzer.

As the story goes, there was a rumor about a school superintendent in the Bronx who had misappropriated a baby grand piano from a school and given it to a pastor-community activist. This caused quite an uproar, and there was considerable speculation as to whether this had occurred. Breslin wasn't one for rumors. He marched up to the Bronx, knocked on the pastor's door, and said, "Show me the piano."

It speaks to Breslin's ability to get to the heart of the matter. But it also makes the point that there is no substitute for seeing something with your own eyes. If I wanted to know whether Earl Karlinsky was cruising the parking lot, slapping tracking devices on cars, I'd have to find a way to set up there and check it out.

I couldn't very well use my car. My Malibu was too conspicuous.

The water in the shower shut off. That's when an idea came to me.

"Hey, can I borrow your car today?" I asked.

"That depends," Tina said. "Can I borrow a towel?"

"That can be arranged," I said, exiting the bathroom for a moment to fish a towel out of my linen closet.

I returned as she slid the shower curtain back. I took a few seconds to leer at Tina's naked body.

"You know you're gorgeous, right?" I asked.

"Towel," she said.

I handed it to her.

"What do you need my car for?" she asked as she went through a drying routine made more complicated by her baby bump.

"I just wanted to do a little snooping on a source and I need a change of vehicular appearance."

"Okay, just try not to get any bullet holes in it," she said. This, sadly, had happened to my Malibu. If you looked carefully enough, you could still see where the holes had been patched up.

I returned to my bedroom to give my wardrobe its usual 1.3 nanoseconds of consideration. I came away with pleated slacks, a button-down shirt, and a patterned tie—an ensemble that was a completely different fashion paradigm from the day before, because the shirt was pale blue, not white, and the slacks were slightly darker.

If I ever write an erotic novel, its title will be inspired by my closet. I'll call it *Fifty Shades of Khaki*.

I went downstairs to the kitchen and fed Deadline, who was nervously pacing in front of his bowl, anxious to get on with another busy day of eating and sleeping. I then poured myself a man-sized bowl of a children's cereal and checked my e-mail.

The one from Buster Hays was the first to catch my eye. Buster still struggles with e-mail etiquette and has yet to master where the salutation belongs. Hence I clicked on an e-mail with "Dear Ivy," in the subject line.

The good news is he has recently overcome his affinity for Caps Lock, so I could at least peruse the body of the e-mail without feeling like he was screaming at me. It read:

> According to task force, another carjacking last night, approx. 12:30 A.M. in the 100 block of Washington Street. Vehicle was white Cadillac CTS, three years old. Driver was shot in neck but managed to walk to hospital. Assailant ID'd as a young black male wearing blue ski mask.
> Buster
> P.S. Don't thank me. Just send scotch.

I absorbed that news for a moment. The man in the blue ski mask—who may or may not have been following me the day before, and who may or may not be working in a crew with Earl Karlinsky—had a busy night. I wondered if the Cadillac belonged to a Fanwood Country Club member. Cops would not usually share the name of a victim who had survived an assault, but if anyone could coax it out of them, it would be Buster. I replied to his message, asking him to do just that, promising a second bottle of scotch as a thank-you.

The other e-mail of interest came from Doc Fierro. It was a list of every member of Fanwood Country Club, along with a pointed suggestion I not misuse the information or say where I had gotten it.

I replied with a quick thank-you, along with an acknowledgment that I owed him a debt of more than just gratitude. Then I redacted his name from the e-mail and forwarded it to Buster Hays with a request that he ask his guy on the carjacking task force to check it against their database of recent victims.

About the time I was done with this, Tina appeared, with damp ringlets of hair brushing against yesterday's blouse.

"I'm starving," she said. "Do you have anything resembling berries or citrus in this house?"

"That depends, do Froot Loops count?"

"You realize you're going to have diabetes by the time you hit forty," she said.

I grinned. "Yeah, but if you go by my maturity level, that's still at least twenty-eight years away."

She just shook her head. We swapped car keys. She leaned in, kissed me on the cheek, then left Deadline and I to our usual breakfast silence.

For as much as I was eager to get on with the business of investigating Earl Karlinsky, I had two promises to keep: one, that I'd visit Sweet Thang in her do-gooder headquarters at ten o'clock; and two, that I'd turn that visit into a readable puff piece by 5:00 P.M.

I knew I could put off the whole thing, being as Brodie wasn't going to be in much shape to know or care that I hadn't turned the story in. But that hardly seemed like the honorable thing to do under the circumstances. If the true measure of a person is what he does when no one is watching, I didn't want to come up short.

Giving Deadline one final pet, I locked up, hopped in Tina's Volvo, and started toward Newark. There is a certain theory of journalism that says in order for a story to be considered real news, there has to be at least one person who would rather not see it in the paper. And, sadly, the person forced to write it doesn't count.

By that standard, the story I was about to slap together was not real news. But the crossword puzzle isn't real news, either, and people would get mighty pissed if we didn't run that. Besides, a newspaper owes it to its readers to be a reflection of the community it covers. So I resolved to just get this over with, quickly and quietly.

The address Sweet Thang gave me led to a featureless box of a one-story brick building that made it clear to me the Greater Newark Children's Council was not wasting donor money on posh digs. Or signage. Next to the front door, there was a small plastic plaque with black-and-white lettering. It couldn't have cost more than ten dollars. It was a grim marker to what was promising to be a grim place.

Then I walked inside and it was like entering a cheer factory. There was framed children's artwork covering every available wall space: gleeful stick figures with explosions of hair, dots for eyes, and overlarge smiles; bright, bold suns with rays of light that reached practically to the ground; rainbows that took up the whole sky; houses fronted with purple flowers, pink bushes, and lollipop trees.

Some of the scenes depicted were idyllic panoramas these children—with lives bounded by concrete, asphalt, and poverty—

probably had never seen themselves. But they dreamed about them all the same. Their optimism fairly burst off the walls.

"They're wonderful, aren't they?" I heard a familiar voice say.

I turned around, and there was Sweet Thang, all bouncy blond hair and big blue eyes. I knew, from experience, that she was also probably wearing a dress, one that rather nicely displayed her commendable feminine aspects. But I had established a strict no-look policy when it came to anything below Sweet Thang's chin.

"When I got here the walls were bare and I was like, 'This will *not* do,'" she said. "So every time a kid in one of our programs made a drawing and I happened to be there, I asked if they wanted to bring it home or if I could keep it. Most of them were happy anyone even wanted their picture. After I had collected a bunch of them, I found a frame shop that was willing to mount them for us at cost and a donor who was willing to fund it. A year later, this is what you get."

She smiled and so did I. I'd defy anyone, male or female, to spend more than ten minutes around Sweet Thang without falling in love with her, just a little.

"Anyhow," she said, "I'd like you to meet Jawan Porter. Jawan, you can come out now, honey."

From an office door just behind Sweet Thang, a little boy of perhaps six peeked out. He had perfect brown skin and a mop of an Afro atop his little head.

"Come on, Jawan," Sweet Thang urged. "Jawan, this is Mr. Ross. Shake his hand just like I taught you."

Jawan walked toward me and held out a waifish arm. I grabbed the small hand at the end of it.

"Don't forget to look him in the eye," Sweet Thang instructed.

Jawan and I exchanged meaningful eye contact and then I smiled at him. He smiled back, showing off two gummy gaps where his front teeth should have been.

"Ah, looks like someone has just gotten a visit from the Tooth Fairy," I said, because it seemed like the thing you should say to a toothless six-year-old.

Then I caught that Sweet Thang was shooting me a cautionary glance, accompanied by a small head shake.

"Jawan lives in a residential home on Avon Avenue," she said. "He's got eleven brothers and sisters there."

And that's when I got it. Tooth Fairies didn't necessarily visit group homes in Newark. Jawan probably had some vague conception of who the Tooth Fairy was. He did not necessarily have firsthand knowledge of her magic.

Sweet Thang quickly changed the subject. "You know something I learned about Jawan? He's a really, really fast runner."

Jawan's smile stretched from the bottom of his face right up to the top. "Yeah, some of the big kids are faster. But I'm the fastest of the little kids."

"Show Mr. Ross how fast you are, Jawan."

He looked around nervously. He had probably been told—perhaps repeatedly—not to run inside. "It's okay, Jawan," Sweet Thang assured him. "You can run to the end of the hallway and back."

Jawan tore off down the carpeted hall, reached the end, then launched himself back toward us. He stopped in the exact spot where he had started, then looked at me for approval.

"Wow," I said. "How did you get to be so fast?"

"It's because my shoes are so fast," Jawan said, showing off his kicks, which appeared to be brand-new.

"Let me see one more time, Jawan," I said. "I can't believe how fast you were."

Jawan repeated his mad dash to the end of the hallway and back. His chest was heaving just slightly when he was done.

"I can go even faster if I'm outside," Jawan said. "I can go like a rocket."

Jawan made rocket noises, to emphasize his point. As he did so, I pulled a camera out of my pocket. Most of our photo staff had been laid off, so for a story like this—where, frankly, the artwork wasn't absolutely crucial—I was expected to snap a few pictures. There was no question a real photographer could do much more with the subject, but the paper could no longer afford real photographers for such simple jobs.

I snapped a few shots of Jawan posed like a Usain Bolt about to explode from the starting blocks. Then I took two more of Jawan showing off his gummy smile.

"Okay, Jawan, thank you. You can go back to Mrs. Rohne now," Sweet Thang instructed. "Jawan is enrolled at Stephen Crane Academy. It's a Montessori charter school that we run."

She waited until Jawan had departed, then added, "Those shoes were purchased with proceeds from the Chariots for Children program. Everyone in Jawan's group house got a new pair."

I couldn't have tamped down my smile if I wanted to, because I knew exactly what Sweet Thang was doing. She knew it, too. Having lured me into coming to do a story, she was now spoon-feeding me its contents.

"Jawan Porter with the fast shoes, huh?" I asked.

If I couldn't turn that into a heartrending anecdotal lede, I might as well turn in my press card.

"Just trying to be helpful," she said. "Let me show you the repair shop."

She led me through a back exit to a paved area ringed by a series of brick buildings, all of them larger than the office we had just departed. This had obviously once been a manufacturing complex of some sort that the Greater Newark Children's Council had taken over and rehabilitated. Newark had many such properties. Most of them had not been put to as good a purpose as this one.

Sweet Thang pointed out the buildings they used for their charter school, which appeared to have been relieved of their grime by a vigorous power-washing. She chattered about the school a bit. Like many charter schools, they were outperforming comparable public schools. I nodded politely through her presentation. At some point, she would probably try to strong-arm me into writing about them, too.

Then she steered me toward the repair shop. It was surrounded by old cars—most of them junkers—and still had its grime very much intact.

"Most of the Chariots for Children program is staffed by volunteers," she said. "Over the last year, we've developed a network of mechanics who come in and work for us when they can. We get a whole crew of them on Saturdays and Sundays. They are just the nicest guys. When I first started there were only one or two of them and now there are more than a dozen. They say it's because I make sandwiches for them, but they're just being nice. My sandwiches aren't that good."

Somehow, I doubt it was the sandwiches they were coming for. Unless we were applying that word euphemistically, in which case I am sure the mechanics found Sweet Thang's sandwiches very appealing.

She entered the building and I followed. It had a warehouse-like feel to it, lit from above by an array of caged halogen bulbs that hung from the twenty-foot ceiling. From somewhere inside, a television kept a low chatter going.

There were two hydraulic lifts, a long workbench filled with tools, and a pegboard behind it with even more. On the floor I recognized several tanks that likely fueled acetylene torches, motors for powering speed wrenches, and other tools of the mechanic's trade. Beyond the lifts there was an open area filled with various pieces that had once been inside the cars they served. The whole thing sort of looked like a chop shop.

"When a car gets donated, we make an initial assessment about whether we should try to fix it up for the auto wholesaler's auction or whether we should just sell it for parts," she continued. "This obviously isn't my area of expertise, but there are some parts on a car where there's a good secondary market. Like, catalytic converters or something. Actually, don't write that down because I have no idea what I'm talking about. The point is, sometimes the car is worth more in pieces than it is whole. Our goal is to wring every dime out of each donation that we can. Oh, there's Dave, come on."

She led me toward a man whose most prominent feature was a white handlebar mustache that he had greased up to fine points on both ends. He was bent over the open hood of a red Dodge Caravan, doing something with a wrench that was surely very wrenchly—auto repair not being my area of expertise, either.

"This is Dave Gilbert," she said. "He is the director of the Chariots for Children program. It's supposed to be a part-time position but he's here, what, sixty hours a week? I swear, it's like he lives here. He's just a total sweetheart. Dave, this is Carter Ross, my friend from the *Eagle-Examiner*."

Gilbert nodded at me. The mustache nodded with him. It really was an impressive piece of facial hair. Like a human version of a water buffalo's horns.

"Nice to meet you," he said.

I reached out to shake, then he held up his right hand. It looked like something that could have belonged to a chimney sweep.

"Yeah, maybe we can just wave," I suggested, and that seemed to suit him fine. He returned his attention to his work.

And then, for the first time, I focused on the car that was on the lift next to the Caravan. It was a white Cadillac CTS. And while I can't say I was an expert, it looked to be about three years old.

Just like the one Buster Hays said had been carjacked in Newark the night before.

I tried to keep my tone of inquiry casual. "That's a nice Caddy there," I said. "When did that one come in?"

Gilbert pulled his head out back out from under the hood. He looked over at the car, then at me. I worked at making my face the very study of neutrality.

"Couple of days ago," he said.

"Wow. Do people ordinarily donate cars that nice?"

"It happens," he said. "Depending on your tax bracket, the write-off you can claim can be more valuable than the car."

"Not my tax bracket," I assured him.

"Mine, either."

"I take it you're fixing that one up for auction," I said. "I bet the resale value on that thing is at least forty grand."

Dave and his mustache just nodded again. I studied the car for a moment. The car had no license plates, so there went one easy way to tell if it was stolen. The VIN number was also out of my reach: the car was high enough on the lift that I wouldn't be able to see it, much less be able to write down its seventeen letters and numbers without arousing suspicion. Then another idea occurred to me.

I turned to Sweet Thang and said, "Lauren, maybe I can interview the person who donated this car. It's such a generous donation, they deserve to get some publicity for it. That would make a perfect addition to my story."

Sweet Thang was just opening her mouth to reply when Dave cut her off. "No can do," he said. "They wanted to keep it anonymous."

Well, that was sure convenient.

I was trying not to get ahead of myself too much. Was I just getting delusional, seeing would-be carjacking rings everywhere I turned, whether it was Earl Karlinsky's parking lot or Sweet Thang's charity?

After all, a white Cadillac CTS was a reasonably common car. I'm sure General Motors produced several hundred thousand of them. It was not unreasonable to think that one could be carjacked while another was being donated.

Then again, what better front for an operation that resold stolen cars than a charity that benefited needy children? Maybe the reason this place looked like a chop shop was that it really *was* a chop shop. Gilbert could hide his illicit work among the legitimate stuff and no one would be the wiser. It was the last place the auto theft task force would ever look for hot merchandise.

Gilbert again returned to his work. Sweet Thang rambled some more about the program. I wrote down enough to be able to fake my way through the article I owed Brodie.

But when I got her back outside, my mind was still churning.

"Hey, this may seem like a weird question," I said. "But are you sure Dave Gilbert is legit?"

She looked startled. "Well, yeah. I mean . . . yeah. Why?"

"Because a white Cadillac CTS just like the one he had up on his lift was carjacked in Newark last night. Do you guys run criminal background checks on your employees?"

"Uh, I have no idea," she said. "I'm sure we're required to do them on the people who work with kids. I don't know about the people who work with cars."

"Do you know his full name, by any chance?"

She knew this meant I was going to run his name through a variety of databases to uncover any possible wrongdoing in his past. To be honest, I do this quite frequently: with people I've just met on the job; with my female friends' new boyfriends, particularly when they seem too good to be true; with sources who might not yet have been fully vetted. That they don't turn out to be criminals 98 percent of the time doesn't stop me from checking. Because that 2 percent sure does make things interesting.

"Carter, he's a sweet man who dedicates his life to helping the children of Newark. He's not a felon."

"Well, then there's nothing wrong with me looking into his background a little. If he's clean, it's no harm done. If he's not, then we'll talk again. I'm not sure I can do the Chariots for Children story without at least checking."

She twisted her face a little, her best attempt at a scowl—not that she could really carry one off. Then she said, "His middle initial is 'I.' He told me once that it stands for Isaac."

"Date of birth?" I asked.

"I have no clue and I'm *not* looking it up for you," she said. "I'm sure Dave is not a criminal."

I wasn't. For as much as I liked Sweet Thang, her assurances in this instance meant little. It was one of the things that had made her ill-suited to newspaper work: she assumed everyone was as pure of heart as she was.

And they weren't. They just weren't.

CHAPTER 22

When I returned to my car, I e-mailed Kira O'Brien, one of our librarians and a fleeting romantic interest during my prepregnancy life. Kira and I had our fun, but her idea of a major life commitment was agreeing to attend a party more than a week ahead of time. When I learned I was going to become a father, I informed her of my retirement from dating and my intention to seek a more permanent solution with Tina. She had happily moved on to less complicated options.

We had since returned to an amicable professional relationship, with no hard feelings on either side, which meant I could prevail on her to investigate my hunch about David Isaac Gilbert. I was reasonably certain there would only be one person with that name in New Jersey, but just in case I told her to look for a date of birth that made him roughly sixty years old. It's too bad Kira couldn't do a public records search on handlebar mustaches.

Once that was done, I decided—since I was already in the neighborhood—to make a quick detour to Tujuka Okeke's house. As I made the short drive, I thought of the critically important work of Dr. Duckworth.

One of the big buzzwords in educational circles over the past few years is the word "grit." Teachers and researchers are figuring out that the students who go on to become successful aren't necessarily the ones with the highest IQs or the ones from the wealthiest families—smart kids and rich kids underachieve all the time. The real can't-miss high performers? They're the ones who are willing to keep bashing their head against a problem until they solve it, the ones who refuse to be cowed by repeated failure. That's grit.

The pied piper of the modern grit movement is a University of Pennsylvania researcher named Angela Lee Duckworth. She and her team have gone to a diverse array of challenging environments, from the U.S. Military Academy, to an inner-city Chicago public school, to corporate America. In each of these very different settings they asked: Which cadets would make it through the grueling first year? Which students would beat the odds and graduate? Which salespeople would post the best numbers?

The team tracked the population over time, looking at their success or failure, and seeing if it correlated to an array of traits: intelligence, social skills, family income, race, and so on. But the trait that kept coming back as being the most significant predictor of success was not any of those things. It was grit. It was the people who set a long-term goal for themselves, then had the passion, perseverance, and work ethic to see it through.

I first learned of this research when Tina forced me to watch Dr. Duckworth's TED Talk—Tina's chief concern being whether or not she was nurturing a gritty enough fetus. But what immediately struck me is that most reporters would be able to independently confirm Dr. Duckworth's results after just a few months' hard time in the newsroom.

The best way to crack a source was often just to keep after them and make them realize, in the most polite and respectful way possible, that you weren't going away. As long as you didn't cross the line into pissing them off—and made them realize the necessity of your persistence—most of them eventually caved.

I hoped Tujuka Okeke would be one of those. In addition to wanting to talk with her about her ex-husband generally, I still had the specific question about why her insurance company might have been withholding payment. I hadn't necessarily been in the market for a story about the evils of the big, bad insurance company making life difficult for the poor widow, but I also wasn't going to turn one down if it gifted itself to me.

And so, once again, I parked next to her home, walked up her short driveway, and knocked on her front door.

When nothing happened, I knocked again. The Toyota was in the driveway, just as it had been the day before, leading me to surmise she was home.

After a minute or so of staring at her front door, it finally opened. Tujuka Okeke appeared.

"Mrs. Okeke, I'm sorry to bother you again, but I—"

"I work the night shift at University Hospital," she said testily. "I have to sleep during the day. Please leave."

And, in short order, I was again staring at her door. A lesser reporter might have viewed this as failure and defeat. A gritty reporter did not. This was one more necessary step toward establishing a working relationship with Tujuka Okeke. In a strange way, I knew it was progress.

Because now I had a chance to prove what a sympathetic fellow I was. There was a small mailbox bolted next to her door. I removed a business card from my wallet and turned to a clean sheet from my notepad. I wrote:

Ms. Okeke,
I'm terribly sorry to have woken you. I was unaware of your work schedule. That must be difficult.
I would still like to speak with you about Joseph and, in particular, any trouble you might be having with your insurance company. Please understand I mean you

and your family no ill will. My interest as a reporter is only to write the truth.

I would be happy to talk at whatever time is convenient for you. Please call me or e-mail me to set up a time.
Sincerely,
Carter Ross

Satisfied, I tore off the sheet, wrapped it around the business card, and placed both in her mailbox. I let the lid down slowly, so as not to make any undue noise.

Dr. Duckworth would, I hoped, be proud.

I was just turning to walk back down her front steps when my phone rang. It was Chillax. I answered it as quickly as I could so the noise didn't disturb Mrs. Okeke.

"Hey," I said.

"Hey, brah, what's up?"

"Just making friends and influencing people."

I was reasonably certain the Dale Carnegie reference was lost on him. But he replied with, "Tchya, beast."

Beast, in this instance, was like boss. Only better. I think.

"What's happening with you?" I asked. I was now back in my car.

"That MILF editor said I'm supposed to work with you again today," he said. By "that MILF editor" I assumed he meant Tina. MILF is an acronym I could not spell out around my mother without blushing.

"Great," I said. "How are we feeling about the Kevin Tiemeyer side of this story? Do we have enough stuff in our notebook to begin writing?"

There was quiet on the other end of the line. Its volume built all the way to silence.

I decided to be helpful. "Okay, so writing a story is sort of like . . . taking a shot in a lacrosse game. Now, you can take a shot almost any time you have the ball, of course. But if you're too far away or if you don't have the right angle of attack, the chances are pretty slim it's going to go in. You follow me so far?"

"Yeah, like there was this time against American—"

"Don't interrupt me, son, I'm building a metaphor here," I said. "Now, as I was saying, you want to take the shot when the time is right. But you also don't want to wait too long, because the defense will come along and knock the ball away. The defense, in this case, is the other media. You can't give them the chance to catch up with you and take your angle away. There's always a balancing act, right? So, first things first, let's see what our shot would look like if we took it right now. If you had to write Kevin Tiemeyer, what would your lede be?"

"Uh, that he was, you know, carjacked and . . . we got that, you know, that family statement from yesterday."

"And what did the family statement say?"

"That they're really bummed because Kevin was a good dude and that they're asking the media to give them privacy during this difficult time. I have it written out, but that's the main idea."

"I see, and let me ask you: who else got that family statement?"

"Uh, well, everyone. Why?"

"Because that means it's been on every television station, radio station, and Web site in the known universe by now. So it's sort of already played out, you know? It's like if you tried a trick play in the second period and it didn't work. You can't try it again in the third."

"I feel ya, brah."

"I'm . . . so glad," I said. "Anyhow, I was back at Fanwood Country Club last night, chatting up some of the members. You had mentioned the neighbors said he was mowing his own lawn and had stopped going out to dinner all the time. The word from the country club is that he suspended his membership for a few months. He was clearly going through some kind of life change. Let's try to figure out what it is. I think when we do, we'll be ready to take our shot."

"All right," he said.

"And now you want to know how to do that."

"Tchya."

I thought about the key participants in Kevin Tiemeyer's life. Family was out: everyone with a logo-covered microphone in the New York area was trying to get Tiemeyer family members right now, and they had gone into duck-and-cover mode. I had mined the country club as well as it could be mined. The neighborhood was already picked over as well. That left his job, which sounded like it was where he spent most of his time anyway.

"Everyone is calling him a banking executive," I said. "Where did he work again?"

"USKB."

"Oh, right. I knew that." United States Kinship Bank was either the third- or fourth-largest bank in America—it was always hard to keep track, what with all the mergers and acquisitions in that industry. When it opted to relocate some of its sprawling operations to Park Place in Newark a few years back, it was a big win for the city.

"You want me to go over there and ask some questions?"

"Yeah, but here's how you're going to do it. Don't go inside. If you do, they'll push you to some flak who will give you a canned statement about what a tragedy this is for the entire United States Kinship Bank family but how they won't let it deter them from first-rate customer service in Kevin's memory. We need that like we need a five-minute major."

I was proud of myself for my lacrosse knowledge, which I thought had already been exhausted.

"Stay outside," I continued. "I feel like every time I go by that building I always see people smoking outside. Smokers make for great targets. Most of them are pretty social and for five minutes or so, they're going to have nothing to do besides talk to you. One of those smokers had to know Tiemeyer. Just play it cool and chat them up and see what shakes out."

"Got it," he said. "Dude, I'm gonna crush this."

"Yeah, it'll be just like that time against Dickinson," I said.

"Brah, you were at that game?"

"As far as you know," I said. Then I ended the call, turned the Volvo's ignition key, and started driving toward Fanwood.

CHAPTER 23

The white man in the tie was back. Only this time, he was not driving his lousy old Malibu. He was driving a new-looking Volvo station wagon.

Scarface Sammy sat up when he saw the man. It was so interesting, after weeks of nothing noteworthy at the Okeke house, to see this man a second day in a row. Sammy knew that setting up on Tujuka Okeke's house would eventually give him something to chase. Maybe this white man was that something.

Then Sammy remembered how easily this man had spotted him the day before, and he hunched back down. Sammy knew his scars made him recognizable. He stayed low and observed.

Malibu man—or maybe he should call him Volvo man now—was walking in the same proud manner, like he was someone important, like he feared nothing but also like nothing feared him. That made him even more interesting to Sammy. It was a demeanor he didn't see very often.

But who was this man, exactly? And why did he keep coming to see Tujuka Okeke? And what was his role?

Tujuka and Volvo man once again had a very brief interaction. They spoke a few words to each other. Then Tujuka slammed the door. Like she was angry.

But that could have just been an act. Had she spotted Sammy, too? Did she realize she was being watched? Did she know she had to keep their interactions short, as if she was keeping up a guise he was merely an unwanted door-to-door salesman?

He watched as Volvo man went into his wallet (for cash, perhaps?), wrote her a note (a receipt, maybe?), then walked back down the steps toward his Volvo.

It left Sammy with a dilemma: try to sneak up on the front porch and see what was in the mailbox? Or follow Volvo man and figure out who he was?

In the end, Sammy thought that reading the note was too risky. There was too great a chance Tujuka would see him, possibly even call the police on him. That would be, to say the least, disadvantageous to Sammy.

Volvo man was taking a phone call. He would be distracted. That made him feel like an easier target. Sammy would just have to be more careful about how he performed his surveillance this time.

Sammy watched as Malibu man continued his phone conversation in the car. Then he ended the call, started the Volvo, and drove away.

Ordinarily, Sammy would have just pulled out after him, operating under his usual theory that most people are too oblivious to know they're being followed. But Volvo man had proven himself to be a different animal. So Sammy waited a few seconds.

The Volvo turned right at the end of the street. Sammy held his position until he was sure the Volvo was out of sight, then started his white Ford Fusion and gave chase.

Sammy took a right. Two cars were between him and the Volvo. If he missed a light, he might be done for. And there were a lot of lights in that part of Newark.

His luck held for the first four lights, but not for the fifth. But it was okay. The Volvo had stopped at the next light down. Soon, the Volvo turned right on Irvine Turner Boulevard. Sammy smiled. White people typically found Irvine Turner Boulevard for only one reason: it led to the interstate, the quickest way out of Newark.

Now that he was reasonably certain where the Volvo was traveling, Sammy dared to ease off even farther. He was perhaps two-tenths of a mile back when he saw the Volvo, predictably, take the ramp toward I-78 West.

Then it was the Garden State Parkway. Then it was Route 22. Just like the day before. Except this time, Route 22 did not yet have its usual lunchtime traffic snarl. Sammy made sure there were always at least two cars between him and the Volvo as they continued west.

They were out in the 'burbs now. Sammy kept his tail going as the Volvo turned off Route 22 and headed toward . . . where? Sammy didn't know, of course. He hoped they were going to either Volvo man's home or business. Either one would have told Sammy a lot more than he currently knew.

They were now several turns away from Route 22, traveling along a two-lane state road. They had just passed a country club, when the Volvo turned into the driveway of a suburban ranch house that had, of all things, a cactus out front.

Was this it? Volvo man's home? Sammy just kept driving. He had the house marked. The cactus made it easy to remember.

But then, wait, the Volvo wasn't stopping. As Sammy drove by, he saw the car's backup lights were engaged. Why was it backing up, unless . . .

In his rearview mirror, Sammy watched as the Volvo made a K-turn. It was heading back in the opposite direction. Sammy cursed in Yoruba. Had he been made *again*? How was that possible? He had been so cautious.

He kept his eyes fixed on his rearview mirror, slowing slightly as he continued up a hill, sure the Volvo was about to disappear from his view.

Then it didn't. It was coming to a stop along the side of the road. The last thing Sammy saw as he crested the hill was the backup lights, but this time only a brief flash. Like the Volvo was shifting from drive into park.

Maybe Sammy hadn't been made after all. After he crested the hill, out of sight of the Volvo, he executed his own K-turn. Then he veered off the road, halfway down a bank that sloped down into the woods. He shut off the engine, disembarked, and ran back to the top of the hill, keeping to the fringes of the trees so he wouldn't be spotted.

The Volvo was in the same place. And the white man was still sitting in it. Sammy stayed in place. Five minutes. Ten minutes. Nothing happened.

Twenty minutes. A half an hour. An hour. Sammy was a patient man. It came with his line of work. But why was nothing happening? Why was Volvo man not going anywhere?

And then it occurred to Sammy: he was watching the white man, who was himself watching something else.

But what? And why?

It was time to find out. Sammy returned to his car, retrieved his Beretta from his glove compartment and tucked it into the shoulder holster under his jacket. Then he started off in the direction of the Volvo.

CHAPTER 24

My trip out to Fanwood was uneventful and traffic free, giving me a chance to ponder my current predicament.

For whatever reason, I do some of my best thinking while driving. I guess it's because the conscious mind is minimally engaged in a task, meaning it doesn't get in the way of the subconscious, which is where all the good stuff comes from anyway.

Or maybe that's absurd psychobabble. I just knew there was nothing like some good windshield time to organize your thoughts. And I found myself thinking about Earl Karlinsky and what I was or was not about to see.

If he was in the parking lot at all, that was a strong indication something was amiss. Country club general managers had no business rambling around a parking lot. If I saw him bending over cars and inspecting their wheel wells, that was a dead giveaway. It would be my equivalent of Jimmy Breslin finding the piano.

I could then match that behavior with the other convincing evidence that Buster Hays was hopefully going to produce for me: that according to the Essex County Auto Theft Task Force, an unusually high percentage of Fanwood Country Club members and their guests had recently been victims of carjackings.

None of it would get Karlinsky convicted in a court of law. But it would be enough for me to put a story in the paper. The authorities, who had advantages I did not—like search warrants and subpoena power—could likely handle it from there.

That left me only with the problem of how to best spy on the parking lot. I had been out to Fanwood enough times to have a rough sense of its grounds. As I recalled, the parking lot was toward the edge of the property, with only the practice range—a large, open grassy area dotted with yellow golf balls—separating it from the road.

The end of the practice area had a large net for catching any balls that happened to be hit by future Masters champions. Then there were a few trees, but not many. Then the road.

I was reasonably certain I could peer through the trees, over all those golf ball dots and into the parking lot. The distance was a little over three hundred yards, give or take.

More than likely, I'd be able to see just fine with the naked eye. If not, the camera I had used to snap a picture of Jawan Porter had a 10X zoom. I couldn't use it to locate the moons of Jupiter, but when it came to spotting treacherous country club managers, it would work just fine.

When I reached the brick pillars of Fanwood Country Club, I saw the layout was just as I remembered. I cruised past the entrance, turned around in the driveway of a house that, quite incongruously for this part of the country, had a cactus in the front yard. Then I eased the Volvo off to the side of the road, just beyond the aforementioned netting and strip of trees, and began my stakeout.

My perch was elevated slightly, midway up a decent-sized hill, which helped my vision. I was glad for the trees, which kept me from feeling too obvious. The Volvo helped in that regard as well.

Being as there was nothing immediately happening in the parking lot, I settled in and began my wait.

As a reporter, I spent a lot of time waiting: for bad people to do bad things, for sources to talk to me, for flaks to call me back, for documents I had requested from public agencies, for editors to give me feedback on stories, whatever.

There were times when I hoped, at the end of my life—say, age eighty-five or so—I would have all that waiting time gifted back to me. I figured that would get me to ninety, at which point I would happily accept a quick, painless death.

Naturally, if I happen to reach that ripe age and still enjoy breathing, I reserve the right to change my mind about all this. But I don't think I will. Ninety seems like a more than fair number of years to have used the Earth's ever-dwindling resources. At that point, it's someone else's turn.

These were the kind of cheery thoughts with which I passed the time as the same lack of noteworthy events continued to unfold in the Fanwood Country Club parking lot. There was no sign of Earl Karlinsky. The only club employee I saw was Mr. Haughty in his little golf cart, buzzing up to people as they drove in and offering them a ride to the clubhouse, lest they actually get any exercise by walking.

Sometimes, Mr. Haughty helped them with their golf bags, which they kept in their trunks. A roughly equal number of members did not require his assistance with anything. Either they stored their sticks at the club or were only coming to Fanwood for social reasons, in which case Mr. Haughty served as their chauffeur.

I watched this routine for a while—twenty, forty minutes maybe, long enough that my thoughts started wandering even further afield, to things like the economics of fossil fuel extraction as compared to the rising price of milk. And, really, someone is going to have to explain to me how a nonrenewable resource that takes millions of years to form and is only found deep within the rocky folds of our planet costs less per gallon than the mammary gland secretions of the world's most populous domesticated ungulate.

And that's when my subconscious, working on some level I didn't understand, spoke up and told me: Mr. Haughty was part of it.

Of course he was. He had unfettered access to the parking lot, all day, every day. He drove an endless number of laps through it while ministering to his duties. When he stopped behind members' cars, they popped their trunks for him and he dove right in.

Meanwhile, the drivers of those cars were still inside the car's cabin, futzing with their sunglasses, fumbling with their phones, taking a final sip of coffee, whatever. They weren't worried about the kid rifling through their trunk. He was just pulling out their golf clubs, after all.

How easy would it be for Mr. Haughty to size up the car, decide it was worth a sufficient amount, and then slip a tiny tracking device of some sort into the trunk? There were no shortage of places. He probably tucked it under the mat, next to the spare tire; or, if the trunk was cluttered, he could toss it in the back, where it would stay undetected until the car could be swiped.

It wouldn't take him more than five seconds to do it. Then he could go about his business, smiling his haughty smile, knowing his future victims were completely unaware he had just set them up.

Hell, they probably even tipped him for it.

How I would prove this, I didn't know. Again, it might be another one of things that would be left to the authorities. When they carried out their well-planned raid on Fanwood Country Club, they would discover a bag filled with tiny GPS chips in Mr. Haughty's locker.

In the end, the kid would probably flip on Earl Karlinsky faster than a champion gymnast. But that was as it should be: as I had the scheme figured out, Karlinsky was the mastermind. He deserved to take the hardest fall. Or maybe Karlinsky was just another minion and the real boss was somewhere else.

And it all started in the parking lot.

From a storytelling standpoint, I could place Kevin Tiemeyer and Joseph Okeke in that parking lot, in preparation for their seemingly innocent round of golf together. Within a month, I had them both dying in violent carjackings. Then I could list the other Fanwood-connected victims, interview a few of them, and package the whole thing quite neatly. Then, there would be the matter of follow-ups for the arrest, the inevitable indictment, and so on.

And in each story, I'd get to write that glorious sentence, "Authorities learned of the carjacking ring after a report in *The Eagle-Examiner* . . ." Because, yes, sometimes newspapers like reminding you of just how damn important we still are.

I brought up my phone to check my e-mail. There was one from Buster Hays. The subject header was now "Re: Dear Ivy," and the body was brief: "I've got some information for you but I'm too thirsty to tell you over e-mail. Maybe if I had seen any evidence you were going to do something about that thirst, I'd feel differently. Buster."

In other words, I was going to have to pay my scotch bounty before he gave up anything. Typical Buster.

There was also an e-mail from Kira O'Brien. She had found David Isaac Gilbert, associated with several addresses in and around Newark. But what I found infinitely of more interest was where he had lived previously: a federal penitentiary.

Kira had enclosed a link to an article from a newspaper in Massachusetts. Federal prosecutors were announcing that an investigation into billing irregularities at a not-for-profit assisted-living facility in Swampscott had resulted in a plea bargain wherein David I. Gilbert, fifty-eight, of Saugus, the former director of the facility, admitted to Medicare fraud and misappropriation of patient funds. In exchange for an admission of guilt, he would be given an eighteen-month sentence in federal prison, which he would begin serving immediately.

About midway down in the article, there was Dave Gilbert's mug shot. Being as this was before his incarceration, he was a few pounds heavier. The pointy handlebar mustache looked like it weighed the same.

Phrases like "Medicare fraud" and "misappropriation of patient funds" were too vague to know exactly what he had done. The article didn't go into detail, probably because the prosecutors hadn't given any. But it sounded to me a lot like Dave Gilbert was bilking the federal government out of taxpayer funds *and* a bunch of unwitting senior citizens out of their hard-earned retirement savings. Nice. I wonder if he kicked his residents on their way to church, too.

The article was three years old. So it was easy enough to assemble a time line: he served his eighteen months, got released, then settled in New Jersey, far enough away from Massachusetts that no one would have heard about his old scam. Then he quickly began constructing a new scam.

As a convicted felon, there was a huge swath of employers who wouldn't even consider hiring him. But that still left the Greater Newark Children's Fund, where they were all as naïve and trusting as Sweet Thang and didn't bother with background checks. Once installed as the director of the Chariots for Children program—where he could masquerade as one of the good guys—he could find a way to twist it for his own profit.

Had he then hooked up with the Karlinsky crew? Or was he a separate cell in a criminal syndicate that kept its parts ignorant of each other? Or was he, in fact, completely independent and just happened to be running what appeared to be a chop shop?

I didn't know at this point. All I knew is that Gilbert had been a crook and, for as much as I wished I could believe in rehabilitation, my experience—to say nothing of the stubbornly high rates of recidivism in this country—told me how unlikely that was.

Once a crook, always a crook. Even Sweet Thang would have to concede that. I forwarded her a link to the article, just barely resisting the urge to add an "I told you so."

Instead, I just wrote, "Call me when you have a moment." I would need her help to unravel Gilbert's role in whatever was going on.

Finally, I looked up from my phone. Little had changed in the Fanwood Country Club parking lot. Mr. Haughty was still there, waiting in his golf cart, poised to swoop down on whatever unsuspecting pigeon came in next.

CHAPTER 25

Scarface Sammy picked his way slowly down the hill, one deliberate movement at a time, his eyes fixed on Volvo man the entire time.

Stalking people was something of an art form and he had made a study of it through the years: what worked, what didn't.

Ultimately, he felt his best teachers were the great cats of his native Africa. He loved watching animal documentaries just so he could watch them do their work. They would lie there, almost entirely obscured in the long grasses of the savannah. They would take one step, then wait. Smell the air. Let the grasses sway. Watch the gazelles graze. Only then did they take another step.

Patience was absolutely critical. The great cats didn't leap out and begin sprinting toward their prey until they were certain of success.

The fact was, if you just ran up to people, they would see you coming easily and make a decision about whether they were going to stick around. And many of his targets, particularly the ones who knew Sammy and what his job entailed, chose not to.

Sammy understood the impact his face made on strangers, particularly white strangers. His skin was not like the black people they knew. It was much darker. His scars, which were given to him in childhood to ensure his good health, only added to the effect. They made him that much more foreign—and, yes, scary. They were not the kind of tiny lines favored by modern Yoruba, if they even practiced scarification at all. No, Sammy's scars were the old-school kind: deep and, for those from cultures unaccustomed to them, shocking.

If Sammy just walked up to the man in the Volvo—or ran up to him, for that matter—all he would get in return was a face full of mud, sticks, and leaves that the Volvo's tires spun up as it fled. Especially if Volvo man noticed that the bulge in Sammy's jacket was the size and shape of a shoulder-holstered Beretta.

So Sammy kept himself hidden, carefully gliding from one tree to the next, never exposing himself for more than a fleeting instant or two. The closer he got, the slower he went. When he got within two hundred feet, he would count to ten before he let himself move again. At a hundred feet, he started counting to twenty.

It certainly helped that Volvo man wasn't paying any attention to his surroundings. His entire focus seemed to be on the parking lot of the country club. When a car passed by on the road, Volvo man didn't even swivel his head to watch it.

The first time he even looked down—to look at his phone, perhaps?—Sammy had just closed the gap to about eighty feet. Sammy didn't dare go faster. But he was getting more confident.

He was maybe fifty feet away, still neatly hidden, when he suddenly realized he wasn't the only person interested in the man in a Volvo.

Another car was pulling up. A big SUV. Sammy stopped his counting, checked to make sure his hiding place was adequate, and watched for what came next.

CHAPTER 26

Mr. Haughty had disappeared to who-knows-where, leaving the parking lot devoid of activity for the moment. I was essentially just staring off into the distance—to the point where I was probably less aware of my surroundings than I ordinarily would be.

So I didn't pay particular attention that a large SUV had left the parking lot and was cruising up Fanwood Country Club's long driveway; or that it turned left out of the pillars, in my direction; or that its driver and passenger were giving me the evil eye as they passed.

I only really started noticing it when it turned around—in the driveway of the cactus house, just like I had done—and was coming back in my direction, pulling over to the side of the road as it did so.

And then, in very short order, it became something I couldn't have ignored if I wanted to. It was rolling up like it didn't even see me, accelerating at a time when it should have been easing to a stop. That's when it occurred to me: the SUV was going to ram me.

My hand went for the Volvo's ignition. The gesture was as automatic as it was futile. Even if I could get the car started in time, there was no chance I'd be able to get it in gear and on the move. The roar of the SUV's engine was coming at me too quickly.

I made a sound that was some undignified mix of a squeal and a shriek. It wasn't my well-being I was worried about. It was the car's. Tina's only instruction when I asked to borrow her Volvo was for me to "try not to get any bullet holes in it." I doubted she would consider having her entire back bumper crumpled much of an improvement on that.

There just wasn't anything I could do to avoid it. My hand was moving too slowly toward the ignition. The SUV was moving too fast.

Then it braked, sliding to a stop on the soft ground just inches short. The only thing filling my rearview mirror was an oversized, polished chrome grille plate.

In my rearview mirror, meanwhile, I could see two people get out. From the passenger side came Mr. Haughty, wearing a Fanwood Country Club polo shirt. From the driver's side, there was Earl Karlinsky, dressed in the same logo jacket as the day before, although his gray hair struck me as being extra bristly on this day.

Mr. Haughty was hanging back, somewhere around my bumper, doing I-don't-know-what. Karlinsky stormed up to my window. I composed myself for the coming confrontation. Bullies like Karlinsky love it when they make you nervous, and I wasn't going to give him that pleasure.

He glared at me through the closed window. I waited a beat before lowering it.

"Mr. Ross," he said, his face pinched and firm behind his wire-rimmed glasses. "You are currently on Fanwood Country Club property without an invitation and are therefore trespassing. If you do not leave immediately, I will call the police."

I would have yawned—to signify how worried I was about his threats—except his musk had crawled into my car. I feared that if I inhaled too deeply it would make me gag.

Instead, I realized this might be my best opportunity to interview Karlinsky before my story ran. Unlike cops, who can get search warrants and ask questions later, reporters had to ask questions first. We don't get to surprise anyone with what we put in the newspaper if it's a story that accuses them of wrongdoing. If I was going to intimate that Earl Karlinsky was involved in a carjacking ring, I was going to have to ask him about it. That's another way in which journalists are unlike law enforcement: we have to give the criminals equal time.

With this in mind, I said, "Hang on, Mr. Karlinsky. I want to make sure I get this on tape."

I reached into my briefcase and pulled out my digital recorder, which I kept well-charged for occasions like this.

"This is . . . this is outrageous!" he sputtered. "This is harassment!"

I thumbed the record button before I spoke.

"No, trust me, I know harassment laws very well, Mr. Karlinsky, and this doesn't even come close. If anything, you're harassing me. I had a perfectly legitimate reasons for being at your club twice yesterday, including once when I was explicitly invited by one of your members. Yet you tried to chase me away both times. The second time, you grabbed my wrist, which I did not want you to do and which made me frightened. That's assault and battery right there, and I have a bar full of witnesses. So if you want to get into a legal pissing match with me, by all means, let's do it."

Since he wasn't a cartoon with a thought bubble over his head, I didn't know for sure; but I was reasonably certain he was thinking, "Oops."

Meanwhile, Mr. Haughty was still near the back of my car. It was a strange place to be. And I couldn't very well pay attention to whatever he was doing while simultaneously fighting a verbal battle with Karlinsky.

"Now," I continued, "the reason I'm watching your country

club is because I believe you are part of a criminal enterprise that is identifying high-worth vehicles and planting tracking devices on them so that your Newark-based associates can then carjack them. Would you care to comment on that?"

His face pinched some more. "That's . . . that absurd. That is the most ridiculous thing I've ever heard. And if you print that—"

"Then you're denying it."

"Damn right I'm denying it. Are you out of your mind?"

"So it's just a coincidence that Kevin Tiemeyer and Joseph Okeke played a round of golf together at your club about a month ago, and both of them are now dead after carjackings that turned violent."

He stomped his foot—to what end, I'm not sure—and pointed at me as he spoke. "I have no idea what you're talking about. And I don't know what would possibly make you think I have anything to do with that. That's the most absurd and unbelievable and outrageous and—" He stopped there, apparently out of words to express his incredulity.

"If it's so unbelievable, then when I check your club roster against recent carjackings in and around Newark, I'm not going to find an inordinate number of your members having recently been victimized by that crime?"

"Are you insane? You're absolutely out of your mind. This is outr"—he stopped himself, perhaps aware he had already used the word "outrageous" twice already—"I have no idea what you're talking about. And I'm not going to listen to any more of this. You have to leave. Now."

He removed his phone from his pocket. His hand was shaking as he jabbed at it with his finger.

"So, again, you deny any knowledge of or involvement in a carjacking ring operating out of your club?"

By that point, he was either pretending not to hear me or actually not hearing me. Mr. Haughty was still behind me somewhere, though I couldn't see him unless I looked in my rearview mirror.

"Yes, this is Earl Karlinsky, the general manager at Fanwood Country Club. There is a man named Carter Ross who is sitting alongside Fanwood Road on the edge of club property in a gray Volvo. I have asked him to leave and he has refused. Could you please send a car out here and—"

I had already seen what I needed to see. I had also heard enough of Earl Karlinsky's blather for the time being. I rolled my window up and drove off, leaving Karlinsky and his cabana boy behind.

Frankly, Karlinsky's presence had vexed me a lot less than Haughty's. Why had he come? To provide his boss some backup? To intimidate me?

Or to put a tracking device on my car?

Just in case, I went about a mile down and then pulled over to the side of the road to give the Volvo's back bumper and rear tire well a thorough inspection. I hunched under the car and looked for something that didn't seem right. Then I used my hands to feel for it.

I found nothing. I was probably just being paranoid, sure. But there were at least two recent visitors to Fanwood who would have been well-served by a little more paranoia in their lives.

My first priority, as I finally got heading back toward Newark, was Buster Hays and his apparently ferocious thirst. He had information I now needed more than ever and, knowing Buster as I did, he was not going to give it up until I paid my ransom.

Not being much of a scotch man, I wasn't sure if Ballantine's— Buster's scotch of choice—was a common brand or if it was considered more exotic. But, again, I knew Buster. He took pride in his Bronx roots, public school education, and common man's sensibilities. When he called me "Ivy," he didn't mean it as a compliment. I suspected that just about any dispenser of intoxicating liquids would carry it.

My trip to the newsroom involved passing at least one such store along Broad Street. Or, maybe, more like three of them. I opted for the second.

If you are seeking a cure for depression—or want to feel uplifted about your fellow man—stopping at a Newark liquor store is not something I'd recommend. The one I chose was an excellent example of its type. It was housed in a building that exuded ugliness from a chipped, sooty, tile exterior that may have once been yellow but had since faded into something less than that.

Its defensive structures were depressingly impressive. The top of the walls were protected by sharp, outward-curling metal ramparts whose purpose was to prevent would-be thieves from scaling up to the roof. The windows—or the portals where there perhaps had once been windows—were covered over in concrete. All other conceivable points of access, everything from the door to the heating and cooling vents, had bars on them. There were fifteenth-century Moorish fortresses that were easier to penetrate.

Populating the sidewalk were three professional drunks who looked like they had scraped up just enough money to buy their poison of choice, then hadn't bothered to stumble more than a few feet outside the door before they began administering it.

The insides were dim and musty, and most of the decoration—if you could call it that—had been provided by the producers of the beverages being sold. The motif, if it could be summed up in two words, was garish neon. The floor had a pervasive sag to it; as if it, too, had simply given up.

I am no one to lecture on the evils of alcohol. I have certainly been known to enjoy its pleasures from time to time. But I'm also mindful of not becoming one of those journalists who regularly chases his sorrows with booze. I've heard stories about how that method of self-soothing eventually turns out. Most of the time, it's not with the protagonist turning into one of the skid row professionals I had just passed outside. Instead, they end up as guys who somehow hold on to their jobs and houses, but who can't get out of bed in the morning without a shot of vodka. Frankly, I'm not entirely sure which is worse.

After a diligent, two-minute search, I eventually found the Ballantine's. (For the record: it's near the rotgut, one aisle over from the firewater, and one shelf up from the hooch.) I grabbed two bottles of it, and took them up to the register.

There, I found a charming, linguistically fractured sign that read: WE DONT EXCEPT CREDIT CARDS. THERE HAVE BEEN TO MANY FRAUDULANT CHARGES. CASH ONLY.

I dug into my wallet and managed to find two twenties, which I passed under a small slit in the bulletproof glass to a man who accepted—yes, accepted—the bills, which were not, in fact, fraudulent. He handed me my change without comment, then slipped me two brown paper bags with the unspoken understanding that I would likely be joining his other patrons outside.

My WASPish instincts compelled me to disabuse him of this notion, so I lobbed up a lame, "I sure hope my friend likes this scotch."

The man behind the counter looked at me like he neither believed me nor cared. I left the store, withstood some halfhearted panhandling from the men outside—who couldn't exactly claim they weren't going to use the money for booze—and completed my journey back to the office.

Once inside the building, I quickly checked in on Tina, who informed me she was fine and her morning was fine and the baby was fine and everything else was fine. But she was saying it in a way that led me to believe that if I didn't leave her alone, I would very quickly not be fine.

Her stress, I could guess, was Brodie-related. I had only been in the newsroom for a few minutes, but it felt like his heart attack had projected gloom on all who entered.

Most of it was concern for a revered man's health, of course, but a small part of it was uncertainty about the future as well. Brodie's stalwart presence was one of the few givens in the ever-changing multivariable equation that was the newspaper industry. He was our rock.

I think we all understood there was no guarantee a seventysomething-year-old coming off a major heart attack would return to work. And even if he did, his aura would never be quite the same. There was no pretending the old man was invincible anymore. Our rock had been fractured.

Then there was the even more pressing question: in the likely event Brodie stepped aside, who would our new boss be? The leading inside candidates would have to be Eberhardt and Looper. They had been around almost as long as Brodie and would be able to carry on his legacy, albeit without his legendary stature.

An outside hire would be a far more menacing proposition. My fear, of course, is that it would be some Web whiz we lured away from Google, a tablet-toting, pulp-loathing technophile who would be given some odious title like "Director of Content" and lecture us about the importance of search engine optimization.

The mere idea of it made me want to run back to the liquor store and double my order.

Given where my thoughts had wandered, I found comfort in locating the prehistoric Buster Hays in his usual spot: sitting at his desk, injuring his keyboard.

He had a pair of granny glasses perched on the end of his nose. I was able to distinguish his paisley tie from the one he had worn the days before because the stains were in different places.

"Okay, I have traded my shame for these two bottles of devil spirits," I said. "Talk to me."

With great ceremony, I presented him the brown paper bags. He peered inside both. Satisfied, he placed them next to his briefcase on the floor.

He returned his attention to the keyboard and delivered his findings in typically brusque fashion. "I got a name for you on the driver of the Cadillac CTS."

"Really?" I said. "I don't mean to underestimate you, Buster, but I didn't think your guy on the task force would give that up."

"I told him you'd get the driver's permission before you put his name in the paper."

"Yeah, but, still, aren't they worried about witness intimidation if we print the vic's name?"

"Think about it, Ivy: whoever stole that car already knows the victim's name and address. It's printed on his insurance card and registration, which ninety-eight percent of Americans keep in their glove box."

"Good point."

"Plus, it doesn't sound like there was much to witness," Buster said, then tore a sheet from the notepad next to his keyboard. "Here."

The paper contained the name Justin Waters and an address in Chatham, a well-to-do town to the west of Newark.

"Great," I said. "And did they get anywhere with that country club membership list?"

"I gave it to my guy. He said he'd run through it and get back to me."

"Thanks, Buster," I said. "Enjoy the scotch."

"I will. Now go away."

I obliged him, returning to my desk and pulling up my own list of Fanwood members. The name Justin Waters was not on it. Then again, neither was the name Joseph Okeke. Chatham wasn't very far from Fanwood. Mr. Waters could have been another Fanwood guest who had unwittingly driven his GPS-tracked car into Newark and the waiting arms of a gang of carjackers.

After a few keystrokes, I had Waters's home telephone number. I called it and heard a chipper voice telling me he wasn't home. I left a message.

Chances were good he was still in the hospital. The fact that he was healthy enough to walk there suggested he wouldn't be there for too long. Still, he had been shot in the neck. The emergency room doctor wasn't exactly going to tell him to rub some dirt on it and go home.

I played a game of what-if that I sincerely hoped I would never have to participate in: if I were shot in the hundred block of Washington Street, what hospital would I stagger to?

The map in my brain came up with Saint Michael's Medical Center. It was definitely the closest facility. If I struck out there, I'd try another nearby hospital.

I was just about to call it when my cell phone started ringing from a number I didn't recognize.

"Carter Ross," I said.

"Hey, Carter, it's Zabrina Coleman-Webster," I heard.

"Yeah, hey, Zabrina, how are you?"

"I'm good. I've been thinking about our conversation yesterday and wanted to talk some more."

"Okay," I said. "What about?"

She lowered her voice. "I don't really want to talk about it here, if that's okay."

Recalling that she was forced to share an office, I said, "That's fine. I need some lunch anyway. How about we both grab a sandwich and meet in Military Park in twenty minutes."

"That'd be great," she said.

"Talk to you soon," I said, then hit the END button on my phone. Wasting no time, I picked up my desk phone and dialed the number for Saint Michael's.

Mind you, not the number for the public relations staff. Thanks to an irritating piece of legislation know as HIPAA, the Health Insurance Portability and Accountability Act, hospitals couldn't release any information about a patient—or even say whether a patient was a patient—unless they were expressly permitted to do so. I'm sure it was a great advance for the privacy rights of those under medical care. For a newspaper reporter, it was like persistent bedsores.

Thankfully, there was nothing in HIPAA that said I couldn't just call up a patient and hope for the best. I hit the buttons needed to reach an operator, then asked for Justin Waters's room.

Two rings later, I heard, "Hello."

"Hi, Justin," I said, assuming I had reached the man himself. "My name is Carter Ross. I'm a reporter with the *Eagle-Examiner*."

"Oh, hi," he said, as if this was just another part of being in the hospital, not that different from an impromptu visit by the chaplain.

"I wanted to talk with you about your carjacking last night for an investigative piece I'm writing about the subject. Are you up for it?"

"Yeah, sure, I guess," he said, good-naturedly.

I asked how he was feeling—sore, he said—then ran quickly through his background. He was a lawyer who worked at a firm in Basking Ridge. He liked to go into Newark for the nightlife. It wasn't hard for me to deduce why. From his voice, I could tell he was a young black man. Yet the town where he lived, lovely Chatham, tended to be populated by older white folks who like to roll up the sidewalks at 9:30 P.M.

Then I got around to the incident itself. He walked me through the most terrifying five minutes of his life: how he left the bar after "one or two" drinks around 12:30 A.M.; how he stopped at a light along Washington Street, not really thinking about much of anything; how a kid wearing a blue ski mask ran up to him, gun first; how that sight made him react instinctively, and his instincts told him to stomp on the gas.

"It was totally, totally stupid," he said. "I know I should have just given him the car. It's not even my car. It belongs to my firm. I don't know what I was thinking."

He remembered the sound of the gun going off but blacked out after that. His next memory involved staggering into the Saint Michael's emergency room. He was dazed and bleeding from wounds to his face and neck. Luckily, all were relatively superficial. The bullet had only really grazed his neck, just barely missing his carotid artery.

"One inch over and you'd be writing my obituary," he cheerfully informed me.

Instead, he was patched up and awaiting his release from Saint Michael's at any moment. We shared our relief over that fact, and over the vicissitudes of life, which can leave one feeling enormously grateful over something as horrible as a carjacking. The gift of life is never fully appreciated until it's nearly taken away.

We were getting along so famously, I just kept rolling with the questions.

"So don't ask me why I'm asking this," I said. "But have you played golf recently at Fanwood Country Club?"

He hadn't. Likewise, he had never met a man named Earl Karlinsky. But he also wasn't the only driver of the car. His firm was located within walking distance from a train station and had made a deal with its lawyers: take the train to work, bill hours while you ride, and the firm would maintain a small fleet of cars for their personal use during or after work. Any one of five partners and eleven other associates could have used the vehicle.

I would have to check the law firm's Web site for the names of the other attorneys to see if any of them were Fanwood members. If one of them had played as a guest or just visited there, it was going to be beyond my investigative grasp. I didn't have the time or desire to track down sixteen lawyers and ask them about their recent golf outings.

"Okay, so strange question number two: do you have the VIN number for the Cadillac, by any chance?"

He didn't. But before I hung up, he promised he would check in with the office assistant who farmed out the cars and get it from her, then e-mail it to me later.

I didn't even have to tell him I wanted it because I may well have located the vehicle in question. Justin Waters did not seem concerned about justice, vengeance, or any of the other petty desires with which human beings sometimes consume themselves.

He was just happy to be alive.

CHAPTER 27

There are people who live or work near Military Park in Newark for their entire lives without knowing one cool fact about it: when viewed from above, it is shaped like a sword.

I only knew it because it was the kind of tidbit regularly shared with me by the great Clement Price, a legendary, beloved—and, alas, late—professor of history at Rutgers-Newark, who spent the final forty-two years of his life teaching Newark where it came from.

By the time I arrived at Military Park—still driving Tina's Volvo, because I had forgotten to swap keys with her—I could already see Zabrina, who was sitting along the outer edge of the park on a bench.

I parked near her at a metered spot, fed it a half-hour's worth of quarters, then ambled out. Zabrina had a white wrapper open next to her on the bench and smiled as I approached the bench.

"You forgot your sandwich," she said.

"Yeah, I had a quick interview to do, so I didn't have time to grab one."

"You can have the other half of mine if you're interested," she said. "I was just going to bring it home anyway. It's turkey with Swiss cheese. It's delish."

She extended half a sub toward me. It was still wrapped, but I didn't need to give it much of an inspection. While some people think it's congenital, it is, in fact, an acquired characteristic: newspaper reporters are incapable of turning down free food.

"Thanks," I said.

I sat down next to her. We chewed in silence for a moment. Military Park recently received a much-needed face-lift and was now quite the showpiece. Across from the park to the east, there were Newark icons like the New Jersey Performing Arts Center; the New Jersey Historical Society; and WBGO, a public radio station with a small news crew whose work I admired—sometimes grudgingly so, when they beat me to a story. To the west of the park, Prudential Insurance was completing the building that would serve as its new world headquarters.

It made Military Park a part of Newark that felt like a thriving city; a place where you could now sit, enjoy a sandwich, and not have to think about the chronic ills that still wrack other parts of town.

Zabrina broke our brief reverie with, "My mama taught me that when you mess up, you best just say so and apologize for it, so everyone can get on with it."

"I see. And how did you mess up?"

"Yesterday, when you came by, I said some things I probably shouldn't have said to the newspaper."

I didn't groan out loud. Just internally. The backtracking source is one of the more annoying animals in the newspaper forest. Unfortunately, it's also one of the more common. People were constantly trying to take things off the record.

She continued: "I just . . . Joseph really valued his privacy. He was pretty insistent we not be public about our relationship. He always said it wasn't anyone's business but ours and I . . . I pretty much agreed with him. But then you came and somehow you already knew about Joseph and I, and I just started blabbing about it. I think it was because it felt so good to talk to someone about it."

"Uh-huh," I said, opting not to tell her I actually hadn't known a thing about it until she had told me.

"But I really shouldn't have done that. And I apologize for that. It was wrong. Just because Joseph . . . isn't with us anymore doesn't mean I still shouldn't honor his wishes.

"Uh," she groaned. "That was, like, a triple negative. Anyhow, I guess what I'm saying is, it wasn't anyone's business back then and it's no one's business now. Would it be okay if you just leave that part out?"

There are no set rules about how to respond when someone is trying to retract statements they've already made. The hard line is to tell them, essentially, tough luck: you said it; it was on the record at the time; therefore, I own it. The other possibility is, of course, to give them a break.

I usually base my response on the source themselves. If it is, say, a politician—or some other public figure with long experience in dealing with the media—I usually laugh them right out of the room. Because they should know better.

But if it's a civilian—say the local Rotary Club president who seldom, if ever, dealt with the press—I usually cut them some slack. Especially when, as in this case, it was not information crucial to the story.

Plus, she had given me a sandwich.

"Yeah, I guess I can take that out," I said, as if I had already written the piece.

"Thank you," she said, releasing a breath.

"But just so we're clear, what you told me about Joseph's involvement in Rotary is still fair game, yes?"

"Oh, yeah, that's fine."

"And the part about how he was heading to his house to get some documents to prepare for a morning meeting. That's sort of a good detail, because it shows he was just another guy, thinking about work the next day. I can say he had just left a friend's house. That okay?"

"Yeah, sure."

Now for the more important part: "And I can still use what you said about Earl Karlinsky asking him about his car."

That threw her. "Uh, yeah. Sure. Out of curiosity, why does that matter?"

"Oh, I don't know. It just shows that it was the kind of car that other people noticed and took interest in and that Joseph was proud of it and liked to talk about it," I ad-libbed. "It's like if you asked me about my Volvo over there. I wouldn't say more than about three words about it. That would tell you something about me, that I'm not really much of a car guy, and maybe that I don't consider driving a Volvo to be a big part of my personality."

Especially since it wasn't mine. But there didn't seem any point to adding that. It might involve having to explain my rather complicated relationship with Tina. And I was going to follow Zabrina's lead and keep that private.

"Oh, yeah," Zabrina said. "I never thought about it like that. But I guess that's why you're the writer and I'm an accountant."

"Trust me, if we switched jobs, I'd be a lot worse at yours than you would be at mine."

She laughed. "When is your story going to come out, anyway?"

Sources were often asking me this question. I had learned, given how little control I had over the process, to be vague about my answer. "Not sure," I said. "My editors would like it for Sunday. But it could be earlier than that, or later."

"Oh. Gotcha," she said, dabbing a bit of mayonnaise from the corner of her mouth.

"I'll try to let you know before it runs. I may have to call with any other questions I have about Joseph. His widow hasn't exactly been very forthcoming with me."

"Really? Why not?"

"I don't know, since the two times I've been on her front porch she's slammed the door in my face," I said. "Actually, if you happen to chat with her, could you tell her I'm a decent fellow who doesn't have horns coming out of his head?"

"I guess I could but we don't really . . . now that Joseph is gone, we don't really have a reason to talk anymore. I had thought about trying to continue a relationship with Maryam. She really is a lovely girl and I enjoyed the time I spent with her. But the only thing we had in common was her father, and . . ."

She didn't finish the thought. "Okay, I understand," I said. "No big deal."

"What do you need from her, anyway?"

"I'm still trying to track down that insurance thing," I said. "It's that reporter's instinct toward protecting the little guy. If there's an insurance company trying to screw a widow out of money, it's the kind of thing I want to be able to put in the paper."

I emphasized my hunger for this subject by taking a wolfish bite from my sandwich.

"Would it help if I could give you a copy of Joseph's auto policy?" she said.

This was the equivalent of asking a boxer, *Would it help if I pinned the other guy's arms down?*

"Sure would," I said. "How'd you end up with that?"

"He left an accordion file with some papers at my house. I was going through it the other night. To be honest, I wasn't sure what to do with it. It's yours if you want it. How about you drop by my house tonight and pick it up?"

With a copy of Joseph Okeke's policy in hand by the end of

the day, I'd be able to dedicate some time tomorrow to attacking his insurance company with merry abandon.

"Sure," I said. "What time?"

"I'm probably going to be working a little late. Then I wanted to stop by the gym on the way home. Could you come by at eight?"

She furnished me her address. I wrote it down. "I'm not going to have time to clean," she said. "Just park in the driveway and I'll run it out to you."

I could have told her that, as a newspaper reporter who had trekked through his share of tenements and interviewed his share of people who were conscientious vacuuming objectors, I would be very nearly impossible to offend. But I understood a little about certain women and cleaning. Tina had once refused to answer the door for the UPS man because the living room wasn't tidied. So I just said, "Okay. No problem."

We lapsed back into silence for a moment. She had finished her sandwich. We had, for all practical purposes, finished our conversation. Yet there was clearly more on her mind.

Just to get on with it, I said, "What is it?"

"Nothing, I just . . . you're going to figure this out, right? Who did this to Joseph?"

"I'm sure going to try," I said. "With something like this, it's the cops who ultimately nail the bad guy. That makes me sort of like the tour guide. I'm the one who leads them down the path and tells them where to look."

"Good. I don't want to sound like . . . I mean, I was just his girlfriend. But we had something special and it would be . . . I just really hope there's justice, that's all."

"Me, too," I assured her.

At that point, she stood up. She thanked me for listening to her wishes about respecting Joseph's privacy. Soon she was heading back toward the firm of Lacks & Ragland to continue her afternoon's toil.

I sat and finished my sandwich in a park shaped like a sword, feeling like I was soon to be armed with one myself.

When I returned to the newsroom, I went to check in on Tina again, challenging myself to find new ways to ask how she was feeling without her realizing it.

She wasn't in her office. I left her car keys on her chair, relieved to be free of the responsibility of driving a car whose blue book value was beyond three digits. I fished into her purse and found my keys. At least now if anyone tried to rear-end me, I wouldn't have to worry that the real threat to my well-being would come later.

On my way back to my desk, I passed Tommy, catching a glimpse of him out of the corner of my eye. But that was enough. Tommy and I have been friends long enough, and have worked in close quarters often enough, that I have become an expert reader of his moods. People talk about having work spouses, that person in the office who, in a platonic way, looks out for them the way their real spouse does at home. I guess you could say Tommy has become my work husband—and I'm pleased to say that's now legal in New Jersey.

The first thing I noticed is that he had his earphones in, which is not necessarily a bad sign. It just means he's trying to concentrate or to avoid someone. It was the second thing I noticed that made me concerned. He had this little pout on his face. At the risk of bumping up against stereotypes about gays being happy, Tommy is not a pouter.

I sat down in the empty desk next to him. I gestured for him to pull out his earphones, which he did.

"What's the matter," I asked. "Is it about Glenn? He's always had problems with commitment, so don't take it personally that he wants a break."

"No, it's not that. Worse."

"Worse?"

"Remember those skeletal remains I told you about?"

"The ones found at the construction site for the Nigerian embassy?"

"Yeah, those. I had gotten my hopes up that it was some kind of juicy mystery, a horrific crime, a great untold story."

"And?"

"The medical examiner's office determined the body died of tuberculosis a long time ago, back when people died of tuberculosis a lot. Basically, someone buried this guy in their backyard, then the world forgot about him and paved over him. So there's no mystery, no crime. Boooorr-ring."

He said the last word in a singsongy tone, then settled back into his pout. I felt for him. People who become newspaper reporters tend to be talented, intelligent, insightful people who might have been successful in any number of fields but are willing to sacrifice all kinds of comforts—a regular work schedule, an office full of normal people, a career that actually has a future—in exchange for having a job that's *not* boring. We don't deal well with downtime. If trouble does not present itself to us, we'll usually go looking for it.

Lucky for Tommy, and for myself, I seemed to have enough swirling around me that I could share. His boredom was going to be my opportunity.

"What if I said I had a present for you?" I asked.

"A present?" he asked, brightening immediately. "What kind of present? Is it wrapped? Does it have a big, bright bow on it?"

"Well, if I did manage to wrap it, it would be in the shape of a six-foot-three, broad-shouldered former college lacrosse player."

Tommy grinned. "And when I opened it, would it be a super-tasty intern?"

"Well, I don't want to spoil the surprise. But I will say that if you went to the USKB building on Park Place, you might find one of our reporters hanging around outside, trying to interview people who worked with Kevin Tiemeyer, the carjacking victim. You interested in going to help him?"

"Letmecheckmycalendaryes," Tommy said.

I felt a little guilty about using an obviously straight intern as bait. But only so much. Tommy would enjoy the harmless flirting. Chillax would probably be too dim and/or too secure in his sexual orientation to notice and/or care he was being flirted with.

The real winner would be my story. Chillax was untested, and nothing about his production so far suggested he was anything special journalistically. Tommy, on the other hand, was one of the most gifted reporters I had ever worked with. He was especially good at man-on-the-street stuff, turning random strangers into instant friends who told him things. If there was anything of note to learn about the life and times of Kevin Tiemeyer, Tommy would find it.

He quickly grabbed a notepad and went for the elevator. The last thing I heard him saying—or, really, half-sighing—were the words "long stick middie."

CHAPTER 28

The latest job began the way all the others did: with Black Mask getting a phone call.

He knew the number, of course. It wasn't Blue Mask—thank God, that guy was starting to freak him out. It was . . . what had he called them before? Ah, yes: the people with the money.

"'Sup?" he said.

"I got one for you tonight," he heard. "You good with that?"

"Yeah. I'm good."

"Good. I already changed the password."

The password went to the e-mail account they used so that nothing would have to be said over the phone. It was an anonymous account, set up on a public computer so the IP address couldn't be linked to anyone. The details of the job—the type of car, how he could find it, what he would get paid for it when he delivered it—were all written in an e-mail sent to the account. They changed the password with each new job, adding one to the first number in the password, then bumping the first letter down one spot in the alphabet.

"Got it," Black Mask said. "I'll talk to you la—"

"Wait, wait. This one is going to be a little different."

"Yeah? How? You don't want me to do it with . . . you know."

"With what?"

"Not what. Who."

"What are you talking about?"

Black Mask grimaced, frustrated. Not using names, while prudent, was a pain in the ass. "Am I doing this one with that person I been doing the other ones with lately?"

"You mean with my brother?"

Good. At least Black Mask wasn't the one who said it. "Yeah, with your brother."

"Yeah, you're doing it with my brother. What's wrong with my brother?"

"He's trippin', man," Black Mask said. "I know you're trying to help him out, him just getting out and all. But I think prison made him crazy. The last dude, he shot him for his watch. And I was, like, yo, just leave him be. But your brother, he was like, I don't know, he had this look in his eyes. He was stone cold."

"Well, it's funny you should say that, because I actually *want* you to shoot the guy this time."

Black Mask took a moment to swallow this request. "You do, huh?"

"Yeah, you got a problem with that?"

"Kind of."

"Kind of why?"

"Because it's . . . it's messed up is all I'm saying," Black Mask said. "Especially with the cops. You jack a car and it's like, whatever. They let it go. You kill someone and it's just a different . . . ain't you heard the news? This last dude was a banker or something. I mean, who's the new one?"

"It's in the e-mail. I'll pay you double, okay?"

This significantly shortened Black Mask's deliberation. "A'ight," he said.

"Tell my brother to do it if you don't want to do it."

"Why don't you tell him?" Black Mask said. "He's your damn brother."

212

This brought a pause. Black Mask waited for a response, but none came. Then it clicked with him. "Oh, damn, he don't know it's you giving us these jobs, do he?"

The response was quick. "No. And we're going to keep it that way."

Black Mask just laughed. "Now you the one who's trippin'. What, it run in the family or something?"

"You tell my brother I'm part of this, and you're out. This is easy money I'm giving you. I can find someone else to take easy money. We clear?"

"Yeah, I guess so," Black Mask said.

"Good. Now stop being a bitch."

"Ain't no bitch."

"Then stop acting like one. You ain't been caught and you ain't gonna be if you're careful."

"A'ight. Whatever."

Black Mask ended the call. He shook his head again at the absurdity of being in business with your own brother, who didn't know who he was in business with. Then again, the more Black Mask thought about it, the more he realized: if Blue Mask was his brother, he wouldn't say anything, either.

The dude was just off.

CHAPTER 29

As I settled into my desk chair, I finally turned to the dilemma that I knew I would have to confront at some point.

Did I write the Chariots for Children story, knowing its director, Dave Gilbert, had an indecorous past and was quite possibly using the Greater Newark Children's Fund as a cover for a significant criminal enterprise? Or did I renege on the promise I made to Brodie, taking advantage of a man who had practically died the night before?

It was a tough call. Don't get me wrong, we ran puff pieces all the time on organizations or people we later exposed to be corrupt. The difference was, we were unaware of the corruption at the time the puffery appeared in our pages.

Then again, there were possibly innocent explanations for what I knew. Maybe the Cadillac CTS I had seen was not the one that had been stolen the day before. Maybe the Children's Council executive director knew about Gilbert's background, but brought him on anyway. After all, there were parts of Newark where probably half of the adult men had spent time in prison. It was impossible not to hire ex-cons.

I decided the best course of action was to write the piece, then stash it in Brodie's folder in our computer system. That way

I would know I had delivered on my promise, but the piece wouldn't possibly run until some later date, by which point I had already figured things out.

It was three o'clock when I began my typing. I had promised its delivery at five. Two hours felt like the proper amount of time to write the story of Jawan Porter and the fast shoes.

It was the kind of piece that I could have probably spent the rest of my workday crafting if I wanted to get picky with the language. But somehow I doubted my literary legacy was at stake here. Sometimes, a newspaper reporter had to be cognizant of the fact that his product was the vaunted first draft of history, and that future generations of scholars would be scrutinizing his words and debating the intent behind them. Other times, a newspaper reporter had to be cognizant of the fact that his product was going to be used to give current generations of puppies a place to pee.

This was clearly a case of the latter.

I was just getting into the flow, as it were, when my cell phone rang. The call was coming from Millburn and the home of Patricia and William Ross, AKA Trish and Bill, AKA Mom and Dad.

My father, a retired pharmaceutical executive, would never call me during work. He came from an era that frowned on taking personal calls at the office—the days before e-mail, the Internet, and telecommuting rendered the delineation between personal time and work time so hopelessly muddy.

That meant the caller was my mother, a retired schoolteacher, who I might have ignored were this more clearly personal time. Except she only called me during work time when it was important. Or at least important to her.

"Hey, Mom," I said. "What's up?"

"It's time, isn't it?"

I was momentarily stumped. "Time for . . . what, Mom?"

"The baby," she said breathlessly. "It's coming, isn't it? I had a premonition."

Ever since Tina cleared thirty-six weeks gestation, the point at which a fetus was considered fully cooked and ready to enter the world, Mom had been claiming that being C-3PO's grandmother gave her an intuition as to when the child would arrive. She was convinced Tina wouldn't make it to thirty-nine weeks, when the C-section was scheduled.

And maybe Mom really did have some special insight. The more likely truth was that, with three children of her own in their thirties—and exactly zero grandchildren to show for it—she was driving herself (and everyone else around her) crazy with anticipation.

Before we knew C-3PO was upside-down, Mom had actually asked if she could be in the delivery room during labor because, and I quote, "It's not like Tina has anything I haven't seen before."

My mother and Tina actually get along very well. Just not, you know, *that* well. For laughs, I ran the proposal past Tina. She did not find it as funny as I did.

Just as all the books suggested the modern, type A, control freak mother ought to have, Tina had a birth plan. Actually, that's not wholly accurate: Tina now had anywhere from five to seven birth plans. There was her original plan, the one she created within the first hours after she learned of her pregnancy; the plan she developed after she learned the baby was breach; then a series of contingency plans, which anticipated certain points of weakness in the primary plans and grew more elaborate in response to those anticipated failures.

Unsurprisingly, none of these plans involved having my mother in the room with her.

In exchange for my mother withdrawing her request, I had promised I would call her the moment I knew Tina was in labor.

And whereas once my mother, who most of the time loved me like no woman has ever loved a son, would have trusted I would be a man of his word, she had apparently lost all confidence in me.

"No, Mom, nothing is happening," I said.

"I'm telling you, I can *feel* the contractions."

"Mom, no offense, but you're fifteen years past menopause. Are you sure that's not just gas or something?"

My father picked up on another line and said, "I told her not to call."

"Hush, Bill."

"I also told her she was driving everyone crazy," my father said.

Mom ignored him. "Are you sure she's not in labor?"

I turned toward Tina's office, peering at her through the glass window. She was talking with a reporter. Her body language was relaxed. Her face was composed. Her hands were resting on her belly.

"Mom, I'm looking at her right now. I'm telling you, nothing is happening."

"Have you asked her? A woman can be having contractions and not tell anyone. Tina is a very private person, you know."

"Yes, Mom, I know, but—"

"Is she dilated?"

"Excuse me?"

"Her cervix. Has it started dilating? It takes a long time for it to soften up enough to allow a baby to pass through, you know."

"No, Mom, I haven't asked Tina about her cervix lately."

"I was walking around three inches dilated for weeks before I had your brother."

"That's . . . very informational, Mother. But she's not due for two weeks yet."

"I know, I know. It's just with the baby being a breach, and all. You *have* to get her to the hospital, or she could end up being like Patsy."

Mom had a sorority sister from a thousand years ago named Patsy who allegedly "nearly died" after complications from a breach pregnancy. Patsy was now quite healthy, as was the thirtysomething-year-old "baby" in question. But every time I reminded my mother of this, she accused me of being excessively cavalier with the health of her unborn grandson.

"Okay, Trish, that's enough, let him get back to work," my father said.

"Hush, Bill."

"You're driving everyone crazy," he said again.

And, again, my mother seemed not to hear him. "You'll call me the moment you hear something, right?"

"Yes, Mom."

"You won't wait."

"No, Mom."

"Because we might hit traffic on the way to the hospital."

Tina's C-section was scheduled to happen at Saint Barnabas Medical Center, the same hospital where I had been born thirty-three years earlier. It was no more than a ten-minute drive along secondary roads from my parents' house.

"I think you'll be okay, Mom."

"I just don't want to miss it. Your father's not getting any younger, you know."

"Jesus Christ, Trish, I'm not dying," my father interjected.

"I'm just saying," my mother said.

"Goodbye, Carter," my father said. "We love you and we're proud of you and now we're hanging up, right, dear?"

"Don't wait," my mother said one last time.

"I won't," I promised.

I placed the phone handle back on the cradle. From a few desks over Buster Hays rose and began walking in my direction.

He reached my desk, leaned over, and in a low voice said, "Ivy, if I have to hear you talk about someone's cervix again in this newsroom, I'm going to take one of those bottles of scotch and break it over your head."

I had returned to my keyboard for perhaps ten minutes when my phone rang.

"Carter, it's Armando Fierro," he said tersely.

"Hey," I said, suddenly on edge. Doc never called himself Armando. At least not around me. Then again, I'm not sure I had ever talked to him when he was pissed off, which it sounded like he was.

"I have to ask you something, and I had better get a straight answer," he said.

"Go ahead."

"Did you break into our pro shop last night?"

Uh-oh.

I knew I needed to say something. Unfortunately, the only things going through my head was "uh-oh," and its close cousins, "hoo-boy" and "oh, crap."

"Actually, let me just save you the trouble of answering that," he continued. "I'm going to share with you a little-known fact about our pro shop. We had trouble with some minor thefts a few years back—people going in after hours and helping themselves to shirts and balls and that sort of thing—so we installed security cameras that activate when the automatic lights go on. Earl Karlinsky tells me he has footage of you in the pro shop last night, well after its five o'clock closing time."

The name Earl Karlinsky made my jaw clench. My head now had several more interjections going through it, none of which I would be comfortable saying in church.

Doc went on, making an effort to keep his tone even: "Now,

I haven't been by the club to see the tape yet, but I will later this afternoon. For right now I'd really like to know: why were you breaking into our pro shop last night?"

"Well, I wouldn't say I broke in," I said. "The door was—"

"Don't screw with me," he spat. "I invite you into our club as a guest, then I stick my neck out for you when Earl tries to run you out, then I introduce you to a bunch of our members—I vouched for you, I *vouched* for you. And this is how you act? Like some goddamn criminal? Sneaking around in a place where you clearly don't belong? What the hell, Carter?"

Again, there were no especially useful responses on my tongue.

"Earl said the tape shows you messing around on the starter's computer. You know, when I was in government, I was a big defender of freedom of the press, and I think I've established myself as being pretty friendly to you guys since then. But I have to tell you, it's none of your damn business when someone is playing a round of golf at a private club or with whom. And if you try to put anything you got from your little bit of spy craft in the paper, you better have your lawyers damn close.

"Actually, no. I think I'm going to make sure they're close. I believe you guys use McWhorter and French as outside counsel, do you not? How about I call up their libel person and tell her exactly what's going on? Ordinarily I'd just call Brodie and count on him to be reasonable, but with Brodie on the shelf for a little while I think I've got to bring out the big guns. Maybe I'll just remind them I could use that surveillance footage to get an injunction slapped against the *Eagle-Examiner* printing its next edition. I bet *that* would get their attention."

He was just fuming now. If he calmed down for a moment, he'd realize no judge would stop the state's largest newspaper from printing on such flimsy evidence. Still, the last thing I needed was for Doc Fierro—a man who had connections at every level of the public and private sector—going all jihad on me.

I hadn't wanted to tell him anything about what Karlinsky and his haughty sidekick were doing. Not until I had it better substantiated. But he was giving me little choice. I had to give him something to justify what otherwise looked like absurd behavior.

"Doc," I said softly, too softly to really interrupt him.

"And *then*," he railed, "Karlinsky tells me you were spying on the club earlier this afternoon. He said you were just parked alongside the road, doing God knows what; and that when he pointed out you were trespassing—which you were—you threatened him with some kind of ridiculous assault and battery charges from when he grabbed your wrist? Seriously, Carter, is that really how you want to play things? Because I guarantee you there will be a room full of guys with amnesia if you even try to—"

"Doc," I said, loudly enough that he stopped. "Stop ranting and give me a chance to talk. Karlinsky is bad news, okay? I'll admit I don't have this completely nailed down, but I think he's part of a major carjacking ring in Newark. My theory is that he and another club employee are tagging high-end luxury cars with tracking devices, and that when those cars go into Newark, they get nailed. Tiemeyer was one of their victims. So was a guy named Joseph Okeke, who was killed two weeks ago, about a week after he played a round as a guest at Fanwood. That's what I was on the computer checking. I got another source telling me Karlinsky even asked Okeke details about his car during his visit, like he was casing the thing to steal it."

Now it was Doc's turn not to respond.

I pressed ahead: "The reason why I asked you for that membership list is that I wanted the Essex County Auto Theft Task Force to be able to look it over. I haven't heard back from them yet, but my guess is they'll find several more of your members own cars that have been jacked. Karlinsky is a pestilence, Doc. I might not have been totally forthright with you about what I was up to and I'm sorry for that. But I had a good reason."

Doc stewed on this for another moment. During his many years in and around state government, he had been confronted with the greed and stupidity of humanity many times. They were the cause of at least three-quarters of the problems he had fixed, including the one that had first earned him his nickname. He knew that, at least in New Jersey, it usually made sense to assume people were being driven by their demons and not their angels—and then be pleasantly surprised when you turned out to be wrong.

I thought for sure Doc was going to recognize the higher purpose behind my low actions and give me a full pardon.

But it was not to be. "Look, Karlinsky is a bit of a prick, I'll give you that," he said. "And God knows his cologne could choke a horse. But he's not a car thief. He's just not. To be honest, I don't think he's smart enough to come up with a scheme like that."

"Doc—"

"Look, I can't have you chasing wild theories that cast our club into a bad light. And you have to stop harassing Earl. I can only stick up for you so much before I start losing credibility. And the moment you entered a part of the club where you clearly weren't supposed to be, whether the door was open or not, you crossed a line. You're really giving me no choice. I'm putting the word out among the members that you are no longer welcome as a guest at Fanwood Country Club. If you try to show up there again, Earl will call the cops. And from this point on, you can consider me as serving in the role of the club's official spokesman. If you so much as think of typing the word 'Fanwood' with the expectation that it's going in the newspaper, I better have a chance to comment on it. Are we clear?"

"Doc," I said again.

"Are we clear?"

"Yeah," I said finally. "I guess."

With that, he hung up on me.

CHAPTER 30

Black Mask bounded down the steps of his apartment, hoodie pulled over his head.

He looked both ways when he hit the sidewalk—a well-ingrained 'hood habit—then turned right. He kept his hands shoved in his pockets and felt for his gun, which was shoved in his waistband.

As a convicted felon, Black Mask wasn't supposed to have one. On top of that, it was stolen. If a cop found it on him, Black Mask would have some serious weight over his head.

But there was a saying among thugs in Newark: better to be caught with a gun than without one.

Black Mask hopped in his truck, of which he was the lawful owner. He wanted to spend as little time driving stolen vehicles as possible.

His destination was the Newark Public Library. It was, perhaps, a strange place for a man of his vocation to be going. But the NPL had public computers with those IP addresses that no one would be able to trace back to him.

It was a safe place to check the anonymous e-mail account for the details about the latest job he and Blue Mask had been given. A few clicks and a few keystrokes, and he'd know everything he needed about his next victim, right down to the name of driver and the model of the car.

Black Mask made sure to switch up which branches he used. It didn't help that NPL had been closing branches lately. Damn budget cuts in this city just never seemed to end.

This time, Black Mask went with the main branch downtown. He hadn't been there in a while, but it was perfect. Lots of computers there. No one would notice him or remember another young black man walking in there to spend a little time online.

His drive from the Weequahic section of town got bogged down in traffic as he neared center city. He waited it out—what choice did he have?—and eventually found parking on a side street. With small regret, he stowed his gun in the glove box. The library had this thing that looked like a metal detector at the front entrance. He didn't need to attract that kind of attention.

No matter. He was downtown now. It was safer there.

Five minutes later, he was seated in front of a computer, having signed in under someone else's name. He smiled every time he did it: other criminals had fake passports, fake driver's licenses, whatever; he had a fake library card.

He brought up the Internet, accessed the Web mail site, typed the e-mail and password, being careful to shift the number and letter as needed.

Sure enough, a new unread e-mail was waiting. He clicked on it. His eyes scanned the screen. He frowned at a few of the details. Then he got to the good part.

The car would be a Volvo XC60, for which he and Blue Mask would be paid $3,000.

Then he got to the end. The e-mail always said the name of the driver. Most of the time, Black Mask didn't care so much. It was just another name.

This time it felt a little different. This time, he was going to have to tell Blue Mask to kill the guy, a guy he had never met before, a guy he didn't particularly have anything against.

A guy named Carter Ross.

CHAPTER 31

For the next two hours, I tried to ignore the teeth marks that Doc had just left on my head and hoped none of the threats he made about calling our lawyers would be carried out. I worked diligently on Jawan and his fast shoes, trying to keep to my self-inflicted five o'clock deadline, realizing I wasn't going to quite make it but trying to stay close to it.

I kept my e-mail off and my concentration on. My only interruptions came in the form of texts from Tommy. The first said: "Got some good stuff. Back in a bit to share."

The next arrived perhaps twenty minutes after that: "He is soooo tasty!"

I cackled, if a bit mordantly. Poor Tommy. As if it wasn't bad enough he had to be dumped by my commit-o-phobic cousin Glenn, he was now trying for a rebound that was completely out of reach. I tapped out, "You realize you're crushing on the straightest guy this side of a Heritage Foundation candidates forum, right?"

He soon fired back. "I hope so! You realize they're all a bunch of closet cases, right? Get them in the men's room and it's like a Turkish bathhouse."

All I could do was snort, glad that no one knew why. It

was around five thirty when I completed the story. I shipped it over to Brodie's folder, where it would molder for some time before being discovered. Then I turned my attention to my e-mail.

Justin Waters had come through for me, forwarding a message from his firm's secretary with the VIN number for the Cadillac, which I copied into my notebook.

Then there was one from Tina: "Pop your head in when you have a second?"

Ever the dutiful almost-fiancé, I stood up and followed her instruction to the letter.

"Do you want just my head or do you want the rest of me, too?" I asked when I reached her door.

She looked up from whatever she had been staring at on her screen, momentarily bewildered, having evidently forgotten the exact language of her e-mail.

I helped her: "You said to pop my head in and—"

"Yeah, yeah, sorry," she said. "Come on in."

I sat in my usual chair. "My mother was just asking about you," I said, neglecting to add which part she was asking about.

"Oh, really? That's sweet of her."

Tina stared off into the distance for a moment, almost like she was looking at a piece of her window that was somewhere above my right shoulder. Her hand was resting on her belly. Tina's focus was typically sharp enough to cut glass. It was unusual to see her so distracted.

I decided to prompt some words from her. "Did you want to talk to me or did you just want me to soak in your aura?"

"Yeah, yeah, sorry," she said again. "I'm . . . a little out of it."

"You're not having a contraction, are you?"

"No," she said quickly. "Why would you ask that?"

"My mother was having a premonition you had gone into labor."

I thought that would earn me a laugh. Instead she said, "No, no."

"You would tell me though, right?"

"Of course."

"Because, you know, all those lectures from Dr. Marston about 'negative outcomes' and all that . . ."

"Yeah, yeah, I know. I just . . . I wanted to ask you if you were busy tonight."

"I have to pick up some documents at a source's house at eight, but after that I'm free. Why?"

"There's something I want to talk to you about. But it has to be total cone of silence."

"Uh, all right. Is it work-related cone of silence or home-related cone of silence?" I asked.

"A bit of both. How about we do Indian take-out like you wanted last night? I should be able to clear out of here by eight. I'll see you at your place at eight thirty."

"You're being kind of mysterious," I said.

"When you hear what it is, you'll understand why I have to be," she said.

"Now you're being even more mysterious."

"Yeah, I know," she said.

I stopped myself from asking more. As I may have mentioned, Tina was a challenging woman. Lately, as she slowly—very slowly—let me into her life, I felt like she had been giving me a series of tests. She probably didn't realize she was doing it. And I'm not sure I fully understood how the tests worked. But they seemed to involve trust: whether I had it in her, whether she could have it in me.

It was important to let her tell me whatever she felt like sharing in her own due time. So I just said, "Okay. Indian take-out at eighty thirty it is."

"Thanks," she said.

"And now, let me guess, you want me to pop my head back out of your office."

"That would be great," she said. "Do me a favor and close the door behind you."

I did as she asked, never realizing such a simple act could feel like a metaphor.

As I returned my body to my desk, I similarly returned my brain to work. Now that I was armed with the VIN number from Justin Waters, it was time to figure out what was happening behind the happy facade of the Greater Newark Children's Fund.

This made me realize I had never heard back from Sweet Thang, which was odd. I had sent her the story about Dave Gilbert hours earlier. I knew her duties at the nonprofit, varied as they were, kept her busy. But one of the reasons Sweet Thang could kill the batteries on two smartphones in a day is that she was never out of touch for very long.

I pulled up "Thang, Sweet" in my contact list and hit the send button. It rang, then rang some more, then sent me to voice mail. I shifted over to "Thang, Sweet 2," but got the same result. So I texted her: "Hey, what's up? Did you see the Gilbert thing? Call me."

Less than a minute later, "Thang, Sweet" came up on my phone.

"Hey," I said.

"I'm only calling to tell you I'm not talking to you," she said.

With Sweet Thang, not talking was its own lengthy conversation. It would involve explaining how she wasn't talking to me, why she wasn't talking to me, and what impact her not talking to me would have on shrimp farming in Micronesia.

"Before you don't talk to me, let me just first make sure: you heard about Brodie, right?"

"Yeah. My dad told me. But while I'm not talking to you, let's definitely not talk about that, because I'll start crying again."

"Okay, fair enough. Then let's get onto this whole you-not-talking-to-me thing," I said. "You realize this makes you a PR person who is trying to dodge me. You remember I like to gently braise stonewalling PR people and eat them as mid-afternoon snacks, right?"

"I know, I know, I just . . . back when I was at the *Examiner*, this was the sort of thing I used to talk to you about. I always knew that whatever problem I had, you had experienced it sixteen times before. And you could always talk to me about ten different ways to handle it and then talk to me about the best way to handle it and it would make me feel so much better about things. But now it's, like, I don't know, I'm not the intern anymore and I ought to be on my own. And, besides, you're a newspaper reporter and I'm a flak and there's supposed to be this wall between us. And you can't go over the wall to get advice and then expect to be able to crawl back over to the other side of the wall. It doesn't work that way.

"I mean, really, I'm supposed to ask you to tell me how I can make sure this doesn't turn into a scandal that harms the Greater Newark Children's Council when you're the person whose job it is to turn it into a scandal that harms the Greater Newark Children's Council? I know, I know, it's not actually your job to make it a scandal. Your job is to report the truth. But in this case it turns out that the truth is a scandal and I can't let that happen. So whether you're causing that hurt or are just the messenger is really just semantics. The end result is the same."

She may have actually surfaced to take a breath at this point, but I can't swear to that. When Sweet Thang gets going, it's like she has scuba gear hidden somewhere.

"That's the first reason I can't talk to you," she continued. "The second reason is when I think about Dave . . . I mean, this will, like, ruin him. He'll probably lose his job and no one will hire him anywhere else once the word is out. And on the one hand, it's like, tough luck. You do the crime, you do the time. You make your bed and all that. And if anything, I *should* narc him out, because what credibility do we have—with our donors, with our employees, and most importantly with our kids—if we let someone get away with being untruthful. It's one thing to not know about it. That's bad enough, because it makes us look like we're clueless. But to have it brought to your attention and do nothing that's, like, total negligence and how can we allow that?

"But then I also just keep thinking, I don't know, I've seen him in action, you know? And shouldn't you judge someone based on what you've seen, not based on some mistake they may have made a long ago in a very different context when they may have been a very different person? You're not a Christian if you don't allow for forgiveness. I don't want to turn into one of those fake Christians who talks about forgiveness but really just wants to get all judgy. If Jesus was alive today—and, really, I believe He lives in all of us—He would be preaching in the prisons, hoping to redeem the worst of all the offenders. And, anyway, I don't want to make this all religious. The point is, I *know* Dave Gilbert and he really is the nicest, sweetest man and his heart is just in the right place and he does what he does to help kids. I know that on a deep level, in a way that can't be swayed by some stupid newspaper article. I mean, no offense."

She stopped there. I waited to see if more came out of her, but she was done for the moment. After all, we weren't talking.

The funny thing is, Sweet Thang was right about at least one thing: I had experienced this sixteen times before, give or take. And the first time was probably when I was about her age. This was back when I was working at a smaller daily newspaper in Pennsylvania. I was writing a story about a prominent and wealthy businessman who was leading the fund-raising charge for a badly needed children's center and pledging to kick-start it with a large donation.

During my reporting, I learned he had done some ethically questionable things to amass his fortune and seemingly been sued by everyone he had ever done business with. Still, I didn't want to hurt the chances of the children's center being built. So I wrote a glowing article about him, one that neglected to mention his perpetual shadiness. He had the article framed and mounted in his office, like a prize buck.

Within two years, the guy had disappeared overseas, leaving behind a pile of broken promises and a vacant lot with a sign announcing a children's center that would never come to be. It left me feeling like a dupe and taught me a lesson I had never forgotten.

"Well, let me start by saying I'm glad we're not talking," I said.

"Stop making fun of me."

"And, look, you're right: I have experienced things like this before. And what I've learned is that you have to let the truth stand for itself. If the truth is Dave has done some bad things in the past but is now trying to do good, that's one thing. And I think it can be reported in a sensitive way that stays true to facts but doesn't do harm to the Greater Newark Children's Council. I don't think anyone begrudges a Newark nonprofit giving an ex-con a second chance.

"But if the truth is that Dave has done some bad things in the past and is still doing bad things, that's something that needs to come out, no matter how ugly it gets. And I'll be honest, what often gets politicians, corporations, or institutions in the most trouble is not that they've allowed something bad to happen. As long as they own up to it, the damage usually goes away pretty quickly. It's when they try to cover it up that heads really roll. That's the lesson of Watergate, Bridgegate, and every gate in between."

"I know, I know," she whimpered. I was glad this conversation was happening over the phone, because Sweet Thang was pretty adorable when she was dejected and I didn't need that kind of temptation. Even if there was no chance I was going to act on it, it made me feel guilty all the same.

"So here's what we're going to do. You've got a key to the Greater Newark Children's Council garage, do you not?"

"Yeah."

"Okay. Good. I've got the VIN number for the Cadillac that was stolen last night in Newark. Let's just check it against the one in his garage, assuming it's still there. If it's not a match, that's one thing. If it matches, I think it's safe to say we have a problem that we have no choice but to act on. But let's get all the information first."

She wasn't saying anything, a rarity. Sweet Thang had many qualities. Reticence was seldom one of them.

Sensing her indecision, I played my trump card: "I've got my Chariots for Children story written, but you know it can't run until I check this out. That's life at Harold Brodie's newspaper, whether he's in the hospital or not."

Again, she said nothing immediately. But I did hear her sigh.

"Okay, fine," she said, eventually. "Why don't you come over in an hour or so? Everyone will have gone home by that point and we can be looking around without having to answer any questions."

"Deal," I said.

She sighed again.

"Lauren?" I said.

"Usually, you only call me Lauren when you're trying to be nice," she said. "So why doesn't this feel nice?"

"Because the search for the truth seldom does," I said. "But, trust me, you're doing the right thing."

CHAPTER 32

Having exhausted myself with all that mentoring—and feeling in need of a little alone time—I meandered down the back stairwell.

The *Eagle-Examiner* building is a warren of corridors, half staircases, and mismatched parts, many of which can only be reached via passageways that seem to have been laid out for the implicit purpose of getting people lost.

It's really something like two or three buildings that have been attached in ungainly fashion and made to appear, from the outside, like one edifice. Its blueprint—if one even existed—would look like a jigsaw puzzle whose pieces didn't line up.

None of the floors of the buildings that have been forced together are the same height. None of the support beams are quite where they need to be. There are load-bearing walls in all kinds of inconvenient places.

Those are some of the root causes of the architectural clumsiness. The other is that the facility has been through so many of the typesetting paradigms that have, at various points, held sway over the newspaper business. Hot type. Cold type. Then, eventually, the shift to desktop publishing.

With each new era, the building received a retrofitting that was necessarily inelegant. After all, a newspaper had to be produced every day during the transition, meaning the two technologies existed side by side for a time.

The result of all this slapdashery is such an idiosyncratic mishmash that it took me at least three years not to feel like I was getting lost every time I left the well-worn path from my desk to the soda machine. Eventually, though, I realized it was a wonderful place to explore. The remnants of some of the old equipment were still lying around in nooks and crannies. If you knew what you were looking at, it was like a stroll through your own personal newspaper museum. I tried to enjoy it while I could, knowing our time in the building was running out.

As I descended, I went past the fire door that had not sounded its alarm in at least twenty years, since the building went smoke-free in the midnineties. The newsroom's smokers, who realized the door represented the shortest route between them and a nicotine fix, had disabled it, then thwarted all efforts to repair it.

Reaching the basement, I passed some half-empty rolls of newsprint that had been left behind in the late seventies. That was when the owners realized that since their subscribers had moved to the suburbs it made sense to move the presses there as well.

It was a real heyday for a paper like ours. The *Newark Evening News* had gone out of business, leaving only us, the morning paper, without any real competition. From what I'm told our profit margins were 30 percent and all our business staff had to do to keep them there was pick up the phone when advertisers called. The newsroom didn't even have a budget. It just spent what it wanted.

I was lost in that fantasy as I strolled past the pressmen's locker room. Then my daydreams were interrupted by the sound of . . . giggling?

Clearly, it wasn't any of the pressmen. There hadn't been any of those in the building in a long time. And, besides, pressmen weren't the giggling type.

Tommy Hernandez, on the other hand, certainly was. And that was who I saw as I opened the door. But it was who he was kissing that really shocked me:

A certain tall, broad-shouldered, former college lacrosse player.

"No way!" I blurted.

Two heads whipped toward me.

"Chillax, you're . . . you're . . ." I was so surprised it took me a moment before I could finish with: "You're gay?"

"Yeah, brah," he said, smiling. "Surprised my parents, too. They used to think I read *Men's Health* for the articles."

Tommy leaned his head into Chillax's chest. "At least you weren't one of those poor repressed souls who thought he just hadn't found the right girl yet."

"Naw, I pretty much knew from the time I was, like, five and I played doctor with the Petrocelli twins. Justina Petrocelli getting naked wasn't that interesting to me, but her brother Justin sure was."

"Did your teammates know?" I asked.

"Oh, yeah," Chillax said, like it was no big deal. "I came out sophomore year. They were, like, whatever, dude. As long as I played my ass off, they wouldn't have cared if I wanted to hump the school mascot."

"Huh," I said, then looked at Tommy. "I guess when you texted me and said you got some good stuff, you weren't lying."

"Yeah. Sorry for the little detour here," Tommy said. "We were going to do a notebook dump with you when we got back but you were doing that thing with your computer screen where you're like Superman with the X-ray vision and you can stare right through it."

"No big deal," I said. Tina and I had once nearly consummated our relationship in the pressmen's locker room. It would be hypocritical of me to fault Tommy and Chillax for choosing it as the place to begin theirs. "But before you guys get too busy here"—I made a circular motion with my hand—"would you mind doing that notebook dump now?"

Tommy looked at Chillax, who looked back at Tommy. There was a wistfulness in their glances that made me feel rotten for playing the spoiler. But on the off chance I needed to write this thing quickly, I needed to have those notes.

"I guess not," Tommy said, at last.

"Thanks."

Tommy said, "Let's just go upstairs and type up the notes and then we can—"

"Word," Chillax said, not needing Tommy to complete the sentence.

"Mind giving me the quick headline right now?" I asked as we started walking together back toward the stairway that led up to the newsroom.

"Yeah. Kevin Tiemeyer was about to lose his job," Tommy said.

"Really?"

"Uh-huh. I'm guessing that's why he was mowing his own lawn, not going out to dinner, and ditching the country club," Tommy said. "One of USKB's mergers had basically made his department redundant. I guess there was a question about which one they were going to keep. Kevin's lost. They were letting him stay on for the quote-unquote 'transition' and then he was going to be shown the door."

"Did he find a new job yet?"

"If he did, he hadn't told anyone he worked with. I talked to a few other people in the department. It sounds like they were pretty specialized—don't ask me to explain what they did, because I can't—and that made it harder to find something. You've heard that saying that to find a new job it takes a month for every ten thousand dollars you make? They were all hunkering down for a bit of unemployment."

"I wonder if that's what he and Joseph Okeke were talking about when they played golf," I said. "What I can't figure out is how the two of them knew each other. Banking and Nigerian telecommunications aren't exactly related."

"Unless Tiemeyer had somehow financed a deal for Okeke?" Tommy offered. "All I really understood about Tiemeyer's department is that it involved lending in some way."

"Possible," I said. "I'd love to be able to nail that down. Otherwise my story would just refer to them as two golfing buddies, which sort of begs the question of how they became buddies."

"I got phone numbers for three of his more chatty colleagues," Tommy said. "I could call and ask."

"All right. Thanks. I'll see you guys later."

We had reached the newsroom. Tommy went toward his desk. But my eyes followed Chillax.

I remembered talking with one of our sports beat writers, who once covered Jason Collins, back when the Nets played in New Jersey and before Collins came out as the first gay athlete to play in a major American sporting league. Our beat writer told me that of the fifteen guys in the Nets' locker room, you would have put Collins in about thirteenth place in the Most Likely To Be Gay voting.

On court, he was a plodder whose main role was to set picks that got his teammates open for baskets—which meant he spent a lot of time letting people run into him. Off the court, he was not the least bit effeminate, nor was he flamboyant in speech or action. If anything, he went out of his way to be boring. Especially when it came to how he dressed. He fit none of the gay stereotypes.

Which just goes to prove one of the immutable axioms of

human behavior: you never know what happens when the bedroom door closes.

When I returned to my desk, there was a sheet of yellow paper from a legal pad sitting on my chair. I didn't even need to read it to know: Managing Editor Rich Eberhardt was looking for me.

Eberhardt was a short, kinky-haired, high-strung man whose reading of the paper and retention of that material were famously, if not freakishly, encyclopedic. He devoured the thing cover to cover, right down to the home sale listings, and could often recall the arcane details from stories we had written ten years earlier.

He spent no small part of his day roaming the newsroom with a yellow legal pad. As the keeper of the budget—our tabulation of which stories were slated to appear in the next day's paper—Eberhardt was constantly hectoring reporters, asking them whether their stories would be ready to run. His insistence increased as deadline approached.

One of his other primary duties was to compile the corrections. If you had a story in that day's edition, but nothing scheduled for the next one, you dreaded seeing him and his yellow pad coming at you. It meant you had screwed up and would be publicly shamed with a printed item on page two that would likely begin "Due to a reporter's error . . ."

If I've made him sound like a pain in the ass, it's because he was. Sometimes. On other occasions, he had an easy smile and was quite likable. With Eberhardt, it was sort of a moment-to-moment thing.

In this case, I didn't know what he wanted. Just that the yellow piece of paper said, "COME SEE ME ASAP, PLS.—RICH" in hasty scrawl.

Eberhardt's office was next to Brodie's in the corner of the newsroom. Like all the other top editors' offices, it was walled by glass. As I approached, I could see he was not alone.

He was accompanied by Angela Showalter, the paper's outside counsel from the law firm of McWhorter and French. She was very smart and highly capable and I'm sure if she lived in my neighborhood, I'd enjoy carpooling with her once C-3PO was old enough for swim team.

As things stood right now, however, she was still a lawyer, so I wasn't happy to see her. In the newsroom, we called her Nowalter, because her basic job was to make sure we didn't get sued, which involved saying "no" a lot—no, we couldn't run that story; no, we couldn't include that saucy detail; no, we couldn't quote that anonymous source.

I didn't need to knock on Eberhardt's door. He saw me coming.

"Oh, there you are," he said. "Please come in. You know Angela Showalter, of course."

Nowalter and I exchanged smiles. Mine was perhaps a bit less genuine than hers.

Eberhardt did not waste another moment. "We were hoping you could explain this to us," he said. He clicked his mouse button twice, then swiveled his monitor toward me.

For the next few minutes, I was treated to video of myself in the Fanwood Country Club pro shop. It began with me walking stealthily across the room. Then I slunk behind the starter's desk and started toying with the computer there. Then my head whipped to the left and I dropped behind the counter as Earl Karlinsky came in and tried the handle to the front door. Finding it locked, he departed.

I watched myself rise from behind the desk, looking flushed and anxious, the very picture of guilt. I worked the computer for a little longer, then made my hasty departure.

Eberhardt turned his screen back to its original position. I took a moment to gather myself. My profession is all about divorcing oneself of personal opinions and calling it like you see it. And there was no other way to call this one: it looked bad. Really bad.

I turned to Nowalter. "I take it you've been talking to Doc Fierro," I said.

"He contacted me earlier today, yes," she said. "You're confirming the video is authentic? This is you last night at Fanwood Country Club?"

"I wish I could tell you it wasn't. But I'm afraid it is."

Nowalter shot a dark face at Eberhardt. I immediately began arguing my case. "But I want to be very clear, I was invited to the club and I didn't break into the pro shop. The back door was open. All I did was turn the handle and walk in. What you're watching isn't me breaking and entering."

"I'm sure that's true, but the back door doesn't appear on the video," Eberhardt said. "All we see is the general manager checking the locked front one."

I nodded.

"Who invited you to the club?" Nowalter asked.

"Doc di—" I began and then I stopped myself. My conundrum was becoming painfully, painfully clear to me. The only person who could clear me of wrongdoing was the very person who was accusing me of it. The only evidence I had in support of my innocence was my own testimony. He, on the other hand, had this damning video.

In short, Doc Fierro had my man parts in a vice. But why had he decided to tighten the crank so quickly? As far as he was concerned, there was no story yet. We had established that I would call him if there was. Why the preemptive strike?

Then the explanation walked up and dislocated my jaw. Doc was protecting Earl Karlinsky. They were in on this thing together.

It all made sense. And part of the proof was something Doc had told me, something I should have had sense to know myself: Earl Karlinsky wasn't smart enough to come up with a scheme like this himself.

But Doc Fierro sure was.

As all the rows and columns lined up in my head, Nowalter and Eberhardt hadn't been talking. They were just looking at each other in a meaningful way, as if they were silently rehashing a conversation whose conclusion they had already reached.

Eberhardt cleared his throat. He ran his hand through his wavy hair, which I recognized as one of his nervous tics. I felt like my neck was being lowered on to the chopping block.

"Look, Carter," he said. "If Brodie were here, maybe there would be some possibility of leniency. You've done great work for this paper and that counts for something. And, personally, I believe you when you say you didn't break in. That's just . . . it's not what it looks like on that video and I can't . . . I can't allow harm to come to Brodie's newspaper while he's not here. I'd never forgive myself. You know we can't allow our reporters to run around breaking the law in the name of gathering news."

Then he let the ax drop. "I'm afraid I have no choice but to suspend you without pay until further notice."

CHAPTER 33

Blue Mask was certain—absolutely certain—that he had closed the door to Birdie's bedroom before he crashed on her bed. He was exhausted, having pulled an all-nighter to drive down to the depths of the New Jersey Pine Barrens, bury her, dispose of the car, then get himself home.

He needed sleep. Uninterrupted sleep.

Yet what woke him up? The damn cat. Jumping on the bed. And the door was open. Did the cat know how to turn handles or something? Blue Mask swore.

He'd teach the thing a lesson. Without moving the rest of his body, Blue Mask brought his foot up, which was still clad in a sneaker. The cat was on the corner of the bed, licking its paw, seemingly not paying attention.

Blue Mask kicked, aiming for the thing's skull. The sneaker connected with the cat's belly instead. But without much effect. The cat seemed to wrap itself around the shoe, going from an exclamation point to a parenthesis in an instant. All of the energy from the kick just got absorbed in the middle.

It hopped off the bed, meowed indignantly, and walked off, more irritated than injured. Blue Mask swore again. Maybe he'd just feed the damn thing rat poison and be done with it.

He swung his feet down to the floor, felt a small ache in his shoulder muscles from the shoveling. His left palm had a blister on it.

The hunger hit him right after he stood up. He hadn't eaten since the day before. He wondered if Birdie had anything in her refrigerator. He didn't want to spend down what little money he had. It might have to last for a while.

Then, as if to dispute that fact, his phone rang. It was Black Mask.

"Yo," he said.

"Yo, we got a job to do."

"Yeah? When?"

"Tonight," Black Mask said.

That was good. A job meant money. He needed to build up his nut again. At least this time he knew Birdie couldn't steal it from him.

"A'ight," Blue Mask said. "What kind of car?"

Black Mask always seemed to know what kind of car they were going to jack. Blue Mask had no idea how.

"It's a Volvo. A nice one. Silver. Practically brand-new."

"Cool. And you sure it's gonna be there?"

"Yeah, fool, I'm sure," Black Mask said.

Somehow, Black Mask could also predict where the car would be moments before it arrived. It was uncanny. Blue Mask asked him how he knew, but Black Mask never let on. He would just say the car, say the intersection and, presto, there it was. Like he had conjured the thing.

"Where you want to meet?" Blue Mask asked.

Black Mask gave him an intersection and a time. Blue Mask said he'd be there. They ended the call.

He went downstairs to look in Birdie's fridge. Cottage cheese. Mangy-looking meat for stew. Apple sauce that looked like it had been in there for a while. Some old ham. Nothing he wanted to eat.

Hell with it. He went out to the closest McDonald's and celebrated with two Big Macs and some fries. He was less concerned about saving his money now. He was going to get paid tonight.

CHAPTER 34

If there was one good thing about my retreat from Eberhardt's office, it was that I somehow managed to keep my dignity intact.

I wanted to cry, but kept it in check. I wanted to yell, but didn't. I wanted to make an impassioned appeal for a second chance, but ultimately recognized the fruitlessness of that effort.

Instead, I stoically told Eberhardt that if our roles were reversed and I was presented with the same set of circumstances, I probably would have made the same decision. I may have won points for my maturity with that, or Eberhardt may have just been relieved he wasn't going to have to call security on me. He told me he wasn't sure what the next steps would be, just that I should avoid the premises while it was being sorted out.

The one thing I extracted before I departed was a promise that he would not put the word out among the staff about my suspension until the next day. I told Eberhardt it was because, with Tina's condition, I wanted to be able to gently break the news to her myself as to what had happened and why.

And that was true. But I also wanted to buy myself a little more time when I could continue to operate as a fully functioning reporter, without the rest of the staff realizing I was untouchable.

The fact was, the best way to restore my credibility was to destroy Doc's. And the best way to do that was to prove he and Karlinsky were part of this carjacking ring. If I could do that, it would cast that video in an entirely different light. It would make Doc look like a man with a compelling motivation to lie about its particulars. Even Nowalter would agree our case would get 100 percent stronger. No judge trusts a witness with an obvious agenda.

How I would explicitly tie Doc to the wrongdoing at Fanwood Country Club wasn't yet clear to me. I just knew the stakes had changed. I was no more than a week or two away from becoming a father to a baby I might not be able to support. If I lost my job at the *Eagle-Examiner,* I might never work in journalism again. Correction: I might never work anywhere outside retail. The only hiring most newspapers did anymore was essentially child labor. They certainly weren't hiring someone else's damaged goods.

Neither was anyone else. Once word got out I had been fired, I would literally become unemployable by any of the institutions that provided so many ex-reporters a soft landing. And while Tina still had her job—ensuring C-3PO wouldn't starve—that felt like scant comfort. I don't ordinarily get hung up on macho notions of masculinity. Most of them are horribly outdated and deserved to have been buried around the time humanity left the hunter-gatherer phase.

Yet something hardwired in me, something I perhaps hadn't recognized before, was suddenly telling me that if I couldn't provide for my child, it made me less of a man.

I was now more resolved than ever: Doc Fierro had to go down. Quickly.

And I knew where I had to begin. On my way to the elevator, as I kept an eye on Eberhardt's office, I stopped by Buster Hays's desk. He was pounding his keyboard with the usual ferocity.

"Hey," I said, trying to sound casual. "Did you hear from

your guy on the task force about that Fanwood membership list yet?"

"Nope," he said, without looking at me.

"Would you mind calling him? It's gotten to be sort of important."

"Believe it or not, Ivy, I have other things to do around here than to be your handmaiden."

I stood there for a moment and stopped trying to keep my emotions in check. I failed.

"Buster," I said softly. "Please."

His head snapped upward. My eyes fixed on his.

And then three words came out that I thought I'd never hear from Buster Hays's mouth: "Ivy, you okay?"

I looked down at the carpet for a moment.

"This doesn't have anything to do with why you were just in Eberhardt's office with Nowalter, does it?" he asked.

It occurred to me Buster probably knew more than he was letting on. He often did.

"It's probably better for you that you not know the details," I said. "But, yeah."

"Okay," he said, nodding his head slightly. "I'm a little slammed on deadline right now. But as soon as I file I'll call my guy and put the screws to him."

"Thanks, Buster. I owe you."

"Yeah, you do," he said. "But you know how you're gonna repay me?"

He didn't wait for my response. "You just take care of yourself, okay, Ivy? There are only so many real reporters left in this newsroom. Be a damn shame to lose one of the best we got."

I left before Buster could realize he had gotten me choked up. I was in dire need of some kind of break, and Buster's cooperation felt like a big one.

Then another one arrived. I was just out of the building, on my way toward the parking garage, telling myself this wouldn't be the last time I made that particular walk, when my phone rang.

"Carter Ross."

"Mr. Ross, this is Tujuka Okeke."

I felt myself smiling. Grit had won again. "Good evening, Mrs. Okeke."

"I received your note," she said. "I am sorry I was rude earlier today."

"I'm sorry I woke you up."

"If you would like to come by my house tonight, we can talk about Joseph."

"That would be great. What time?"

"My shift starts at nine," she said. "I have to leave no later than eight forty-five."

"How does seven sound?"

"That would be fine," she said, and we bid each other goodbye.

The smile was still on my face. It felt like my momentum, so irrevocably lost mere minutes earlier, was now returning to me.

I ran through a quick itinerary in my mind. I could hit the Greater Newark Children's Council at six thirty and with Sweet Thang's help be out in fifteen minutes. That would land me at Tujuka's house by seven. I would be rushing it a bit, but I could get what I needed there in forty-five minutes and make it to Zabrina Coleman-Webster's house by eight to grab those insurance documents. Then I could be on time for my take-out date with Tina.

As I drove toward Sweet Thang's place, hope buoyed me. Assuming Buster could come through for me, I thought of the story I'd be able to offer Eberhardt: a carjacking ring terrorizing a well-known country club, perhaps being led by a former state cabinet member, perhaps involving a noted Newark nonprofit; a cast of victims that included a banker who was about to lose his job, a businessman who had been a doting father, and a widow who was being cheated out of insurance money.

It would be more than compelling enough to get him to lift my suspension.

Before long, I was parked alongside the dumpy brick home of the Greater Newark Children's Council and had gotten out of the car. The front door was locked, so I hit the buzzer on a small intercom next to the door.

"Be right there," a squelchy version of Sweet Thang's voice informed me.

She appeared at the front door with her bouncy blond hair tied up in a ponytail, always a sign she meant business. She held the door open for me, and I entered.

"I have just been a *wreck* about this all day," she said as we walked back to her tiny office. "I spent half the afternoon crafting the resignation letter in which I admit this is all my fault and express incredible remorse over the harm I have unwittingly caused an organization I care deeply about."

"I might end up being wrong about all this," I reminded her.

"Yeah, but most of the time you're not."

"We'll see. Come on. Let's get it over with."

She was standing next to her desk, not moving. "I've decided I don't want to be there when you look at the car. I already feel like I'm betraying the GNCC enough as it is. Here. Just go."

She went into her desk drawer and retrieved her keys, which were at the end of a lanyard made from a thin strip of rainbow-colored cloth. I accepted them with a small amount of hesitance. I wasn't sure if I was up for more activity that might later be interpreted as breaking and entering on someone's security camera footage.

"I'd really feel better if you . . ." I started to say, and was about to add *came with me*. But there was a certain set to Sweet Thang's jaw. She wasn't budging on this one.

"Never mind," I said. "I'll be right back."

"You'll let us comment, of course," she said. "I spent the other half of the afternoon preparing statements for our executive director to make about how appalled we are, about how this does not reflect the values of our organization, and about how we acted swiftly the moment we learned about it."

"And I will print all of it and more when the time comes," I assured her.

"Okay. It's just that Dave is—"

"Sweet Thang," I said, cutting off what I recognized would be a long monologue. "Just sit tight. I'll be right back."

The corners of her mouth went down in a manner that would have been adorable were it not for the circumstances. I left her in her office, tracing my way out the back exit we had used earlier in the day and across the courtyard.

When I reached the door to the garage, I held the keys and the rainbow lanyard aloft for a moment, to make sure any cameras registered that I had been provided them by a GNCC employee.

I inserted the key into the lock. It turned easily.

The inside of the garage was still lit from high above, as it had been earlier in the day. The television was still playing, too, providing a ghostly, chattering soundtrack to an empty room. I wondered why Dave hadn't turned it off before he left for the day.

The Cadillac CTS was still up on the hydraulic lift. That solved my first potential problem—I had worried it would have been chopped up and moved away by the time I got back. But it did nothing to solve my second: I had no idea how to get the car down so I could check the VIN number against the one Justin Waters had provided me. Hydraulic Lift Operation 101 was not an offering in the Amherst course guide, nor was it part of on-the-job training at the *Eagle-Examiner*.

I walked toward the Cadillac and was just starting to look for the lift controls when there was a stirring in the corner.

Then I heard a sound that has to rank near the top of the scariest sounds on Earth: that metal-on-metal *chick-chick* of a shotgun slide being racked. I whirled around to see Dave Gilbert.

"What the hell do you want?" he demanded.

Ordinarily, it was Gilbert's handlebar mustache that commanded most of my attention when he spoke. But not this time.

This time, it was the barrel of the shotgun he had aimed at my chest.

CHAPTER 35

For a second or two, my eyes flitted between Dave Gilbert and the shotgun. Both were quite serious, in their respective fashions.

"Sweet Thang knows I'm in here," I said quickly. "If something happens to me, she'll know it was you."

He readjusted the gun, getting a more comfortable grip. He was about twenty feet away. It is a common misconception that it is impossible to miss with a shotgun when firing at close range, because of the spreading action of the pellets. This is not entirely true, inasmuch as a typical buckshot load expands no more than a couple of inches when fired from thirty feet or less.

Yet while it was theoretically possible for him to miss from this distance, I was not especially keen to offer up my own thin flesh for testing.

"Who the hell is Sweet Thang?" he asked.

"Sorry. Lauren McMillan."

"Then why isn't she here?" he demanded. "You're not supposed to be here."

By this point, I had made a more thorough accounting of the garage—mostly to look for something I could dive behind. During that examination, I had seen that over in the corner, near where the TV was droning on, there was an inflatable mat with a sleeping bag on it. There was also a duffel bag, stuffed with clothes; a small heating element perched on a milk carton; and a carton of ramen noodles.

None of it had been there in the morning. I was quite sure I would have noticed. Which told me Gilbert packed it away during the day. Which told me he was hiding it. Which told me Dave Gilbert was more than like squatting here.

What had Sweet Thang said when she introduced Gilbert to me? *I swear, it's like he lives here.* Once again, Sweet Thang's reporter's instincts were even better than she realized.

"Maybe I'm not supposed to be here," I said. "But neither are you, I'm guessing. Does the Greater Newark Children's Council know you're living here?"

I'm not sure if a mustache can twitch. But I think his did.

"I'm guessing the Greater Newark Children's Council also doesn't know you're a felon," I said.

"They never asked," he said. "I applied for the job, and there was nothing on the application about it. It never came up during the interview, so I never told them."

He shifted the shotgun from one side of his body to the other, keeping his finger close enough to the trigger that I didn't get any ideas it had provided me with some kind of opportunity for escape.

"And the Greater Newark Children's Council probably doesn't know you're supplementing your income by running a chop shop out of here," I said.

"What?"

"Come on, Dave. I'm on to you. That Cadillac over there was reported stolen in a carjacking last night."

"No, it wasn't. It was donated to us on Monday by a family who just lost Grandpa and didn't need it anymore. They gave us the title and everything. It's legit."

"Just stop," I said. "You've basically got two choices right now. You can run away, knowing I'm not going to come after you and hoping the authorities won't be able to catch you, either. Or you can name names and cooperate with the investigation that—"

"What investigation? I seriously have no idea what you're talking about. That car is not stolen."

"Yeah? Prove it," I said. "I've got the VIN number of the stolen car in my pocket. Let me take a look at that one over there."

And then Dave Gilbert did something I absolutely did not expect. He set the shotgun down on the concrete floor, with the nasty end pointed away from us, and walked over to two red buttons against one of the walls.

The next thing I knew, the Cadillac was being lowered to floor level.

"This is ridiculous," he was fuming as the car came down. "This is part of the reason I left Massachusetts. Once people know about your past, it's like everything is your fault. If something goes wrong, blame the ex-con. If something goes missing, blame the ex-con."

He turned to look at me as the Cadillac neared the end of its descent. "Look, I spent time in prison, okay? You got me. But I didn't do what the government said I did. They made it out like I was tricking old people out of their retirement money and stealing money from Medicare. All I did was get sloppy with how I did the accounting and screw up some of the Medicare billing. But, seriously, have you ever *seen* the Medicare regulations? They're incomprehensible. I bet ninety percent of the assisted living facilities in the country are committing fraud in at least one way, not because they mean to, but because the whole system is so damn confusing it takes a Ph.D. in bureaucratic bullcrap to figure it out."

The Cadillac was down on the ground now. I walked over to it and pulled out the pad where I had the VIN number recorded.

Gilbert was still ranting. "I wasn't making myself rich, okay?

The funny thing is, if I really had been stealing money I could have afforded the kind of lawyers I needed to defend myself. Those cases are so complex, one of the firms that specialized in them wanted a hundred-thousand-dollar retainer just to look at it. And they said it would probably be another two hundred grand if it went to trial. The feds offered eighteen months in exchange for a guilty plea. If we went to trial I was looking at a minimum of ten years."

I looked at the VIN number on the dashboard. I looked at the VIN number in my notebook.

"It doesn't match," I said.

"Of course it doesn't match. Look, I'm doing my penance here, okay? One of the terms of my plea bargain is that I can't go anywhere near a facility that gets money from Medicare. So I figured, I can't work with senior citizens anymore, I'll try to help out kids. That's all I'm doing here. I'm being paid nine dollars an hour for twenty hours a week, but between cutting up the cars and the administrative stuff I do, I'm working way more than full time. And, yeah, I'm not making enough to afford my own place, so I crash here. I don't see who's being hurt by it."

Neither did I. I also realized that, of all the problems in Newark, the fact that a part-time worker at one of the city's nonprofits was keeping a secret from his boss did not quite rise to the level of something our readership needed to know about.

"Sorry about the car," I said. "I just . . . I jumped to conclusions."

"Are you going to write a story about me?" he asked. I could hear the pleading in his voice.

"To be honest, I've got better things to do," I said.

"Who else knows?"

"Just Lauren. But I think you probably know she's got a heart the size of Asia, and it's got a big place in it for forgiveness. Just tell her what you told me. She's all about second chances."

"Thanks," he said. "I owe you one."

He held out his hand. It was still a little grimy from his day's work. I didn't care. I grasped it and gave it a good pump.

I thought about telling him he didn't owe me anything. But you never know in this world when you're going to need a favor.

Having retraced my steps across the courtyard and reentered the office, I found Sweet Thang sitting in her desk chair, bouncing her legs.

"Well," she asked?

"No match," I said.

Her legs stopped bouncing. "Oh, thank goodness," she said, bringing her hand to her chest. "So what do you think I should do about Dave?"

"Just talk to him sometime. Tell him you saw the article but that as a former newspaper reporter, you understand that's just the government's side of the story. Ask him for his."

I wasn't going to mention that if she really wanted to, she could ask him right now. There seemed to be no need to complicate matters any further.

Sweet Thang was looking up at me with eyes that were big and blue and grateful. "Carter Ross, you are so amazing. I could kiss you."

I felt a little tremor in my stomach and quickly yanked my phone out of my pocket. "Oh, my goodness, look at the time," I said.

Then I took a second to *actually* look at the time. I realized Sweet Thang wasn't really going to kiss me and that it was just a figure of speech. But, you know, just in case.

My eyes finally registered the numbers: 6:46 P.M. "Quarter of seven," I added. "I gotta run."

"Actually, can I ask a quick favor? Except maybe it's not so quick?"

"Sure."

"You can totally say no if you want. But if it's really, truly not a big deal, would you mind giving me a ride to the train station?"

"Where's Walter?"

I wish Walter was her boyfriend, but it was actually her BMW. It had been a graduation gift from her father. Given the neighborhoods she now frequented, it was a minor miracle I wasn't writing about her carjacking.

"In the shop," she said. "I could try to catch a bus to the train station but the last time I did that at this time of night the bus was like a half-hour late and everyone kept stopping at the bus shelter to ask if I was okay. It was nice, but it was also embarrassing. The entire neighborhood watch turned out just trying to make sure the white girl didn't get mugged. At one point I had five grandmas sitting there with me."

"Yeah, let's spare them that trouble. Only thing is, I need to do an interview, like, right now. Mind tagging along?"

"Oh my goodness, that would be so much fun! It'll be just like old times."

Sweet Thang was beaming. So was I, just on the inside. This may have started out as me doing her a favor. Very likely it would end the other way around. One of Sweet Thang's talents that made me wish she had stayed at the *Eagle-Examiner* was her ability not just to listen to people, but to make them feel heard. The result was that they opened up to her, telling her things they never planned to tell anyone.

It was a gift. And in this case I would be the beneficiary. Having Sweet Thang by my side when I interview Tujuka Okeke could only help.

"Great. I hereby deputize you as *Eagle-Examiner* intern for the evening," I said, ignoring the fact that I wasn't technically an *Eagle-Examiner* employee myself at the moment. "Hang on a sec. Let me just take care of one thing."

I pulled out my phone. Having to drop Sweet Thang at the train station fouled up my time line a little bit. But it was worth it, and I could still keep on schedule, if Tina would be willing to stop at Zabrina's place and pick up those insurance documents for me. I tapped out a quick e-mail to Tina, asking her to do just that, giving her Zabrina's address.

It wouldn't be a big deal. I mean, yes, I was foisting an errand on a woman who was in her thirty-eighth week of gestation. But it's not like I was asking her to dig ditches for me. Zabrina's place was on the way out to Bloomfield. It would involve only the shortest of detours. Tina wouldn't even have to get out of the car, because Zabrina said she'd run it out. Tina would even be driving the car Zabrina expected to see in her driveway, because it was the one I had taken to our lunch date earlier in the day.

I sent the message with the necessary details, then saw that Tommy and Chillax had e-mailed me their notes from their interviews with Kevin Tiemeyer's colleagues.

"Here," I said to Sweet Thang, handing her my phone. "Read these on the way. You might as well get up to speed on everything. Now let's get out of here."

Sweet Thang followed me out and hopped into the Malibu. Once she was done silently digesting Tommy and Chillax's contributions, I gave her the CliffsNotes version of everything else I knew, finishing as we reached our destination.

The only parking spot outside Tujuka's place was perhaps three whiskers longer than my Malibu. But being a veteran of bumper car parallel parking, I made it work, finishing with a whisker and a half on each side of my car.

I had just shifted into park and shut off the engine when I saw that a man was walking at an odd angle toward our car. It took a moment for my eyes to focus on him, another moment for my brain to make sense of the information it was receiving. Then, in one terrifying moment, it all clicked in.

It was Scarface Sammy. His jacket was flapping open to reveal a shoulder holster, with the butt of a handgun peeking out. And the Malibu was too hemmed in to even consider escape.

CHAPTER 36

After the incident outside Fanwood Country Club—where he had come so close to the white man in the Volvo but came up empty again—Scarface Sammy had decided he was done playing around.

He was going to get his man. Because that's what he did, what he was paid to do.

Sammy returned to Tujuka Okeke's house, to continue his stakeout there. He was still convinced she had something to do with what was going on, even if he didn't know quite how.

Once he was in place, he went to work figuring out who the man in the Volvo/Malibu was. Sammy did not have access to the kind of databases that law enforcement people did, of course. But he knew someone who knew someone, as tended to be the case with these sorts of things. And, for a price—too high a price, in Sammy's mind—that someone could tell him who owned a car connected to a certain license plate.

The first plate Sammy asked that someone to run was the one on the Volvo. Sammy was operating under the belief that was more than likely the white man's primary vehicle.

After a delay of a few hours, he got back the result. It was registered to Christina J. Thompson.

Clearly, that was not the person who he had seen driving the car. So who was she?

Sammy was able to narrow down three possible addresses in New Jersey. But the name was too common for any of the databases that Sammy had access to. So he resorted to googling random variations of the name, along with geographic identifiers to help narrow it down.

It was when he finally got around to googling "Tina Thompson Newark" that he learned she was a newspaper editor. But why would a newspaper editor have anything to do with what was happening at Tujuka Okeke's house? And who was the man driving her car?

Sammy realized he was still stumped. So he again paid the needed bribe, this time asking his source to run the Malibu's plates. Sammy worried his employer would balk at the expense if he didn't produce some significant results. But what choice did he have?

It took some time again, then the information came back: the Malibu was owned by Carter M. Ross.

Another common name, but not as common. Sammy was able to find a current address in Bloomfield; a previous address in Nutley; and an address in Millburn that, judging from the dates of birth of the owners, appeared to be Carter Ross's parents.

Sammy smiled in a way that pulled at the scars on his face. There was no way this Carter Ross would escape him this time.

Still, there was the question of who Carter Ross was. This time, Google was quickly forthcoming.

The answer puzzled Sammy. Carter Ross was a reporter for the *Eagle-Examiner*, a fairly prominent one. His work had won a host of awards, even been named a finalist for the Pulitzer Prize.

It only gave Sammy more questions. How was Carter Ross hooked in with Tujuka Okeke? Why did he keep coming back to her house?

Sammy was pondering all of this and more. Then he watched in surreal amazement as the Malibu drove up and parked two cars down from him.

Carter Ross had once again materialized, as if Sammy thinking about him had resulted in his summoning.

CHAPTER 37

Let the following not be mistaken for altruism:

When I saw Scarface Sammy coming toward my door, my first words—after the perfunctory yelp of panic—were, "Sweet Thang, get out of the car and run. Now."

This was not, to be clear, because her well-being was foremost on my mind. It was because, with Sammy closing in on the driver's side, and with the Malibu a minimum of twelve turns away from being free of its parking spot, my best chance to get away was out the passenger side. And it would be a lot quicker if I didn't have to climb over Sweet Thang first.

Alas, I hadn't told Sweet Thang that I had been followed by a menacing Nigerian man the day before, or that I feared he was the man in the blue ski mask who had been pulling the trigger during these carjackings. And the alarm in my voice, was not, by itself, enough to compel her rapid movement.

"What's going—"

I didn't have time to write her an annotated five-year vision statement. I was already unsnapping her seat belt and reaching across her to open the door. "Just move!" I screamed, my voice cracking.

But by that point, it was too late. Sammy was already next

to my car. I turned back just in time to see Sammy reaching into his pocket to begin the rapid chain of events that would seal my fate: reach for gun, remove gun from holster, aim gun, fire gun. I turned away and hunched down. Not that he could miss me from point-blank range, but maybe he wouldn't be able to shoot me in the head. Sweet Thang still hadn't budged. Sammy loomed over me.

"Mr. Ross, please do not be afraid," he said. "My name is Hakeem Kuti. I am a private investigator licensed by the State of New Jersey, working for the Obatala Insurance Company."

When I turned back toward him, I saw what he had produced from his pocket. It was a bronze shield emblazoned with the words AUTHORIZED PRIVATE INVESTIGATOR wrapped around an eagle emblem.

My thoughts caught up slowly. A private investigator. He was a P.I. And P.I.s, while they sometimes carry concealed weapons—as Sammy, uh, Mr. Kuti was doing—they do not often use those weapons to shoot newspaper reporters.

Finally, with my senses returned to me, I turned to Sweet Thang. "Never mind. False alarm," I said. "But we seriously have to work on your reaction times."

Sweet Thang was still mystified as to what was going on. I removed myself from the car and stuck out my hand toward Kuti.

"Sorry about that," I said. "I thought you were . . . someone else."

"I know my face is sometimes frightening to people," he said. "I apologize."

"No, no," I said, now feeling like the white guy who was caught being afraid of the black guy with scars. In other words: a racist. "It's not that. It's that I just . . . you were following me yesterday and . . . never mind. Anyhow, yes, my name is Carter Ross. But you seem to know that already. What can I do for you?"

"You are an investigative reporter, are you not?"

"Yes, that's correct."

"Can you tell me, what are you investigating with regards to Mrs. Okeke?"

I considered this for a moment. Hakeem Kuti was not there to kill me. But he still may have had an agenda in conflict with mine—chiefly, that he represented an insurance company that was trying to cheat Tujuka Okeke out of her claim.

"No offense, Mr. Kuti, but we just met and I don't know why you're here. So, no, I cannot—"

"I apologize. Of course, of course. If I tell you why I am here, maybe you can tell me if you are here for the same purpose."

Kuti's face, scars and all, did not suggest any ill will. Still, all I offered was, "Maybe."

"Very well," he said. "Perhaps you are unfamiliar with my employer, Obatala Insurance. It markets itself to the Nigerian expat community here in the States. It is a relatively small underwriter. Allstate or Prudential measure the number of policies they write in the millions. Obatala measures it in the thousands."

"I understand."

"Because it is small, it notices claim irregularities faster than the larger insurers. Prudential has billions of dollars in assets. When it pays a seventy thousand dollar claim, it is of little consequence. Obatala cannot afford to be so casual."

"I'm following you," I said. Sweet Thang had also gotten out of the car and walked around until she was by my side. I was glad she was hearing this.

"My employer began to notice an unusual number of claims related to carjacking. Obatala is like all insurers, in that it bases its rates on actuarial tables. This is not my area, of course. My background is in the military. I cannot describe how this calculation is made. But the man who hired me said Obatala's number of carjacking claims were six thousand percent higher than what the tables suggest it should be."

"Wow. Yeah, I guess that would get anyone's attention."

"They hired me to investigate. And that is what I have been doing for several months now."

"Because Obatala suspects fraud?" I asked.

"Correct."

"But how could Tujuka Okeke's claim possibly be fraudulent? I mean, her husband was killed. You can't exactly fake that."

"That is why I am here, watching the Okeke house," Kuti said. "Mrs. Okeke could have submitted a claim. She was named the beneficiary in the event of Mr. Okeke's death. But she did not submit anything."

I thought back to the notation made in the prosecutor's office file, the one Kathy Carter told me about. All it said was "insurance disbursement not made." I never paused to consider it was because no one made a claim.

"But . . . why not?" I asked.

"We don't know," Kuti said. "That is why I have been watching her for the last two weeks. Mrs. Okeke distinguished herself by not making a claim when she was entitled to. Obatala sent a claims adjustor to speak with her, but she did not explain her actions to him. Obatala's executives think she knows more than she is letting on. They have ordered me to watch her.

"You were the first unusual visitor she received," Kuti continued. "I thought you could lead me to the answers. That's why you saw me following you yesterday. Then I learned you are Carter Ross, the great investigative newspaper reporter, and now I am hoping you can help me."

He bowed his head slightly when he said it. I had to give him credit: there are few better ways to woo my assistance than to describe me as "the great investigative newspaper reporter."

But in this place, his faith in my alleged greatness was misplaced. I didn't have any more answers than he did.

* * *

Into the midst of this shared confusion, there came a phone call that filled me with the hope that things were about to became a lot more clear.

It was Buster Hays, actually using his cell phone—a rare occurrence for a man who detested any technology introduced after the Ford presidency. I knew that meant it was important.

"Give me a moment," I said to Sweet Thang and Kuti. "I have to take this."

I walked down toward the end of the street so I had some privacy.

"Hey, Buster," I said. "What's up?"

"Well, I don't know if this is good news or bad news for you. But I talked to my guy on the task force. He ran through every name on that membership list. Other than Tiemeyer, you got nothing."

I responded the only way I could at the moment: with dead silence. It was the last thing I expected him to say and my mind wasn't fast enough to catch up.

My mouth soon started moving. "But that's . . . that's not possible. Are you sure?"

"I didn't stand over him while he did it, Ivy. But, yeah. I'm sure. I've dealt with the guy before. He doesn't always tell me everything, but what he does tell me? It's gospel."

"So just to make sure I've got this right. As far as the Essex County Auto Theft Task Force is concerned, the only Fanwood Country Club member to have been carjacked is Kevin Tiemeyer."

"Yeah."

I felt my shoulders sink toward the street. I started sputtering again. "But how could that . . . that's not—"

"You want to close your eyes and have me write it in Braille for you?" Buster said. "I'm just telling you what the guy told me.

275

And, no, before you ask, this is not a guy with any reason to mislead us. He's as straight as they come."

"Okay. Thanks, Buster."

He hung up. For thirty seconds or so, I watched a plastic bag blow along the street. Eventually, I began coming to the conclusions I should have been reaching the moment Buster started talking. In order for my theory to have been true, there should have been at least a half-dozen hits, if not many more. Two carjackings did not a criminal enterprise make. Doc Fierro wasn't my guy. Earl Karlinsky wasn't my guy.

No wonder Doc was trying to get me fired. I thought about my behavior toward Fanwood through the lens of this new information. Me sneaking into the pro shop. Me skulking around the perimeter. Me making a wild accusation about the general manager to a board member. Doc probably thought I was mentally unstable and was just trying to protect his club from whatever undiagnosed paranoid schizophrenia was afflicting me.

I couldn't blame him. I had screwed up. If apologies were planets, I owed him Jupiter.

Yet where that door had been closed, I realized a new window had opened up, one involving insurance fraud. Was that really what was going on here? Was that what Joseph Okeke and Kevin Tiemeyer had discussed on the golf course that day at Fanwood Country Club? A scheme to defraud their insurers? Had Okeke been recruiting Tiemeyer in the scheme? Or was it the other way around?

But, if that was the case, why did they both end up dead? And killed by the same blue-ski-mask-wearing thug, no less?

There was still much to learn. Toward that end, Tina had already e-mailed me back, saying she would stop by Zabrina's house to pick up insurance documents—paperwork I might now use to prove the opposite of what I had originally thought.

Either way, it would be useful. And even if my understanding of recent events had been turned upside down, there was one thing that remained unchanged: I needed to give Rich Eberhardt a story if I wanted my employment at the *Eagle-Examiner* to continue uninterrupted.

I walked slowly back toward Sweet Thang and Kuti, who watched my trudge with curiosity.

"You look like you've seen a ghost," Sweet Thang said.

"Yeah, unfortunately, it might be my journalism career," I said.

"Huh?"

"Nothing, I've just . . . remember all that stuff I told you about how I thought this was a scheme being operated out of Fanwood Country Club?"

"Yeah."

"I was wrong. That was just Buster Hays calling. The only Fanwood member to have been victimized was Tiemeyer. Whatever is happening has nothing to do with Fanwood."

Sweet Thang's head cocked to one side. Kuti was just watching the two of us go back and forth like it was a tennis match.

"So what's going on?" she asked.

"I have no idea," I said. Then I pointed toward Tujuka Okeke's house. "But maybe some of the explanations are in there."

I turned to Hakeem Kuti. "I'm afraid you're going to have to excuse us," I said. "Depending on what we learn, I may end up being very interested in talking to your employer."

"And my employer to you," he said.

"Deal," I said. Then I looked at Sweet Thang. "Let's go."

CHAPTER 38

As Tujuka Okeke opened the door, the smell of something savory and delicious wafted over us.

"Good evening, Mr. Ross," she said without smiling. She was dressed in pale blue nurse's scrubs that set off her dark skin dramatically.

"Please, call me Carter," I said. "And this is my colleague, Lauren McMillan."

I gestured toward Sweet Thang, who asked, "Is that iyere?"

"It is," Tujuka said.

"I just love iyere," Sweet Thang gushed. "Where did you get it? I have the hardest time finding it."

Trust Sweet Thang to know a spice prominent in Nigerian cooking. Tujuka Okeke smiled for the first time.

"There's a market called Makola on Lyons Avenue," Tujuka said. "They always have it."

"It's just so fragrant," Sweet Thang said. "What are you making with it?

"Suya," Tujuka said.

Whatever that was. All I knew is that Sweet Thang had now bonded with our host. Naturally. Easily. Perfectly.

"Why don't you have a seat," Tujuka said, pointing us toward a room inside and to the right.

Sweet Thang and I grabbed spots on the couch. Tujuka took an easy chair that was across a coffee table. The entertainment center was to our left. The furnishings appeared Scandinavian. The electronics were Korean. The artwork on the walls was African. It was, in other words, the typical American family room.

"I understand you spoke with Maryam yesterday," Tujuka said.

"Yes. I hope you don't mind I didn't ask your permission. You were—"

"Maryam has a good head on her shoulders. I trust her to make her own decisions."

"She seems like a lovely girl," I agreed. "And I understand her father was very proud of her."

"Oh, Joseph," she said, shaking her head.

That was how we launched our conversation on Joseph Okeke. I asked Tujuka about her ex-husband's background, his business, and so on. It was much of the same material Maryam and I had been over the day before, although Tujuka covered it with more adult precision about details and dates. It wasn't necessarily anything I was going to write, but it was good to have correct.

Besides, it got her talking. Sweet Thang interjected questions now and then, and I got the sense that Tujuka was getting comfortable with both of us. And that was important for where I was soon to shift the conversation.

First, it was the day of the carjacking itself. Then, more important, it was what came afterward. Or, rather, what didn't.

"I understand you didn't submit a claim for Joseph's carjacking," I said. "If I may ask, why not?"

Here Tujuka paused for the first time in what had previously been a free-flowing conversation. She smoothed her scrubs pants, not that they needed it.

Finally, she said, "Because I don't want to go to jail."

"What do you mean?"

"When you came here yesterday, I told you Joseph got what he deserved," she said.

"I remember."

"That was harsh of me. But it is also somewhat true." She looked down at her pants again and, finding them sufficiently wrinkle-free, continued. "This is very difficult for me to talk about. But I try to teach my children the importance of telling the truth, so I must model the same behavior."

Neither Sweet Thang nor I said a word. This was her confession. Might as well let her spit it out on her terms.

"Our son is at Duke, as Maryam may have told you. Maryam starts college in the fall. We get financial aid, of course, but it is never enough. Joseph and I believe in giving our children the best education they can possibly get, regardless of what it costs. It is the best way to get ahead in this country. It is why we came here, for the opportunities our children would receive."

She took a deep breath and went on. "We had our savings, but that is gone now. We were worried about how we were going to cover the next bill from Duke. And then there's Maryam. She has applied to Princeton. I do not understand how these financial aid formulas work, but between Joseph and I, we make enough money that we are expected to be able to pay tens of thousands of dollars a year. How we would be able to do that and not lose our houses, I could not say. Joseph and I worried about it frequently.

"Then two months ago, Joseph came to me with this wild scheme. He said if he let someone rob him of his car, he could get us fifteen thousand dollars."

"How exactly would that work?" I asked.

"Are you familiar with the concept of a replacement automobile policy?" Tujuka asked.

"I think so," I said. "But maybe not."

Sweet Thang hopped in: "My dad actually got me one for Walter. It's something that can be smart to have for more expensive cars."

"Yeah, that's not something I'd know about," I said.

"Okay, so normally when your car is totaled, the insurance company just gives you what the car is worth, right?" Sweet Thang said.

"Right."

"But in the case of a replacement policy, they give you the amount needed to actually replace the car. It can be a big difference if you're talking about a new car."

"Oh, right," I said. "Because of the whole a-new-car-loses-a-quarter-of-its-value-when-you-drive-it-off-the-lot thing."

"Exactly," Sweet Thang said, and now she was looking at Tujuka. "Now, I don't know about your policy. But with mine, it basically said that if you were driving a car that was six months old or less and it was totaled or stolen, they would pay a claim equal to whatever you paid for the car. Is that what Joseph had?"

"Yes," Tujuka said.

"I'm still a little confused," I admitted. "I'm assuming Joseph probably financed the car with very little down, based on what you guys were laying out in tuition. That meant he still owed almost the entire value of the car in a loan he'd have to pay off. How would Joseph make any money out of being carjacked unless . . ."

And that's when it clicked in my wee little brain. "Oh, I get it. He was going to use the insurance money to pay off the loan. And the people he had carjack him were going to give him a kickback from their sale of the car. That's where the fifteen grand came from."

"That is my understanding, yes," Tujuka said.

All I did was shake my head. For two days now, I had figured the Okekes' insurance company was the perpetrator of wrongdoing. It now appeared it was the victim.

"I tried to talk him out of it," Tujuka said. "I said to him, 'Joseph, isn't this illegal?' And he said, 'Tujuka, don't worry about that.' I begged him not to do it. But my husband could be very stubborn. He said there was no choice. I thought perhaps he had decided not to go forward with it. Then I got that awful visit from the police, saying he had been murdered while his car was being stolen."

She now had her pants bunched tightly in her fists, like she was just trying to hang on to them. "The police spoke as if it was a random event. But I knew it was not. So you asked me why I did not submit an insurance claim and that is why: because I knew it would be a false claim."

"Did you tell Obatala Insurance that when they sent a claims adjustor to speak with you?" I asked.

"No," she said. "I did not want to tell anyone at first. I was worried what it would do to Joseph's life insurance policy. But I have since spoken with a lawyer, and he assured me the policy would still have to pay out. Regardless of the fraud he was involved in, his death was still a homicide. And that is covered under our policy."

"And you are the beneficiary of that policy?" I asked.

"Yes," she said. "It will be enough to cover our children's tuition. I am thankful for that."

As was Joseph Okeke, if he had managed to find a place where he could still appreciate such things.

We spent a little more time discussing the bucket of financial slop Joseph had left behind. Naturally, the fifteen thousand that was supposed to come from the carjackers had never materialized. Tujuka said she wouldn't have accepted it if it did. "Blood money," she called it.

There was also the matter of his car loan and town house

mortgage. It was looking like Joseph Okeke had left this life in a hole his estate would never get out of. There would be no inheritance. The life insurance was all he was leaving behind.

As we spoke, I kept my eye on a digital clock that was on one of the devices in her entertainment center. The numbers were creeping closer to eight. I didn't want to rush things. But, at the same time, Joseph Okeke's lingering credit card debt was not among my chief concerns.

Finally, I was able to work the conversation back around to what I considered to be the big question.

"From everything I've learned about your husband, he wasn't the sort to go around dreaming up scams to defraud insurance companies. Somebody obviously put him on to this or even recruited him for it. Do you have any idea who?"

Tujuka shook her head. "I'm sorry, I do not."

"Did he know the people who were going to rob him?"

"I don't know. All he told me was that he would drive to a certain place at a certain time, and that's where the robbery would happen. He made it sound like it was a very simple thing."

I thought back to what Johnny, the convenience store clerk, had told me about Joseph Okeke stopping for a green light. It hadn't made any sense at the time, but now it did. That was where he was supposed to rendezvous. He would have stopped no matter what color the light was, because it was where he had agreed to get himself carjacked.

He just didn't plan on some guy with a blue ski mask shooting him in the head. Neither had Kevin Tiemeyer. Yet there they were: bonded in life by their shared round on a golf course, bonded in death by their shared murderer, bonded somewhere in the middle by a shared motivation to commit insurance fraud.

Obviously, Tiemeyer had been lured into the same deal as Okeke and was planning to make the same kind of easy money—or, if anything, more of it, since his car was more valuable. He drove to his own predetermined location thinking he'd be relieved of his car but ultimately got a lot more trouble than he signed up for.

Like Okeke, Tiemeyer had been desperate for money. He had known he was about to lose his job and probably suspected he had a long and arduous search for new employment in front of him. He was already cutting back on expenses in other ways. Getting himself carjacked would have been a great way to not only give himself some padding for the lean months ahead, but also to get rid of a car payment he could no longer afford.

That brought me back to the question I had yet to answer to any satisfaction, and that now loomed with even greater importance: how did Okeke and Tiemeyer know each other? Going back to that electrician's metaphor: what was their first contact point?

"Did Joseph ever mention knowing a man named Kevin Tiemeyer?" I asked.

"Yes. When he first told me about the scheme, he mentioned he had discussed it with Mr. Tiemeyer. It sounded like they were approached by the same person, whose identity he did not tell me, and now they were both considering taking part. They discussed it over a round of golf, if you can believe that. I think they were working up the courage to participate."

"So how was it they first met, Joseph and Mr. Tiemeyer?"

"That, I cannot tell you," Tujuka said.

Sweet Thang immediately perked up. "Oh. I thought they met at Rotary."

I felt myself swiveling toward Sweet Thang in slow motion. "Wait, Kevin Tiemeyer was in Rotary?" I asked.

"Yeah. It's in the notes Tommy sent you."

"Oh. I hadn't read them yet."

"Well, it's in there," Sweet Thang said. "One of Tiemeyer's colleagues was talking about what a normal, reliable guy

Tiemeyer was, the kind of guy who, quote, never missed a Rotary meeting."

"I wonder why Zabrina never mentioned that?" I asked.

And then Tujuka Okeke said the two words that changed everything. "Who's Zabrina?"

CHAPTER 39

Black Mask had done enough of these jobs by now. Ten? Twelve? Enough to establish distinct patterns.

Enough that Black Mask knew there were aspects of this particular job that didn't feel quite right.

The first thing was the time. Always before, it had been later. Eleven o'clock. Midnight. One in the morning. Times at which carjackers ordinarily operated.

This one was eight o'clock. It was still dark, yes. But it was a time that felt riskier. There might still be a few ordinary citizens out. And while most of them wouldn't go to the police and say they had witnessed a carjacking—people in Newark knew it wasn't worth it, for the most part—you never knew if one might decide to get brave.

Another thing was the place. Always before, it was an intersection with a traffic light. The corner of Mulberry and East Kinney. The corner of Bergen and Avon. The corner of Central and 10th.

This one was just an address. The man, Carter Ross, would supposedly drive the Volvo XC60 up to the house and pull into the driveway.

And then—lastly and most significantly—there was the

instruction to kill the guy. Yeah, Black Mask wasn't the one pulling the trigger. Blue Mask would do that.

But still. Even for double the money, Black Mask was feeling uncomfortable with it. It's not like he was a Quaker or something. Not in this line of work. He had watched two men get killed in the last month.

The difference was, he didn't know it was coming. This time, he did. And it was making him feel a little queasy.

Nevertheless, there he was, at seven thirty, plenty early. He liked to have time to look around. He had told Blue Mask to be there at seven forty-five. For the kind of money they were making, an extra fifteen minutes didn't seem like much of a sacrifice.

He surveyed the scene, liking what he saw. The homes were larger and a little more spread out than in other parts of the city. The street was draped in large trees that had obviously been planted a long time ago. They would provide perfect cover for what was about to happen in the driveway.

Despite all the logistical differences in this job, he wanted to get it set up the way they had done all the others. Find two good spots to lay in wait. Then, with one sharp whistle, strike.

It was important to do it real professional like that. Even though the drivers knew what they were getting themselves into—after all, they had signed themselves up for it—he had been told to keep up a good front. If anyone did happen to see it and say something to the cops, it had to look like a real carjacking, every time.

Black Mask had just finished his little tour of the area when Blue Mask walked up. His ski mask was on his head, but not yet pulled down over his face.

"'Sup," Blue Mask said.

"Hey. Nice place, huh?"

"Yeah."

"I'm thinking about buying me a place like this someday. But I think you gotta be rich."

"Yeah," Blue Mask said. "Wait. You know who lives here, right?"

"No. Why? It matter?"

Blue Mask just stared at him for a moment, then said, "Naw. Guess not."

"Okay," Black Mask said, slightly mystified. "You got your piece?"

"'Course."

"You good with using it?"

Blue Mask acted offended the question even needed to be asked. "Yeah, dawg. You know I'm good."

"A'ight. 'Cause we're supposed to kill this one. We'll get paid twice as much."

"Yeah?" Blue Mask said. A small smile had come to his cheeks.

"Yeah."

"A'ight. I'll do him."

Just like that. Like he enjoyed the prospect of it. Black Mask felt even more sick.

But there wasn't time to linger on it. They needed to get settled in their places. Black Mask had decided Blue Mask should hide between two parked cars and approach from the right side of the car, like usual. Black Mask would set up around the side of the house and attack the left. His last instructions to Blue Mask were to wait for the whistle—and roll down his ski mask.

Black Mask donned his, then went around to the side of the house. He stood there, perfectly still, and waited.

It wasn't long before a car slowed and began turning in to the driveway. The headlights strafed the side of the house.

It was a Volvo. Make that *the* Volvo. Black Mask whistled sharply, then pulled out his gun. He walked up to the Volvo, now idling in the driveway. With his free hand, he banged his palm on the window. "Out of the car," he ordered. "Out of the—"

And then he actually looked at the driver.

It wasn't who he was expecting. It was supposed to be a dude, a guy named Carter Ross. This was a woman, with brown curly hair. And she didn't look scared, like the others did. She looked pissed.

And something else.

Black Mask could see her stomach bulging out so wide she couldn't really close her legs and so far it was nearly brushing the steering wheel. Yet the rest of her was skinny.

Then Black Mask figured it out. This woman was pregnant.

CHAPTER 40

It says a lot about the speed at which my mental processor works that, at first, I didn't even realize how much the revelation about Kevin Tiemeyer being in Rotary—along with those two words out of Tujuka's mouth—really did change things.

Because I answered her "Who's Zabrina?" with, "You know, Zabrina Coleman-Webster. Joseph's—"

I nearly said "girlfriend," then adherence to an ancient male code of honor—Do Not Get Thy Fellow Brethren in Trouble by Saying Too Much—stopped me. Instead I said, "You know, the Rotary Club president."

Then the significance of those two words started catching up with me.

"Wait," I said. "You seriously don't know Zabrina Coleman-Webster?"

Tujuka's brow had a crinkle that told me she did not. "No," she said.

"The day after Joseph was killed, you didn't get a phone call from a woman named Zabrina, asking where Joseph was?"

"Certainly not," she said.

I pulled my phone out of my pocket and found the photo of Zabrina and Joseph together, the one that had me pondering the vagaries of the universe a little more than twenty-four hours earlier.

"This woman," I said. "Have you ever seen her before?"

I leaned across the coffee table and held out my phone. Tujuka took it for a moment and tilted it until she hit the sweet spot on the LCD screen. Once she had it right, it didn't take her long to decide.

"No," Tujuka said, handing me back my phone.

"That is Joseph with her, right?"

"Yes. Of course. But I have never seen that woman. I am sure of it. Who are you saying she is?"

I paused. Clearly, this was a case where ancient male code needed to be set aside. I'm not sure one's rights under that code superseded death anyway.

"The woman in that photo has been telling me she was Joseph's girlfriend, that they met several years ago, and eventually started dating," I said. "She said they were planning on getting married."

I never realized it was possible for a woman as dark as Tujuka to blanch. But I swear she had lost some of her color.

"No," she said. "Absolutely not. Joseph did not have a girlfriend."

"Mrs. Okeke," I said, as gently as possible, "are you sure that maybe Joseph hadn't told you because he was afraid it would upset you? You wouldn't be the first woman who didn't know her ex-husband was in a new relationship."

"Joseph had been trying to reconcile with me," she said definitively. "He had been trying for two years. He said he was tired of being divorced, tired of living under a different roof from his family. He wanted to be closer to Maryam before she went off to college. He wanted us to share holidays when our other children came home. He wanted us to grow old together, like we planned all along.

"At first I told him no, absolutely not. We were divorced and that was it. Going through it the first time had been too painful to even think about the possibility of going through it again. But lately I admit I had been . . . rethinking that. He had started spending nights here again. He was spending the night here when he got killed, but then he went and did this crazy thing with his car."

"Wait, wait, the night Joseph was killed, he was *here*?" I said.

Zabrina had told me she was with Joseph that night and that he had only left her to retrieve some papers for an early meeting he had. But I was starting to recognize that—like apparently everything else out of her mouth—was a lie.

"Yes, he was here," Tujuka said. "Right up until he left. As I said, I begged him not to."

"Zabrina said she was with him," I said.

"Unless Joseph had learned to split himself in two, I do not see how that is possible. He was here until eleven that night. Maryam would remember. Hold on."

Tujuka rose from her easy chair and walked just out of the room, to the base of the stairs. She called up, "Maryam, could you come down here please?"

"Coming," Maryam said, and I could hear her bounding down the steps. She entered the room just behind her mother.

"Oh, hi," she said, when she saw me. "Mama, this is the reporter I was telling you about."

"Yes," Tujuka said patiently. "Maryam, the night Daddy was killed, you remember it, yes?"

"Of course I do."

"And where was Daddy that night, before he left?" Tujuka asked. "Mr. Ross would like to know."

"Well, here, of course," she said, like it was the most obvious thing to her.

"And what was he doing?"

"What he always did. Bother me about my homework."

The lack of guile that struck me about her the first time I met her was there once again.

"Maryam," I said. "Do you know a woman named Zabrina? Zabrina Coleman-Webster?"

Maryam looked appropriately mystified. "No," she said.

"Have you ever seen this woman?" I asked. I got off the couch and handed Maryam my phone, which still had the photo of Zabrina on it.

"No," Maryam said. "Who is she?"

"She claimed to be your father's girlfriend."

"Well, then she's on crack. Daddy didn't have a girlfriend," Maryam said, with that marvelous teenaged certitude.

I accepted my phone back from her. The whole exchange was far too natural to have been choreographed in any way. Every reaction was right where it should have been.

What it came down to is that, as is often the case for a reporter, I was getting two versions of the same story. In one, there was Zabrina saying she was Joseph's girlfriend, saying she had various conversations with Tujuka in which they had bonded over being single moms, saying she had thought about trying to continue her relationship with Maryam.

In the other, there were Tujuka and Maryam Okeke saying, in their own ways, that Zabrina was on crack. And I have to admit, that story was feeling a lot more credible.

But why would Zabrina lie unless . . .

Unless she was trying to mislead the reporter who was looking into these two seemingly unrelated carjackings. And the only reason she would do that is if she was hiding something: like being involved in the carjacking-for-insurance ring that was responsible for it—either as the recruiter or as the orchestrator.

Had I known Tiemeyer was also in Rotary, I might have had a chance to see it sooner. I just had the misfortune of learning about that round of golf at Fanwood Country Club first. I had thought Fanwood was the root of the tree, when really it was just a branch. The root was Rotary Club, of which Zabrina was president.

It was like twisting the kaleidoscope. Everything about my interactions with Zabrina looked different. When I had come calling about Joseph Okeke, I now saw she had two options. She could have put me off or pretended to know little about the man, which would have sent me elsewhere in search of answers.

But she was smarter than that. It was the old Sun Tzu advice: keep your friends close but your enemies closer. She wanted to keep close watch on what I was learning, controlling that information as best she could to suit her purposes.

For example, when I had mentioned the name Earl Karlinsky, she produced this story about how, yes, a man with that name had asked Joseph about his car, quizzing him about its features.

Did she know how far she was dragging me in the wrong direction? Of course not. But that was the whole point of drawing me close in the first place. She would have found a way to make a bogeyman out of any name I tossed out there, using her platform as Joseph's quote-unquote girlfriend to do it.

I thought about how easy it was for her to fake that relationship. She knew enough about his work life from casual conversations at Rotary meetings. She knew details about Maryam, because Joseph bragged about Maryam to anyone who would listen—whether it was his next door neighbor in his town house complex or someone who just happened to be sitting at his lunch table.

And then there was that photo, which seemed to confirm the intimacy between the two of them. But that was another piece of evidence that was easily misread. If I attended a Rotary Club meeting—as, say, a guest speaker talking about the newspaper business—and the president of the club asked me for a picture, I would have wrapped my arm around her the same way Joseph did.

Had I bumped across anyone who disputed that Zabrina and Joseph were dating, she had a built-in explanation for it—that they were "keeping it quiet," and therefore the person in question must not have been part of the inner circle.

Later, after she had time to think about it a bit, she probably realized she had gone too far. Which is why she played the privacy card, trying to pull their relationship off the record: she knew if I put it in the newspaper, someone—like Tujuka—would call balderdash on her.

Or maybe she was just using that conversation as a pretext to see what else I had learned and as an opportunity to mislead me even further. I thought of her sitting on that park bench, offering me a sandwich, and then smoothly wallpapering over some of the lies she had told me.

That exchange had ended with her offering me those insurance documents. Was it even possible she had them?

Actually, it was: she might have asked Joseph for a copy of his policy, so she could read it over to make sure he had the right kind of coverage for the scam she was running.

But why would she show them to me? It would only lead me closer to the truth.

And then I felt a wave of panic. Between my interest in the insurance angle—even if I had it completely backward—and my insistence in talking to Tujuka Okeke, Zabrina would have known I was eventually going to figure things out. In her mind, I had gone from curious reporter to serious threat.

Which meant she was either using those insurance documents as bait to bring her enemy even closer, or she was using them to lure me into a trap.

A trap that that I had sent Tina, my very pregnant girlfriend, unwittingly wading into.

A trap that could include a man who wore a blue ski mask and was both proficient and practiced at killing people.

My eyes flashed back to the clock on the entertainment center. It read 8:03 P.M. If Tina was on time—and I never knew her to be late—she would have pulled into Zabrina Coleman-Webster's driveway about three minutes earlier.

I stood up, grabbing Sweet Thang's arm as I did so.

"Mrs. Okeke, I'm so sorry," I said. "But we have to go. I think my girlfriend might be in serious trouble."

CHAPTER 41

Blue Mask had his gun turned sideways, because he thought it looked cooler that way. And he was holding it at head shot level, because that's what he was about to deliver.

He walked around from his side of the car, feeling the smoothness of the trigger with his finger. The driver had opened the door but was struggling to get out of the car, for some reason. As soon as he was clear of it, Blue Mask was going to drop him so they could get the hell out of here.

Then Blue Mask saw the driver wasn't a him.

No matter. The sooner he got this over with, the better.

"All right, all right," the woman was saying. "The keys are in the car. Just take it."

She was finally on her feet now. Black Mask had backed away to give her room to get out of the car. Blue Mask was even with the front tire and had stopped walking. He had his feet wide and braced for kickback. A shooter's stance.

"Yo, this ain't right," Black Mask said.

"What you mean?"

"It wasn't supposed to be no shorty. Especially not no pregnant shorty."

"Don't matter," Blue Mask said.

"No, no," Black Mask said. "You don't understand. The message I got said it was supposed to be a dude named Carter Ross. This ain't—"

"Carter Ross," the woman said.

"Shut up," Black Mask said. "I ain't talking to you. You got nothing to say."

Blue Mask still had the woman's head lined up nicely with the barrel of the gun. One squeeze would be all it took.

"Don't shoot her, dawg," Black Mask said.

"Why not?"

"Dawg, she's pregnant."

"Yeah, so?" Blue Mask asked. He was actually kind of excited by the idea. If killing a white banker had gotten that much attention, imagine what killing a white pregnant lady would do.

"It's just . . . this ain't who we're supposed to be doin', that's all," Black Mask said. "Let's just take the car and—"

Then Blue Mask watched as a large, dark stain crept down the woman's pants, sopping her legs.

"Aw, man, now look what you done," Blue Mask groused. "She pissed herself."

"You dumbass," Black Mask shot back. "She ain't peeing. Her water broke. She's gonna have a baby."

"Like, right now?"

"Yeah. You ignorant or something? Don't you know nothing about babies?"

Blue Mask paused for a moment. A cruel smile appeared out of the oval slot of his mouth hole. "Yeah, I know one thing about babies."

"What's that?"

"That you can sell them."

The woman began screaming, "Help," but no more than the "H" and the "E" had gotten out when Blue Mask leapt at her and jammed the barrel of the gun against her lips.

"You shut your mouth, shorty, or I'll drop your ass right here and we'll cut that baby out of you," he growled.

"You trippin'?" Black Mask demanded.

Blue Mask didn't take his eyes off the woman as he spoke. "I met this dude in prison. He told me that for a healthy white baby, you could get, like, fifty thousand, easy. And that's for, like, a white trash baby. For a baby like this, from a fancy lady in a Volvo? I bet we could get a hundred."

"You definitely trippin'. Don't you know nothing about women having babies? They do all this screamin' and stuff. And it lasts for, like, an hour. Where we gonna go that she can do that?"

"That's why I was asking if you knew who lived here," Blue Mask said. "She can have the baby right here. This is my sister's house."

"Your sister!?"

Blue Mask could hear the surprise in his partner's voice. "Yeah, dawg. But she'll be cool."

Black Mask let out a short, huffing chuckle. "Yeah, I know she'll be cool. She's the one who's been giving us all these jobs."

Now it was Blue Mask's turn to be surprised. He said nothing. Just smiled even wider as he kept the gun pressed to the woman's mouth.

So much for his sister going legit. All that fancy education and all those fancy people she hung around, and all it did was give her a fancier hustle.

"That dude, the one who told you about selling babies. He still in prison?" Black Mask asked.

"Yeah. But I can get to him. He'll make some calls, hook us up."

Blue Mask wasn't lying. There were nearly as many cell phones inside a prison as outside of it.

"Come on," Blue Mask said. "Let's take her inside. We gonna sell us a baby."

CHAPTER 42

I ran down the steps of Tujuka Okeke's house, with Sweet Thang right behind me.

My phone was already at my ear. I had hit the speed dial for Tina's number. After a brief moment of silence, the ringing began.

One ring. Two.

"Come on, Tina," I said.

Three rings. Four. Then voice mail.

We were already at my car, which I unlocked using the remote access button. Hakeem Kuti, Obatala Insurance's faithful private investigator, was ambling toward us with no particular speed.

"I need you to drive," I said to Sweet Thang. "And drive fast."

"Okay," she said.

"Mr. Kuti, I don't have time for questions," I said in his direction. "But if you follow us right now, we'll lead you to the people who have been at the middle of the fraud you're investigating."

"Yes, sir," Kuti said, and immediately began jogging back to his car.

I ran around to the passenger side and climbed in. I jammed the key in the ignition and cranked it hard clockwise just as Sweet Thang sat down.

"Where are we going?" she asked.

"Start driving north," I said, having faith in Sweet Thang's knowledge of Newark's street grid that she would know which way that was. "I'll get you an exact address in a second."

I hit the speed dial for Tina again. As Sweet Thang began the process of extracting the Malibu from its too-tight parking spot, my phone repeated itself: four rings, then voice mail.

"Hurry," I said to Sweet Thang, who still wasn't out of the spot yet. "You're not driving Walter anymore. I don't care about my damn bumpers."

She started getting more aggressive with her maneuvering, tapping the cars in front of us and behind us. I texted Tina a "Call me ASAP 911," then switched over to my phone's e-mail to get Zabrina's address.

There was a new message from Tina.

Walking out the door now. I'll get those documents on the way. Also—and don't freak out—I've been having contractions all afternoon. I just didn't want to tell you because it's not a big deal. They're still eight minutes apart. We don't have to go to the hospital until my water breaks and I'd rather labor at home for a while. Again, don't freak. But it's probably going to happen tonight! See you at your place. XOXO.

The message was time-stamped at 7:43 P.M. If she actually walked out the door at that moment, she would have been at Zabrina's house by eight, easily. God knows what happened to her after that.

"Oh, Jesus, she's in labor," I said.

"What?" Sweet Thang said. She had finally gotten the car out and had swung into traffic.

"She's been in labor all afternoon. I knew it. *I knew it*. Well, okay, I didn't know it. My mother knew it. But that's another story. I just thought Tina was a little distracted so I asked her if she was having contractions. But of course she said no, no, no, and—"

I halted my own rant. It wasn't going to get me anywhere. I turned my attention back to my phone instead and gave Sweet Thang the address to Zabrina's house.

As Sweet Thang plugged it into her phone's GPS and began following the soothing voice's directions to our destination, I turned to the Newark Rotary Club Web site. Given how I had misfired in my suspicion of Fanwood Country Club, I wanted to make sure I wasn't making the same mistake with Rotary. I'd just have to prevail on Buster Hays to help me.

Going tab by tab through the Web site, I pulled names off as fast as I could, pasting them into an e-mail that had Buster's address at the top. Then I went to the Rotary Club Facebook page and stole more names. After a few minutes, I had maybe a hundred of them. That had to be a nearly complete roster of the Newark Rotary Club, or at least a decent enough sample size for what I needed Buster to do with it.

Immediately after I hit the send button on the e-mail, I dialed Buster's number.

"Yeah, Ivy, whaddyuwant?" Buster said in a typically languorous tone.

"Buster, I don't have time to explain anything, but trust me when I tell you this is life or death," I said quickly. "I just sent you an e-mail with names of Newark Rotary Club members. I need you to call your task force guy and ask him if he recognizes any of them names as belonging to carjack victims and I need it, like, yesterday. Can you please help me?"

My performance must have been convincing, because for once Buster didn't use a request for a favor as an excuse to bust my balls.

"Got it," he said. "I'll get right back to you."

Then he hung up. I turned my attention to Sweet Thang's driving, which was too slow and too legal.

"This is not a time to pay attention to traffic laws," I said.

"I don't . . . I don't understand what's going on."

"Zabrina Coleman-Webster wasn't going to give me documents when I showed up at her house tonight," I said. "I'm pretty sure she was going to kill me. And I sent Tina to pick up those documents in my place."

Sweet Thang pressed the Malibu's gas pedal down and within a few seconds we were traveling at twice our previous speed. I assumed Kuti was still close on our tailpipe and could keep up. Following people is part of what private investigators do.

I didn't know what we were going to face when we reached Zabrina's house, just that those carjackings had been carried out by two armed men. I needed to do something to even up our odds.

"Do you have Dave Gilbert's number programmed in your phone?" I asked as she began slaloming through traffic.

"Yeah," she said, and handed me her phone, which had been on her lap. I briefly interrupted the turn-by-turn directions, dipped into her contacts, and found Gilbert. I then returned her to GPS mode.

On my own phone, I called Gilbert and began talking him through my current situation. There were two things about the man that made him appealing to me in this moment of need.

One, that he owed me a favor.

Two, that he owned a shotgun.

CHAPTER 43

Blue Mask rapped on the front door to his sister's house in a series of sharp, insistent bursts. When it opened, he smiled.

"Hey, Zee. Surprise!" he said.

Zabrina Coleman-Webster took a step back. "What are you idiots doing? You're not supposed to—"

"Come on, dawg," Black Mask said. "Just get inside."

Black Mask had his gun to the pregnant woman's back and was using it to push her into the house. He wasn't waiting for anyone's invitation.

"Who the hell is this?" Zabrina demanded as the woman entered the foyer.

"We were hoping you could tell us that," Black Mask said. "Because it sure as hell ain't no Carter Ross."

Blue Mask marched up to his sister, backing her up against a wall. She was a head shorter. He used his height advantage to loom over her. "How come you didn't tell me about your little side business, Zee? You think I couldn't handle it? You think I was gonna dime you out or something?"

She shoved his chest hard, moving him back a few feet. "Look, I cut you in, didn't I?"

"Yeah, but why didn't you—"

The woman moaned, staggered a few steps, clutched the railing of the staircase, and sunk to one knee. She brought her hand to her stomach and made a noise that came from somewhere deep in her throat.

"Oh, Lord. She's in labor," Zabrina said, rushing over to the woman.

"Yeah, you quick," Blue Mask said.

"We need to get her to a hospital," Zabrina said.

"Yes, *please*," the woman grunted. "The baby is a breach. Hospital, please."

"Yeah, sure, that's a great idea," Black Mask said. "We'll drop her off at the hospital so she can have her baby, and then we'll drop ourselves off at prison, because that's where we'll be spending the rest of our damn lives when she tells the cops about this."

The woman began, "I . . . I promise I won't—"

"Shut up," Black Mask said. "I told you, you ain't got nothing to say."

Blue Mask shifted his glance between his sister, his partner, and the woman, who had her eyes closed as she breathed through the rest of her contraction.

"So what's your plan?" Zabrina asked him.

"She's having the baby here," Blue Mask said. "And then we're going to sell it."

The woman made a terrible noise, but it wasn't one that could be confused with a word.

"What?" Zabrina said. "Are you . . . no way, not a chance."

"You sell stolen cars, I sell stolen babies," Blue Mask said. "You got any other brilliant ideas? You're the one who got us into this."

Blue Mask watched her nostrils flare, the way they did when she was a teenager and he was a little boy who had pissed her off somehow.

"What I got you into was hustling insurance companies that

308

have more money than they know what to do with anyway," Zabrina said. "What I got you into was making a little flow on the side so we could get Mama out of the projects. What I got you into was something where no one would get hurt. *You're* the one who got us into this mess when you started killing people."

"So when you was telling us to shoot that Carter Ross dude, that's your idea of no one getting hurt?"

"He's a newspaper reporter who wouldn't have gotten interested in any of this if you hadn't killed that Nigerian guy and that banker."

Black Mask intervened: "Can y'all stop the family squabble and focus here for a second?"

Zabrina exhaled noisily and paced around toward the woman, who had crumpled onto the floor and was lying on her side in a fetal position.

"Come on. Let's get her in bed or something," Zabrina said, bending down toward the woman. "Girlfriend, you think you can get up? We'll help you upstairs and get you in a bed or something."

The woman's eyes were closed. Slowly, she opened them. She was making an effort to take deep, steady breaths, not always having success.

"No stairs," she huffed out between gasps. "I'm about to have another contraction."

"Damn," Zabrina said. She looked up at the two men. "This baby is coming soon. Why don't y'all boil some water and lay down some garbage bags and some sheets on the couch in the living room?"

"Boil water?" Blue Mask said. "What is this, *Little House on the Freakin' Prairie*?"

"Just shut up and do it," Zabrina shot back.

"You know how to deliver a baby?" Black Mask asked, his tone more curious than challenging.

"No. But at least I had one once. So just help me out here, bitches."

The woman huffed out, "Breach. The baby is breach." No one paid much attention.

Blue Mask turned to his colleague. "Sheets are in the closet at the top of the stairs. I'll get the water going, then get the plastic bags."

Black Mask went for the stairs. Blue Mask walked into the kitchen. His ski mask was making his face hot and itchy, so he took it off and stuffed it in his pocket. It's not like he had to worry about the woman in the other room identifying him.

He was never going to let her live that long.

CHAPTER 44

Sweet Thang turned onto the street where Zabrina's house was located and slowed when she was about halfway down the block.

"This is it," she said as we passed a rambling Victorian house perched on a small ridge. The steps leading up to the front porch were maybe five feet above street level. The porch itself was another five feet above that. It gave the house a fortresslike feel.

Tina's Volvo was still in the driveway. It was empty, but seeing it gave me some hope. If her car was here, chances were good she was here, too.

I was operating under the assumption that the two men who had killed Joseph Okeke and Kevin Tiemeyer had been waiting to ambush me the moment I pulled into the driveway. There would have been some confusion when the person in the driver's seat was not some white guy, as they had been told it would be, but a pregnant lady.

What would they do at that point? I didn't know, of course. That was just the start of where this whole operation got tricky.

"Okay. Drive down to the corner," I instructed. "I don't know if Zabrina is here, or if she has a crew here or what. But if they are, I don't want them to be alerted we're coming."

"Shouldn't we just call the cops?" Sweet Thang asked.

"And tell them what, exactly? That my girlfriend isn't answering her cell phone? We don't know anything for sure."

"All right. So what's your plan?"

It was a good question. Here I was, riding up like the cavalry, with no idea where to tell my horses to charge. It was hard to base a plan on speculation.

Sweet Thang had reached the stop sign at the end of the block. "Just stop here and let me out," I said.

As I spilled out of the Malibu, I was semiblinded by the headlights of Hakeem Kuti's Ford Fusion. I trotted around to his window, which rolled down as I approached.

"The place where I think our carjacking crew might be is about twelve houses up," I said, pointing in that direction. "It's the one with the Volvo in the driveway. Want to come have a look with me?"

Kuti's face was impassive; or, alternatively, the lack of light and his scars made it harder for me to read any emotion. But he nodded his head and pulled his car over to the side of the road, next to a fire hydrant.

We walked up the block together and I gave him a quiet briefing on what I knew and what I suspected. When we reached Zabrina's place, I veered out into the street and crouched behind a parked car. If anyone was inside the house, I didn't want them to be able to see us.

Kuti followed my lead. I listened for a moment, heard nothing. I popped my head up slightly over the hood of the parked car to look at the house. There were lights on inside.

"Okay. First of all, please silence your cell phones during this movie," I whispered, pulling mine out to make sure it was on vibrate.

This brought a smile from him. "Good policy," he said.

I raised my head to take another glance at the house, but it wasn't exactly going to start talking to me. We needed more information and to be more proactive about acquiring it.

"What do you say you go around to the right and I'll go around to the left," I said. "Look in windows as you go, see what you can see. I'll meet you back here in five."

He didn't say anything, just rose from his crouch and walked up the driveway, angling toward the right corner of the house. As he melded into the darkness, I envied his clothing and skin color, both of which afforded him a lot more camouflage than I had at the moment. This was one of the few circumstances where being a white man in a blue shirt and khaki pants actually disadvantaged me.

I stood up and aimed for the left corner, studying the house as I went. If you put a place like this in the suburbs it would be worth a million dollars, easily. In Newark, they went for less than a third of that. Most of them had been subdivided into three-family houses. This one was unusual in that it remained intact.

The first structure I came across was one of those typically Victorian sitting rooms that had three bay windows jutting out toward the street in a semihexagon. It was dark. I passed by it with only a cursory inspection.

Moving along the wall, staying low next to some shrubbery, I reached what was likely a bathroom, judging from the height and size of the window. Again, no light came from it.

Further back, there was a glow coming from one of the rooms. The ground sloped away as I neared the back of the house, exposing more of the foundation and making the house seem like it was even taller and more fortresslike.

When I drew even with the room, I could see only the upper parts of some cabinets, enough that I knew it was the kitchen. Wanting to inspect the room a little more, I eased my way into the shrubbery. Once I was next to the house, I grabbed the narrow windowsill and pulled up, giving myself a glimpse inside.

My handhold being somewhat tenuous, it was not a position I could hold for very long. All I saw during my brief inspection was a narrow, galley-style kitchen. There were no people, just a pot on the stove with steam issuing from it.

I lowered myself and continued around the corner to the backyard. There was a small back porch butting up against this part of the house, with nine steps climbing up to it. The porch led to what might have been a mudroom or a laundry room. There were no lights on.

The room next to it, on the other hand, was well-lit. But this part of the house was well above ground level. From where I was standing, it was difficult to see much inside.

I continued my clockwise navigation of the perimeter and eventually joined Kuti, who was looking intently at the well-lit room, which extended to the far corner.

"I think she is in there," he whispered. "There are people coming in and out, a lot of activity."

"Makes sense," I said. "I haven't seen much in any other part of the house."

Only the upper portion of the wall and ceiling were visible from where we were standing. I had to get a better view of the room somehow. The closest window was about nine feet in the air, higher than the kitchen window by at least a foot. It was not an insurmountable distance by any means. But it was high enough that I would have to jump to grasp it and I didn't want to risk making noise when my body thudded against the siding.

"You think you can give me a boost up to that window over there?" I asked Kuti.

He nodded once. We approached the wall and he threaded his hands together like a stirrup.

"Step here," he said.

I followed his instruction and he lifted me, until I was able to grasp the windowsill and pull myself up. My eyes were just over the bottom of the windowpane.

What I saw took my breath away. There were three people

in the room. Two were young black males with guns in their hands. The other was Tina.

She was semireclined on a plastic- and sheet-draped couch with several pillows behind her back that kept her propped at a roughly forty-five degree angle. There was a heavy-looking metal tray next to her with ice water on it. Her feet were resting on a coffee table. Her legs were splayed wide. They were covered by another sheet, but she appeared to be bare from the waist down.

Which was really strange.

Unless they were planning to have her deliver the baby right there.

Of course. The boiling water was to sterilize whatever instruments they planned to use. The ice water was to keep her hydrated while she labored. The sheets and plastic were on the couch because they expected all the bodily fluids associated with birth.

They had obviously come across her in the car and, despite their murderous intent toward me, decided they couldn't do her in. But they also couldn't just let her go. Hence, she was now half-naked on the couch, getting ready to push out our baby.

The panic ripped through me. Did they know the baby was a breach? Did they have any idea what they were doing? Even Dr. Marston, who had years of medical training and did this for a living, warned us that breach pregnancies could get very complicated, and that it was best not to even attempt a vaginal delivery. I remembered her lecture about negative outcomes. Would these thugs take her to a hospital if she started having real difficulty?

I saw Tina's pants, crumpled on the floor. I could tell they were soaked. Which meant her water had broken.

Tina had her eyes closed. The two guys with the guns did not seem to be paying attention to her until she began moaning slightly.

"She's having another one," one of the thugs hollered to

someone outside of the room, his voice only slightly muffled by the thin pane of glass that separated us.

I soon recognized that by "another one" he meant a contraction. Zabrina strolled into the room wearing a blue workout suit. Her hands were empty. She turned slightly, and I could see the gun she had tucked in the back waistband of her pants.

Zabrina checked her watch. "Three minutes since the last one," she said.

I felt another surge of terror. Three minutes was close. And her water had broken. This baby was coming. Soon. Whether Tina wanted him to or not.

Zabrina knelt at Tina's side, but did not touch her. Tina didn't seem to notice. I could see her chest heaving. Her legs twitched a little.

Just watching it made my stomach clench.

The windowsill was so narrow, I couldn't stay up there very long. My fingers were starting to cramp and I could feel Kuti's arms getting wobbly. Once Tina's contraction subsided, I decided to come down.

"Okay," I said softly to Kuti.

He lowered me part of the way and I dropped the rest. I pointed in the direction of the street and started walking that way. He followed me. We skirted the driveway, staying out of the direct line of sight of anyone inside the house until we were back out in the street.

Sweet Thang was perhaps a hundred feet down, standing on the sidewalk with someone who I could only see in silhouette. Then I realized the silhouette had a handlebar mustache. Dave Gilbert.

As I approached, I saw he had his shotgun at his side, its muzzle pointed toward the pavement.

"Hey. Thanks for coming," I said.

"Hi," he said. "Is she in there?"

"She is. With three armed guards."

Gilbert held out the shotgun for me. "Then you're going to need this," he said.

I didn't move to accept it. I'm not a gun guy. Quite the opposite. I've never owned one, never shot one, never wanted one in my house. I'm all for the Second Amendment, when applied in moderation, but I abhor what illegal handguns have done to our inner cities. Interview as many mothers who have lost their babies to gun violence as I have, and you'd feel the same way.

Dave sensed my reluctance and took another step toward me with the gun. "Look, I know I owe you a favor, but this is where it has to end," he said. "I'm a felon. I shouldn't have this. If you're going to be using it, I can't be anywhere nearby. As far as I'm concerned, it's yours now."

He held it out. I eyed it. Then I grabbed it with both hands. Tina needed me. My baby needed me. That mattered a lot more than my own personal feelings about firearms.

"Thanks," I said.

"It's already loaded: one in the chamber, two in the magazine. You can bet my fingerprints aren't on them," he said. "And you should know this weapon is untraceable and I bought it from someone who probably stole it. I wouldn't let the police know you have this."

He reached into his pocket and pulled out a clear plastic bag with a handful of cartridges inside. He handed me the bag.

"They're buckshot, just like the ones in the gun," he said. "This is just in case you need extra. But three should be all you need."

"Got it," I said, pocketing them.

"Have you ever fired one of these before?"

"No."

317

"Keep it braced against your body, because it'll kick like a donkey," he said. "If you have to shoot someone, just aim for the middle of their chest."

"Thanks."

"I'm out of here," he said. "Good luck."

He walked off into the night. Kuti had joined our little gathering in the middle of the street. Sweet Thang's eyes were fixed on me, all large and lustrous.

"Are you okay?" she said.

"Not particularly," I said.

"You're going to call the cops now, right?" she asked.

Kuti answered the question for me. "I would not recommend that," he said.

"Why not?" she said.

"Because I understand their policies and procedures," Kuti said. "This is a hostage situation. And in a hostage situation, their priority is to get everyone out alive. In this case, Mr. Ross's priorities are a little different. I believe he is focused more on the safety of two people in particular, one of whom is very small."

I didn't say anything, just nodded slightly.

"I have two children," Kuti said. "If it was my fiancée and my baby, I would want to take care of it myself."

My phone buzzed in my pocket. I pulled it out and saw it was Buster.

"Excuse me for a second," I said, taking a few steps away from Sweet Thang and Kuti and keeping the shotgun pointed away from them.

I answered with: "Hey, what do you got?"

"It's more about what you got," he replied. "My guy on the task force didn't even need to run that list through his computer. He recognized seven names at first glance."

Seven out of a hundred. That sealed it. The Rotary Club was firmly at the center of this conspiracy and Zabrina Coleman-Webster was either running it or involved very deeply.

"Okay, thanks," I said.

"My guy was very curious to know what is going on at the Newark Rotary Club," Buster said. "Is there anything you want me to tell him?"

I took a deep breath and held it. This was the moment. If I wanted a mob of Newark Police on this street—and a full-blown hostage situation, with helicopters and dogs and God-knows-what-else—all I had to do was say the word.

Then I thought about some hostage negotiator telling me to be patient even as I knew Tina and our unborn child were in dire need of medical assistance; about one of those hoodlums inside using Tina as a human shield as he tried to make an escape; about some nervous young cop with an itchy trigger finger firing when he shouldn't; about all the things that could go horribly wrong.

I imagined some police captain apologizing to me for some unforeseen mishap that he insisted couldn't have been avoided. And I might have been in a mood to listen to him, except in the version I was seeing in my mind, we were having this conversation in front of a tiny casket.

Suddenly, I knew for sure: I didn't want that all in the hands of a bunch of people I didn't know and who could never possibly care on as deep a level as I did. For them, it was a job. A job they wanted to do well, yes. But still, it was a day's work that was either going to go well or badly.

For me, it was my whole life.

I looked through the darkness at Kuti, who seemed to understand exactly what I was feeling and who struck me as both calm and competent. I felt the weight of the shotgun. My lungs finally released the breath I had been holding.

"No, I'm good for now," I said. "But, Buster?"

"Yeah?"

"Thank you," I said with all due sincerity. "I really owe you one."

"No," he said. "Not this time."

. . .

I walked back toward Sweet Thang and Kuti, who were in the midst of a muted conversation.

"... absurd not to," I heard Sweet Thang saying.

When Sweet Thang saw I was rejoining them, she said, "Carter, seriously. Let's call the police. This is what they're trained to do. This is why we have police."

"For someone else's child, you're absolutely right," I said. "But not for mine."

She started to say something, then rethought it. She settled on: "Okay."

I turned to Kuti. "We're looking at three armed assailants," I said. "You said your background is in the military?"

He nodded.

"Well then I'd really like your thoughts on how to plan this operation."

"If it was one man, we could try to get a shot through a window," he said. "But not with multiple targets. And not with the guns we have. They are effective as close range antipersonnel weapons. They are far less useful at greater range. Even if we could get two of them targeted at once ... I am gathering you are not an experienced marksman?"

"That's an understatement," I said.

"Then it might be prudent simply to wait. We know they have to come out eventually. We pick them off when they do."

"No good. The baby is a breach. Tina's water has broken and the contractions are less than three minutes apart. We have to get her to the hospital now or we could lose the baby."

Just saying the words—"lose the baby"—made my throat constrict.

Kuti thought on this for a moment or two. "Then we need to find some way to flush them out. It is the only way. As long as they are inside the house, they have too great a tactical advantage on us."

"Flush them out," I repeated. "How do we do that?"

He stared at some unfixed point beyond me. There was a streetlight nearby, but almost nothing on Kuti's ebony face reflected back its dim light.

"If the woman were not pregnant, I would say we set fire to the house," he said, after a while. "But that is too great a risk. We need to do something to force action from them, get them to want to leave the safety of their dwelling. Then we ambush them on the way out."

"Okay, what if we don't set fire to the house. What if we make some kind of explosion outside and . . . what?"

I had become aware that Sweet Thang was watching us go back and forth with this look of disgust.

"You guys are morons," she said. "You have Zabrina's cell phone number, don't you?"

"Yeah," I said.

"Then why don't you just call her? Tell her you're coming over to get those documents. That'll force them to act. At the very least, one of them will have to come out and move Tina's car."

Kuti and I smiled simultaneously. He said, "There is an African proverb that says, 'If you're looking for good strength, look for the chief. If you're looking for good sense, look for his wife.'"

"Americans have a proverb, too," I said. "It comes from the classic film *White Men Can't Jump*. And it goes, 'Listen. To. The. woman.'"

"It's certainly easier than setting a house on fire," Sweet Thang said curtly.

"Okay," I said. "Give me a moment. Mr. Kuti, could you please keep an eye on the house while I make the call?"

"Of course," he said, and began walking back up toward the street.

I walked perhaps a hundred feet in the other direction, far enough that I was sure Zabrina wasn't hearing my voice in stereo. I took a few deep breaths to calm myself, then dialed.

After three rings, she answered. "Hello?"

"Hey, Zabrina, it's Carter Ross from the *Eagle-Examiner*," I said, breezily.

"Oh, hi," she said, matching my tone.

"Hey, this may sound like a strange question, but have you seen my fiancée, Tina Thompson? I asked her to go over to your house to pick up those insurance documents, but I haven't heard from her in a little while."

"Huh, that's strange."

"So you haven't seen her?"

"No, not at all. I was actually starting to wonder where you were," Zabrina said, not too quickly, not too slowly. If she had been surprised at all by my calling, she was already over it. It was chilling how smooth she was.

"Yeah, I asked Tina to pick them up because I was running late," I said, then forced a laugh. "But she's pregnant. So she probably stopped for ice cream and pickles or something."

"I guess. If she comes by, I'll be sure to tell her you're looking for her."

"That'd be super," I said, then sighed as if I was being terribly inconvenienced. "Well, I guess I better come out and get those documents myself. I should be there in ten minutes or so."

There was no hitch in her reply. "Actually, would you mind waiting until tomorrow? I'm beat."

It was a nice try. But I had anticipated her attempt to delay and was ready with a response. "I would, except I need to write this story tonight and Tujuka Okeke still isn't talking to me. Without the documents, I can't write. And I promised the story to my editors first thing in the morning."

"Oh. Well, I'm sorry, but I'd really rather you didn't come by. The thing is, I'm not dressed."

"No problem," I said. "Just leave them on the front porch. I promise I'll avert my eyes from the house as I grab them. I'll be right over and then I'll be out of your hair."

I prepared myself to bat down her next flimsy objection, but she had finally run out of them. Perhaps she realized too strenuous a protest against a fairly reasonable request would have seemed out of place.

"Okay, fine," she said. "Just don't knock on the door, because I won't answer."

"You got a deal," I said. "Thanks for helping me."

"No problem," she said, then hung up.

I trotted back up the street, flashing a thumbs-up at Sweet Thang. "She bought it," I said.

"Okay. What's the plan now?"

"You're going to get in my car and wait for me to text you. In ten minutes, you might have to pretend to be me, pulling into the driveway of Zabrina's house and retrieving insurance documents from the front porch. There's a baseball cap in my backseat. Just put it on, tuck your hair up in it, and make like you don't have hips or boobs as you walk. Hopefully the darkness will do the rest for us."

"Got it. What are you going to do?"

I shook my head and said, "I wish I knew."

CHAPTER 45

After thirty-three years on this planet—one-third of a century, if you want to make it sound more profound—I thought I knew myself pretty well.

The guy I knew had taken a respectable amount of God-given smarts and chosen to apply them to a job with low respect and even lower pay because it was a field that allowed him to fully explore—and even, sometimes, to explicate—the human condition. Folks sometimes found him a little too glib for his own good. Or just a bit overwhelming. But most of the time they recognized that the reason he engaged in the world so thoroughly is that he liked people, in a very real, very genuine way.

He once, long ago, broke a kid's nose during a playground scuffle. He didn't particularly like how that made him feel inside. You could call him a pacifist; or, if you hadn't grown up much since your own playground days, you could call him a wimp. All I know is that the guy had never intentionally harmed anyone since then. At least not physically.

I never thought that guy would have ended up crouched against someone's front porch lattice with a shotgun cradled in his hands.

Yet that's where circumstance had pushed me. I still didn't

quite understand it, even though I had lived every step of the journey. And the only thing that kept it from being utterly surreal—like, how the hell did this happen to *me*, the peace-loving wimp?—was that I had to stay incredibly focused on the moment.

To my immediate left, close enough that our elbows kept brushing, was Hakeem Kuti. We had huddled briefly out on the street and decided that there were two likely scenarios: one, they would send out one person to move the car, in the hopes that I would simply come and go; or, two, they would all come out and evacuate the house altogether, moving their entire operation elsewhere.

We decided if one person came out, Kuti would jump him. If they all came out, we'd both jump them.

It was not an especially elegant plan, I suppose. And it relied almost totally on the element of surprise. But it was the best we could come up with in the minute we had allotted ourselves.

The only good thing was that Zabrina didn't have much time to plot, either. The clock had started ticking the moment I hung up the phone with her. She thought I would be there in ten minutes. Between the one minute I spent talking to Kuti and the one minute we spent getting in place, there were now eight minutes left.

I began counting seconds, one-Mississippi, two-Mississippi-style. For the next two hundred Mississippis, there was no discernible activity within the house. No lights had gone on or off. No noises had escaped.

Then, from the porch, I heard the sound of wood scraping against wood. The front door, which was old and swollen with time, was opening.

The click of metal and the whooshing of a pneumatic piston came next. It was the screen door. As the wooden door slammed noisily shut, the screen door hissed softly back into place. I couldn't see who was coming out. But I could hear sneakers sliding on old grit over the porch floor.

Make that: one set of sneakers. There was definitely only one person. The door hadn't been opened long enough for two people to come out and I didn't hear more than one pair of feet moving. It was a man, judging from the heaviness of the footfalls. I held up one finger in front of Kuti's face. He nodded.

The sneakers stopped for a brief moment at the edge of the porch. By turning to look over my shoulder, I could now make out the chilling sight of a man with a black ski mask pulled over his head. He bent down and set a thin sheaf of papers on the porch floor. Then he straightened and descended the steps, his knees pumping quickly.

He went left, passing directly in front of us without turning his head. His focus was on Tina's Volvo, still parked in the driveway. He had the keys in his right hand. He was moving with the alacrity of a man under time pressure and the obliviousness of one not expecting company.

Kuti let him go by, then leapt out from our hiding spot. The rustling of some dead leaves caused the man with the black ski mask to swivel his head in Kuti's direction, but he was far too late. Kuti was already on him. In what looked like a move he had practiced, Kuti clamped his hand over the man's mouth and stuck the gun barrel in his ear.

"Quiet," Kuti said softly. "If you make a sound, I will kill you. If you make a move I consider threatening, I will kill you. If you follow instructions, you will live. Nod once if you understand."

The man bobbed his head.

"Very good," Kuti said. "Are your instructions to get in the Volvo and drive away? Nod once if yes."

The man's head dipped again.

"Are the others coming out behind you? Nod if yes, shake if no."

This time, he shook. There was no way to know if he was telling the truth. We could only hope he was too scared or too shocked to lie.

"Very good. Now walk at a moderate speed to the car's

driver's side door. You will receive further instructions when they are needed."

The man began walking in a normal pace, with Kuti moving behind him and keeping the gun trained on the man's head the whole time.

Kuti stopped to give more directions when they reached the Volvo. I couldn't hear them by that point, but I watched as they simultaneously opened and then closed their respective doors—the man the front, Kuti the rear. Obviously, he had them synchronize both actions so that anyone inside would only hear one door opening and one door closing.

The Volvo's engine came to life. Its headlights turned on automatically. Its white backup lights followed. Soon, it was backing out of the driveway and turning in the direction of where Sweet Thang had parked my car. Then it left my sight.

There was no sign that anyone inside the house had been aware that one of their teammates had been hijacked. The whole exchange in front of the porch had taken thirty seconds and had been very quiet, so I wasn't worried about anyone hearing anything unusual. Nor was it likely they had seen anything. The rooms with the lights on were all in the back part of the house. Assuming Zabrina and her other associate had stayed there—and they would, since they were anticipating I was going to show up any moment—we were in good shape.

Now it was Sweet Thang's turn. Keeping my cell phone low against the side of the porch, where no one would see its little light come on, I checked the time. It had been eight minutes since I called Zabrina.

"Go in two minutes," I texted her.

No more than ten seconds later, I received her reply. "Got it."

I slipped my phone in my pocket and settled back against the porch, listening intently but hearing nothing of interest until the Malibu's engine came into earshot exactly two minutes later.

As instructed, Sweet Thang pulled into the driveway. She got even with the path that led to the front porch and quickly got out of the car, leaving the engine running and the headlights on. I can't say she looked particularly masculine as she walked up toward the porch. But she didn't look particularly feminine, either. I was really banking on the fact that no one would be watching.

I'm not sure if she saw me as she crossed in front of me. If she did, she was smart enough not to acknowledge me. She climbed up two of the front porch steps, just far enough that she could reach the sheaf of papers that had been left there, and grabbed them. Then she whirled around and retraced her steps back to the Malibu.

Moments later, she was backing down the driveway, just like the Volvo moments before her. Other than her inability to transmogrify into a six-foot-one man, she did it as well as it could have been done.

Her departure brought silence back to the house. It was about this time I suddenly realized one glaring omission from our plan:

We hadn't discussed what to do next if only one person left the house.

I assumed Kuti would stay somewhere nearby, but he would be busy keeping watch over the man with the black ski mask. Which meant I was now on my own.

And neither Tina nor our child had much time for me to decide what to do next.

My feasible options, as far I could figure them, were limited. My good options were nonexistent.

I was one man with a shotgun against two people, both of them armed, who were somewhere inside a large, three-story dwelling. I harbored exactly zero fantasies about trying to shoot one of them through the window. There was little chance I could get a clean shot—they were too high up in that fortresslike house—and even if I did, I had no empirical evidence I possessed the skills to shoot the side of a barn from ten paces, much less a human being from thirty yards. The thought that I could miss and hit Tina was too horrible to contemplate.

Plus, there was still the matter of what to do about the person I didn't shoot, who would then be alerted to my presence.

I was out of time to do the safe thing, which was to wait them out. There was really no choice. I had to force the action. I had to go in. One against two.

The last thing I did before leaving the safety of my hiding spot was text Sweet Thang, dictating what was essentially my backup plan: "I'm going in. Stay close. If you don't hear from me in twenty minutes, assume I'm dead. Call the cops."

I stood up halfway, staying crouched low enough to keep my head below the height of the porch. I crept around to the steps and climbed them, one by one, then softly walked across the porch. I kept my shotgun pointed at the door. If anyone came out, they were going to get a mouthful of buckshot.

My first real barrier was the screen door. Thankfully, it looked to be fairly new, not some rusty thing that would creak a lot. Taking my nontrigger hand off the shotgun, I slowly lowered an L-shaped brass handle until I felt the catch come free. I pulled, doing it gradually enough that the pneumatic piston did not hiss.

Once the door was open wide enough, I slid my body behind it. The next barrier was the old wooden door. I tried its round knob and was relieved to feel it rotate in my hand. The guy in the black ski mask hadn't bothered locking it.

Now I worried about noise. I remembered the sound the door made as it rubbed against its jamb. The last thing I needed was to announce my entry with the squeal of wood chafing against wood.

Fortunately, having grown up in an old house—and having maybe, possibly, snuck out of said house on one or two occasions—I knew a little something about keeping old doors quiet. The squeaking always came from the left, as a result of moisture-related swelling; or the bottom, as a result of the door settling on its hinges.

Having already turned the doorknob, I pulled as hard as I could to the right, toward the hinges, so the left side wouldn't rub. Simultaneously, I lifted it slightly, so the bottom wouldn't chafe, either.

Then I put some weight behind it. I held my breath as it swung quietly open. I entered the house, keeping my non-gun-hand on the screen door until it eased shut. Then I swung the wooden door back, leaving it slightly ajar so I wouldn't have to risk that horrible wood-on-wood sound as it closed.

The foyer was unlit. In front of me there was a staircase heading up. To my left was the sitting room with the semihexagonal bay windows. To the far right was a formal dining room. To my more immediate right was a hallway, perhaps thirty feet long, that extended to the back of the house and my laboring fiancée.

And that, of course, was where I had to go. I brought the shotgun up, letting its barrel lead the way. I was thankful, as I tread on the old hardwood floors, that I wore rubber-sole shoes—a concession to durability and comfort that now seemed prescient.

I had crept perhaps ten feet down when a throaty moan began emanating from the room on the back right. I halted. As soon as the noise started, Zabrina flashed across the hallway, having come from the room on the other side—the kitchen, if I recalled correctly.

Her passage through the hallway was so fleeting and she was moving so fast I didn't really have time to react. I did have time to look at her, though; and, in particular, look at her gun, which was still tucked in the back of her pants.

The moan built in volume. Tina was having another contraction. It made my heart ache I wasn't next to her, comforting her, encouraging her, rubbing her back, letting her yell at me—all the things fathers were supposed to do for the mothers of their children.

I used the noise she was making as cover to continue my slink down the hallway. My right finger remained on the shotgun's trigger. By the time Tina stopped, I was at the end of the hallway, still with no brilliant plan as to what to do next.

"Two minutes thirty seconds that time," Zabrina said.

"A'ight," a man replied.

From their voices, I could tell the man was at the edge of the room, just on the other side of the wall from where I now stood. Zabrina was closer to the couch, near Tina.

I could only aim at one of them as I went in. I decided to target the man. He was the one with his firearm in his hand, or at least he had it there when I glimpsed him through the window earlier. He was the greater threat.

The script in my head went something like this: leap into the room, shoot the man, then turn the gun on Zabrina. I would have to pump the shotgun to eject the old cartridge and put a new one in the chamber. That would give her the opportunity to get her own gun out of her waistband and turn it on me.

We'd probably end up firing simultaneously. I'd take a round, but so would she. It was probable neither of us would survive.

But Tina would. She could crawl to one of our corpses, dig out a phone, and call 911. Her contractions were still just barely far enough apart. She would have time to get to the hospital and have the baby safely cut out of her. No prolapsed umbilical cords. No negative outcomes.

But only if I acted now.

And that's when I realized I had reached that dreaded question, the one all parents hope will never be anything more than hypothetical:

Would you give your life for your kid?

It is, as I said, a question every parent contemplates at some point. But at least in my case, the answer was only worth pondering for some minimal fraction of a second.

Because—even for a child who I never met, even with a full understanding of the consequences, even with all I would be giving up—the answer was so obvious.

Hell yes.

Wanting my enemies to be at least minimally distracted, I waited until Tina's next contraction to move.

She began with the low moan, just like last time. I counted to three. Then I whirled around the corner.

I suppose the humane, merciful thing to do would have been to yell "freeze" and at least give them a chance to surrender without bloodshed, to let them see that they were not outnumbered but they sure were outgunned. And maybe the guy I thought I once knew—the peace-loving wimp—would have done that.

But he was gone. So was his sense of humanity and mercy. They had been replaced by more brutish impulses, instincts that urged me to protect my own at all costs.

I didn't even look at the face of the man I was about to shoot or consider that what I was aiming at was a fellow human being. He was just an object at that point. I stared at the middle of his chest, because that's what I was aiming for.

Then I pulled the trigger.

I felt the gun slam into the crook of my arm. There was heat from gases being propelled at supersonic speed out of the barrel. There was a bright flash of light, followed an imperceptible moment later by a roaring blast.

It is, as I may have mentioned, a misconception that it's impossible to miss with a shotgun from close range. But it turns out it's pretty damn easy not to miss.

The buckshot tore into the man's chest and sent him hurtling back against the wall. But I neither took the time to appreciate my marksmanship or survey its final effects. I was too busy swinging the gun barrel toward Zabrina.

She had been kneeling next to Tina with her back to me. But she was already rectifying that. She had turned toward me, grabbed the gun from her waistband, and was bringing it forward.

With my right hand, the one that had just pulled the trigger, I grabbed the shotgun's slide and, with every bit of strength I had, racked it back toward my body. It made that sound, that *chick-chick* noise that I previously had found so terrifying. Now it was positively symphonic.

From there it was a pretty simple race; a race to the death that, in this too-violent country of ours, had been run everywhere from the streets of Newark to the Wild West. And the winner would be determined by one thing: who could aim and pull the trigger faster?

Tina was in midmoan, her eyes closed.

And then she wasn't. And they weren't.

I was catching this in my peripheral vision. And in real time, I'm not sure I fully appreciated what was happening. It was only later, when I was able to slow it down, that I really understood what she was doing.

Tina continued moaning, but she had opened her eyes. With an alertness that belied the undertaking her pregnant body was in the midst of, she twisted to the right. With both hands, she grabbed that heavy metal tray, the one that had been holding her ice water.

Then, with a savage yell, she slammed its edge into the side of Zabrina's head.

Zabrina's arms went into the air. She toppled over on her left side. My target—her chest—was now on the floor, obscured by the coffee table. Her head was sticking out just beyond the table. I couldn't tell where the gun had gone but I wasn't waiting to locate it. I took two long strides, wound up, and kicked her skull as hard as I could.

If Zabrina had any hold on consciousness before my foot met her cranium, it certainly was gone by the time it impacted. I raised up the stock of the shotgun, ready to bludgeon her if she made any move, but her lights were out. Blood was starting to ooze from the contusion Tina had inflicted.

I looked over to the corner of the room. The man I had shot was crumpled in his own rapidly expanding pool of blood. His body had been spun to the side, so I could see that a blue ski mask was sticking out of his pocket.

He was the one whose predilection for murder had started it all, but he wasn't going to be trouble to me or anyone else; except, perhaps, for the county medical examiner who would have to perform his autopsy.

Zabrina's gun had dropped harmlessly to the floor. I kicked it out into the hallway, on the off chance she began to stir. Then I grabbed a dish towel that was sitting on the coffee table. I quickly wiped down the shotgun, then set it down in the corner. I was leaving that untraceable gun behind without any fingerprints on it, along with a few shell casings I had never touched. Let the authorities just try to prove who pulled the trigger.

Tina, amazingly, was already standing up. I walked over to her and offered her an arm. She waved me away.

"I'm fine, I'm fine," she said. She was grabbing the sheet she had been using as a cover-up and was wrapping it around her bare bottom half.

I just stared at her. "How the hell did you do that in the middle of a contraction?" I asked, pointing at Zabrina.

"Easy," she said. "I wasn't having a contraction. I was faking it."

I was too surprised to summon a reply, so she continued: "I started faking them the moment they brought me into the house. I thought I could trick them into taking me to the hospital. It didn't work. But I figured at that point I had to keep up the ruse. I'm still having a real one every eight minutes. I've been throwing in two pretend ones for every real one."

"So, it's true," I said, "no one really knows when a woman is faking it."

She just smiled and began waddling—and, again, this is not a word I would use around her—toward me.

"Come on, Dad," she said. "Let's go to the hospital."

CHAPTER 46

As soon as we were out of the door, I hailed the Sweet Thang Taxi and Limousine Service by calling her on my cell phone.

By the time we had walked down the front steps, she was pulling the Malibu into the driveway. I helped Tina into the passenger seat, hopped in behind her, and asked Sweet Thang to drive with expedient caution toward Saint Barnabas Medical Center.

For the record, my first phone call as we got underway *was* to my parents. A promise is a promise.

"It's time," I said as soon as my mother answered.

"*It's time?*" she screamed. But I hung up before the rest of what would likely be a very loud, very prolonged exclamation shattered my eardrums or blew out the speaker on my phone.

Tina's parents came next. They live in Florida and had already planned to come up the next week, when the C-section had been scheduled. As I hung up on them, they were making noises about changing plane tickets.

I was about to call Buster Hays when Tina went into a contraction—a real one this time. I knew this for sure because when I asked if there was anything I could do to help, she said she preferred silence. Only she said it with a lot more profanity than that.

When she came out of the contraction, I was about to get

back on my phone when she said, "By the way, there's something I want to tell you before I forget," she said.

"What's that?"

"They want me to run the paper."

"What do you—"

"Brodie is going on a three-month medical leave," she said. "Corporate wants me to serve as executive editor in his absence."

"Oh. Wow. Congratulations."

"He's probably going to retire. No one wants to rush him into it, but that's how it looks. I get the sense this is my tryout. I've got three months to show corporate I can do this job."

"So how are you going to—"

"Carter," she said sharply.

"Yes?"

"I really don't want to talk about this in detail right now."

"Okay," I said.

And, really, it was. We could sort out the intricacies of being executive editor and mom at some later time.

My final phone call during our ride was to Buster Hays. I told him he might want to alert his task force buddy to send detectives to Zabrina's address, where they would discover the Rotary president behind the wave of carjackings in her club and a dead man whose firearm would likely be linked to the shooting deaths of Kevin Tiemeyer and Joseph Okeke.

Later, I would learn the man with the blue ski mask was Zabrina Coleman-Webster's brother, recently paroled from prison. He had gotten involved in his sister's scheme and, for reasons only his twisted brain would understand, started killing the cars' owners. In addition to Tiemeyer and Okeke, he was also believed to be behind the disappearance of his great-aunt, whose house was found empty except for a very hungry cat. The cat had found a place at a no-kill shelter, where he was awaiting adoption. I had a lot on my plate, of course, but I planned to check in a few weeks to see if he found a home. If not, maybe Deadline needed a brother.

I would also learn that Hakeem Kuti had quickly gone to work on the man in the black ski mask, convincing him of the merits of being the first member of a criminal enterprise to turn into a cooperating witness. And it's true: the first person to make a deal always gets the best one.

Certainly, no such offer would be made to Zabrina Coleman-Webster, who took most of the weight and faced a raft of charges. She ended up pleading guilty anyway, not that it helped her much. At her sentencing, she talked about why she did it. The short version was that "Zabrina From The 'Hood," as she called herself, got tired of waiting to collect what she felt the world owed her. She saw this as her shortcut. She expressed profound remorse it had gotten out of control. I'm not sure if her apologies helped the families who would never get their loved ones back. But at least it was something.

Zabrina's cooperation gave Kuti the evidence he needed to uncover a fraud involving policyholders from Obatala and a half dozen other underwriters, all of whom happily paid Kuti a retainer for his assistance. Altogether, more than a dozen of Zabrina's associates—both from Rotary and the firm of Lacks & Ragland—ended up serving jail time for availing themselves of her illicit offer to cash in on their replacement policies with staged carjackings.

My story on the subject was stripped across the top of the Sunday paper a week and a half later. By that point, Doc Fierro had been sufficiently mollified by my long and self-flagellating apology that he dropped his threat to get an injunction against us. That, in turn, had resulted in my being reinstated to my position as a staff writer at the *Eagle-Examiner*.

The only other fallout from the story—or, rather, from the dramatic events that took place during its reporting—was that its writer suffered a minor case of post-traumatic stress disorder. There are people, apparently, who can shoot someone and not feel much remorse. I learned I am not one of those people. I replayed the events of that evening many times, including in a series of therapy sessions. Even though it was clear to all the target in question dearly deserved to be shot, I never really did convince myself to like how it all turned out. Then again, there was never anything I could do to change it. I accepted that, slowly. I suspected it would still haunt me.

The only thing that really helped was that I had something else to occupy my time and attention: a new person in my life, whose arrival was hastened as soon as we reached the hospital that night.

We marched right into the labor and delivery ward, where we had preregistered, and were taken to a room without delay. Tina and the baby really were doing fine, despite the excitement of the evening's activities. Her water had broken on the early side and the contractions were starting to come faster, but she was buttoned up tight enough. The baby was still happily inside mama, with a heartbeat that was strong enough to keep everyone happy.

That said, Tina's attempts to get out of a C-section got exactly nowhere. Dr. Marston arrived, performed a quick assessment, then sent us off to an operating room. There, I was given a mask and scrubs and Tina received an epidural that seemed to have the remarkable side effect of removing the four-letter words from her vocabulary.

From there, it was amazing how quickly it all went. Dr. Marston and her team had obviously done this once or twice before. They put a little tent up so Tina wouldn't have to watch herself get sliced and diced. I got to be on the good side of the tent with her and was thankful for it. Just because I had been urging her to open up around me didn't mean we needed to be literal about it.

I thought there would be more ceremony to it—shouldn't someone say something in Latin? or burn incense? or summon the great animal spirits?—but they went about their task in quiet, workmanlike fashion as I held Tina's hand.

"Just about there," Dr. Marston said. "You're doing great."

Tina had an oxygen mask over her face, so I felt deputized to speak on behalf of the couple. My words, which perhaps should have been more memorable, were something like, "Thanks, Doc."

Then there came this sound. And oh, dear Lord, it has to be the most joyous thing you can ever hear: the squalling of a baby who, having drawn first breath, now wants to tell the world all about it.

The next thing I knew, Dr. Marston was cradling this little human being and laying it on Tina's chest. "Congratulations," the doctor said. "It's a girl."

And, in fact, she was. Not that her gender particularly mattered to me in that moment. I was too busy looking at her tiny little fingers and her tiny little toes and her perfect little nose and these narrow slits where she revealed her blue-gray eyes.

"Hi, baby," I said. "I'm your dad and I love you so much."

I was calling her "baby" because we hadn't picked out a name for a girl. Yet another detail we could sort out later. I reached out with my pinky for my daughter's left hand and she grabbed it with surprising strength and squeezed. My other hand was cupping Tina's head.

"Say hi to your mama," I said. "She loves you, too. She can't say it right now, because she's got this thing on her face. But, trust me, she loves you more than anything."

Tina was just holding on to her daughter, feeling our little girl's skin against her own.

There was apparently a pool at the office over who would cry first during delivery. Let the record show that anyone who put their money on it being Tina Thompson was a blithering fool. My tears were everywhere, welling in my eyes, rolling down my cheeks, dripping off my nose.

I'm not even embarrassed to admit I outcried the baby.

"Oh, Tina, she's beautiful," I choked out. "Just beautiful."

And, yes, I would have died for her. Without question.

But I have to say, in that moment—which immediately put every other moment of my life in a distant, distant second place— it worked out a lot better that I didn't have to.

ACKNOWLEDGMENTS

I do the vast majority of my writing in the corner of a Hardee's restaurant near where I live. I get there by seven or eight each morning—or earlier, if the story rattling around in my head won't let me sleep—and, fueled by free refills of Coke Zero, I stay until the words stop making sense.

Most days, I am joined by Teresa Powell, the longtime manager. Miss Teresa, as a lot of us call her, is the most reliable phenomenon this side of sunrise. In addition to running the show, she pitches in and works the counter, the grill, the drive-through, whatever needs to be done. If the biscuit maker calls in sick, she does that, too.

A lot of authors talk about how hard it can be to find the inspiration to write. Me? I just look at Miss Teresa. I figure if I work half as hard as she does—a single mom putting her son through college on an hourly wage—I'll still be working twice as hard as most folks. And I'm grateful she lets me clutter up the corner of her restaurant, mumbling to myself, day after day.

A note about a few of the names in this book: Kevin Tiemeyer and Armando "Doc" Fierro donated generously to charities—a library and a women's fund, respectively—to have their names used. Thanks for your generosity, gentlemen. Sorry I had to kill you, Kevin.

I have others to thank as well.

That always starts with you, the reader, without whom I would be just a guy muttering in the corner of a Hardee's. I'm particularly grateful to those readers who travel great distances to stalk me, like Candace Perry and my polite Canadian stalker, Amanda Capper. Note to authorities: If I ever disappear under mysterious circumstances, you now know where to start your investigation.

I'm grateful to bookstore owners like Donna Fell of Sparta Books, who always looks for fun, innovative ways to engage her customers. (Not that we're going to talk about what happened at Girls Night Out, right, Donna?)

And of course I remain a big fan of the library scientists who make it their life's work to connect people and books. In particular, I'd like to acknowledge Lindsy Gardner, who is feverishly raising money for a new home for the Lancaster Community Library. If any of you have a spare hundred grand or so, please see Lindsy.

Professionally, I'd like to thank my agent, Dan Conaway of Writers House, giver of great wisdom; my editors, Kelley Ragland and Elizabeth Lacks, who make both me and Carter better than we really are; and the rest of the crew at St. Martin's Press and Minotaur Books, including Hector DeJean, Jeanne Marie Hudson, Matt Baldacci, Talia Sherer, Andy Martin, and Sally Richardson.

I also remain indebted to publicist extraordinaire Becky Kraemer of Cursive Communications for her tireless advocacy on my behalf.

Personally, I need to give a big shout-out to James "Kato" Lum, Tony Cicatiello, and Jorge Motoshige for their never-ending hospitality; to friends at Christchurch School, like Jen and Ed

Homer, who are unswerving in their support and fellowship; to my in-laws, Joan and Allan Blakely, whose enthusiasm for grand-parenting is always so appreciated; and to my parents, Marilyn and Bob Parks, who remain the first people with whom I want to share good news.

Finally, to Melissa and our two children, who bring us so much joy: Thank you for blessing me with the greatest family a man could ever ask for. When I'm with you, all is right.